A New Leash on Life
By Suzie Carr
Edited by T.A. Royce

Also by Suzie Carr:
The Fiche Room
Tangerine Twist
Two Feet Off The Ground
Inner Secrets

Follow Suzie's Blog:
http://curveswelcomed.blogspot.com

Follow Suzie on Twitter:
@girl_novelist

Cover Photography courtesy of T.A. Royce

For Sunshine and Bumblebee

Chapter One

Olivia

The first time Chloe slept over she wore a pink tank top with white lace trim. That first night I stared at the back of her neck and admired the way her shiny, black hair hugged her skin and cascaded down past her ivory shoulders. The soft tickle of her bare legs against mine sent my heart into overdrive. I loved how she didn't seem to mind when I inched up to her. In fact, she cooed when I did, which warranted that I snuggle even closer. She sought me out and pulled me to her. Caught up in the swirl of it all, I cradled an arm around her hips, resting my hand within centimeters of her breast. My breath quickened. My temples pulsed. My skin tingled, connected to the root of ecstasy. She eased into my embrace with a relaxed sigh, placing her hand over mine, acting so cool and collected, like she'd done this a million times before. I pressed my body against her, and she responded with a lovely moan.

This marked the defining moment when I first lost control over my heart to a girl. Well, really, to anyone. Chloe, on the other hand, had already experimented with a soccer player named Devon and a fellow cheerleader, Brianna. She was bisexual and I'd be a bold-faced liar if I didn't admit that this bothered me and

5

caused me massive anxiety whenever her eyes trailed after a handsome guy. I possessed zero control over satisfying that sort of hunger.

Regardless, Chloe and I spent every possible second together. She showcased me as her new best friend, inviting me into her circle of flirty and fun girls. She teased me with her fun attitude and sweet smile, taking me to football games, cheerleader practices, parties, and even drag races at the empty mill parking lots behind the softball fields where I used to score runs as a lanky kid. Chloe painted the world in rainbow colors, and I craved for some of that vibrancy to splash on me.

When we'd separate at the end of a steamy day, I sometimes ached because I missed her so much. I'd lie in my empty bed and think about her silky, black hair, her dark, hazelnut eyes and those creamy legs that stretched on forever. I imagined those legs wrapped around me like a vine, clinging around my body with a gentle force. Then, I'd tuck into a sound sleep only after reliving the moments of the day when she leaned into me with her sweet breath and sent me fluttering with her lips.

My brother, Josh, teased me often. He'd buzz around the kitchen like an annoying gnat laughing at how I had a crush on Chloe Homestead. I'd hit his arm and tell him to shut up. That only set him up to further fan the fire of his antics with more laughing, pointing, and toying with my secret.

When I told Chloe about Josh's joking, she stopped my panic with a soft touch to my babbling lips and a perfectly executed blink. This calmed me, and in fact, even pumped me with a confidence so high that I might've been able to proclaim to my geeky brother that I was a lesbian and damned proud of it. Who wouldn't be with a girl like Chloe? If I had polled every straight girl at Collier High School, I'd bet every single one of them would've loved to be teased with Chloe's plump lips. When she passed through the hallways at school, girls and guys took notice. She unfolded into an exotic, fruity cocktail– luminous, cheerful, and confident.

They stopped mid-sentence to stare. They scanned her from the top of her pretty hair down to her manicured toes. When she claimed stake with me by wrapping her arm in the crook of mine, I floated past them all with an air of supremacy, which evaporated the moment she waltzed away to go to class.

My dull life dissolved the moment Chloe and I fell in love, replaced by a life filled with passion, heat, and lots of euphoria.

I loved how Chloe listened to me. She didn't fiddle with a sink of dirty dishes or tinker with a loose button on her shirt like most of the people in my life. No, not Chloe. She didn't ever nod without looking at me first. She didn't ever stare off into a sink full of suds. No, when I spoke, Chloe cued in on me the way an eagle cued in on its prey – with laser focus. She stared deeply into my eyes and asked me to explain in more detail, asked for my opinion, asked how I would handle things. She hinged on my words.

Chloe needed me in a capacity that no one else in her life could fulfill. She had no family in town. She just had an aunt miles away. Her mother was schizophrenic and living in a mental ward, and her father skipped out on her before she entered this world. She lived with her stepfather and spent most of her time cleaning up after his poker games, cooking his meals, and running away from his insults about how she consistently failed to make his bed the proper way or hang his khaki pants with the correct fold. When Chloe would tell me all of this, she talked with a smile as if none of it bothered her. I would listen. I would nod. I would die inside.

I pitied her and wished more than anything that I could protect her from the dread of her life outside school and my home. I became obsessed with keeping that smile on her face, with sharing my clothes with her, with buying her makeup and hair products with my allowance so she could continue to add light to my life.

She started to spend more nights in my bed, long after she dined with my family and me and after my parents turned off the porch light, locked all the deadbolts, and closed their bedroom door. Her stepfather didn't know I existed, so he never knew enough to come knocking on my front door in search of her. As far as we knew, he never even reported her missing. I wanted to protect Chloe, to be her saving grace, to be that one person she'd always be able to look back on and know I had rescued her.

What her stepfather failed to provide for her in terms of love, support, and a sense of security, I more than offered her. Josh, the conniving clown at our high school, started being nice to her, even attempted to flirt with her whenever she'd turn a blind eye to his charm. Josh needed to be challenged like Chloe needed to be protected. Chloe toyed with him, and he reciprocated by drooling on himself like a lovesick puppy. Even though my blood would boil, Chloe and I would laugh it off later while we cuddled in the glow of moonlight and stars.

For two years, we had a good system. We needed each other in different ways, and this cemented us together through the good and the bad. I dreamt up an entire life together, one where we'd commit to each other on a beach in Hawaii, live out our days in an eclectic city apartment, dance our nights away, and be moms to a set of golden retrievers named Jack and Jill. Our life would be one grand fairy tale.

Then, shortly after waltzing across the stage in our high school auditorium, Chloe met some new friends while working at a dinner theatre. She starred in the play *Oklahoma*. The limelight circled her in love. She snuck me in on opening night. I sat in a folding chair at a table with ten other people. Throughout the acts, I squirmed and shifted several hundred times to see over a monstrous man to see my girl dancing and singing. I strained my neck when the scene called for her to kiss her acting partner, Keith, a blonde guy with handsome features.

I asked her later on if she was attracted to him. She laughed and said, "He's just a friend, silly." A few weeks into the performances, her stepfather investigated her whereabouts and showed up at my parents' house threatening to press charges against her for stealing her mother's diamond ring from his safe. She denied it, and he told her the police had already been by to dust for her fingerprints. She yelled and tossed her heel at him, chasing him out of my living room. My mother huddled behind my father, who just stood tall with his jaw hung low. I later learned that she had, in fact, taken her mother's diamond ring when she left her stepfather's. "My mother wore that ring. Why shouldn't I get it? My mother has no use for it now, and if she were lucid, she'd certainly give it to me."

I felt sorry for her that a diamond ring brought her comfort. She took off, rushing past my parents and Josh, leaving me to worry about her for days until she finally came back. "I have nowhere else to go," she said, her hazelnut eyes tearing up.

I hugged her and promised I'd take care of her, despite the fact that my parents forbade her to sleep at our house anymore out of fear of her dangerous stepfather who, according to them, could come back at any moment with a gun and shoot us all. This prompted me to be straight with her. "You need to return the ring."

"I'm not stepping foot in his house. Are you crazy?"

"I'll go with you."

"He's too strong for us."

Josh stepped in at my request and escorted Chloe back to the house where nothing but bad memories remained. A few hours later, they returned unscathed. He retreated to his room like a whisper. She came into mine, and when I asked her if all went down okay, she started to cry. "I just want to forget that whole part of my life ever happened."

I hugged her and she pulled away. "I'm really tired. I'm just going to go to sleep."

"Okay," I said, watching as she climbed into bed fully clothed. I walked over to her and pulled at the blanket to tuck her in. She rolled over, turning her back to me, still sniffling. Somehow, in my attempt to protect her, I lost a part of her.

The next night, she didn't sleep over. When one night turned into three, and ten unreturned calls turned into twenty, I decided to pay full ticket price at the dinner theatre just to see her. I found her stooped over in the dressing room, tying one of her bootlaces. She wore an ankle length white laced skirt with a blue and white checkered blouse that tightened around her taut waist. She also wore a blonde wig, the front tied back with a blue-checkered bow. She offered me a twisted smile. "I'm just not in a good place right now," she said with the bootlace wrapped around her slender fingers.

Suddenly, her handsome acting partner, Keith, walked in and danced around her chair in bold Sinatra style, singing in a low baritone tone. He bent down and kissed her cheek, offered his hand and swept her away from her chair. He stared at her way too romantically. Her eyes darted away from his, much too nervously for someone with whom she should've been comfortable.

"I'll let you get to work," I said, my voice brittle and crumbling.

She didn't stop me from leaving.

A month and a half had passed after that with only a couple of awkward ice cream dates to catch up. I had taken a job as an animal shelter handler, walking and socializing the dogs who needed a home. So I rambled on about that each time we met up, filling all of the pregnant pauses where Chloe would just stare off to somewhere other than my eyes.

10

The last time she visited me, she showed up at the shelter just as I introduced a family to a cute little hound. I shuffled them into the adoption meet-and-greet room and stood outside the door, staring at Chloe's tilted gaze. She told me a great opportunity had come up for her in New York City. A spot opened up in an off-Broadway production of *Fiddler on the Roof*. After embracing her in a congratulatory hug and wishing her a successful life, I watched her walk away. I blocked my tears from pouring out until she cleared the kennel area.

Since that day, I spent my time hibernating alone in my bedroom petting my basset hound, Floppy. She comforted me. This particular day, I sat on my bed consoling myself by petting her and staring into her adoring brownie eyes. She licked the tip of her nose, oblivious to the cause of my tears. I fell against her velvet fur, and she snuggled up, burying her nose in my hair. I hugged her and swayed, lost in her squishy folds, thankful for her loyalty. "Thank God for you, little girl." I sat up and brushed my hand along the down comforter, the same comforter Chloe and I had slept under a gazillion times.

I looked down at the card she had mailed me from New York City. *I want you to know that I will always be grateful to you and am so sorry for not being the kind of girlfriend you deserve. Your friend always, Chloe.*

I reread her card twenty times trying to find a clue that would glue this scene back together in a way that would add up. After all I had helped her through, she offered me nothing more than a generic goodbye on cardstock?

I sat up and stared out of my window at my mother and father mowing the crab grass. My mother, with her sunhat stretching way beyond her shoulders, raked as my father pushed the gas mower. They laughed about something, both craning their necks back in sync. Twenty-two years together under the same sky, breathing the same air, never tiring of each other, never needing a break to pursue greater things

11

than the other could ever offer. They were childhood sweethearts laced together by the gentle tug of fate and neighborly charm. Neither one had ever been crushed by love; they were virgins to hurt, to humility, to greed. They were untarnished, polished like fine silver, glowing with a sickening sheen to the rest of us who weren't so luckily spared.

Ever since Chloe moved out, I lacked life, like a black hole had taken refuge in the pit of stomach, swallowing everything I had become, everything I would ever be. I faced hell, its flames flickering up to scare any residual joy left for future days. The sun vanished, the birds flew away, the flowers refused to lift their petals in a smile, and the hope of a good day ahead no longer shined its pristine light on me. I stared down a tunnel with nothing more than blackness for my company now. Chloe buried me under a pile of slick mud and skipped off to live her life in the limelight with strangers who couldn't care less about her safety, her emotional well-being, or her past.

I walked over to my vanity and squared off at myself in the mirror. My jaw clenched. My eyes glossed over. Life collapsed inside me. I turned to face Floppy again. She mirrored my sadness. "Fuck her, right?"

Floppy stared up at me and blinked, as if willing me to sit and pet her until the end of days. So, I did. "Never again," I said to her. "No one will ever do this to me again."

She eyed me as if understanding my words. "So, now what, huh? What should I do with the rest of my life?" Her eyes darted back and forth between me and the window, as if at a loss, too. "We could take a long vacation you and me. I can rent an RV, and we can travel across the country. You can sit right up in the front seat next to me, and we can stop at all the great local doggie shops."

I cradled her, and within minutes she drifted off into a heavy sleep. "We'll figure it out. We'll do something worthwhile, something that'll erase Chloe from our lives forever." I rested my head against hers and attempted to drift off to a restful sleep, too, hoping somewhere in my dreams I'd find an answer.

Two days later, my answer came.

My mother screamed out from the kitchen. I flew down the staircase, around the dining room doorway, and into the kitchen. Floppy was lying on her side, stiff as a cutting board. "She's not breathing," my mother screamed then reverted back to pacing and crying.

I ran to Floppy's side and shook her. Nothing. "What happened?"

"I handed her a treat." My mother choked on tears.

I pried open her mouth, stretched my fingers to the back of her throat. I fingered the tip of the treat. It lodged itself deep down. I strained to wrap my fingers around it, and then I yanked at it, pulling out a hunk of string cheese.

I shook her again. Still nothing. I listened for signs of breath, and heard nothing except for my mother's frantic cries. I opened her mouth again and placed my own over hers and performed a series of rescue breaths on her. After several, she opened her eyes in a panic and wiggled under my touch. She coughed and choked and trembled. My mother yelped, which caused Floppy to jump up on her short little legs and circle around us.

I petted her and she whimpered in joy, burying her cute face in between my legs. I couldn't smother her in enough kisses and hugs. I cried, hugging my little girl and reassuring her that her world had corrected itself, and treats, hugs, and long walks would return in full force.

13

When she looked up at me with her brownie, droopy eyes, she thanked me with a heavy blink. I saved her life. My pulse fired up, charged with a purpose far greater than any I'd yet to experience.

I had better things to do with my life than sit around and cry over a girl who didn't need me or appreciate me anymore. A greater mission surfaced now, one that had nothing at all to do with curves, long hair, or pouty lips.

Chapter Two

Thirteen years later

Running a no-kill animal shelter carried a host of troubles, but none powerful enough to launch me into questioning whether or not I walked on the right path. I lived to help animals. I would do whatever it took to ensure they thrived. Animals had every bit as much of a right to inhabit the world as human beings did. Orphanages didn't put children to sleep because no one wanted to adopt them. They took care of them, loved them and protected them. Why should dogs, cats, and other domesticated animals be treated any differently?

When I first took over the shelter, I removed the word euthanasia from appearing anywhere in any form. I fired all the previous workers because none of them believed running a no-kill shelter in Elkwood would last. I refused to cater to this belief. I would just as soon take the needle myself than administer it to any healthy, adoptable animal.

I hired assistants and handlers who mirrored my philosophy that all animals should enjoy the same freedom for life that human beings did. They also lived and breathed their work, working without breaks to round up foster homes and other no-kill shelters with capacity, should we overflow.

15

We scrutinized adoption applicants as if they were adopting a child. We visited their homes. We talked with their neighbors. We performed background checks. We followed up with visits to ensure the safety and well-being of our adopted pets. We refused anyone unfit.

I certainly hadn't entered veterinary school considering money as a catalyst to my actions. I enrolled purely out of my love and respect for animal welfare. Once a full-fledged doctor, the vast amount of purebred dogs that would come in for treatments for illnesses triggered by their unfortunate births to mothers in puppy mills sickened me. Unknowing parents would purchase their adorable puppies from puppy mill supporting pet stores. These puppy mills over-bred dogs in unhealthy, overcrowded kennels. This often resulted in purebred dogs suffering from diseases often too expensive to treat. So, talk of the needle would erupt, and I would cry myself to sleep and curse the day when I decided to become a veterinarian.

After my parents' early deaths, I cashed in my inheritance and bought the town's only animal shelter, a decrepit institution where dogs usually went to die alone.

I'd risk my own life for them, as would my trusty assistants and handlers.

~ ~

An angry storm churned up the Atlantic and headed straight for us. I piled five cases of water bottles onto my cart and steamrolled down the aisles of BJ's. I loaded up on canned kidney beans, chicken noodle soup, and canned peaches. I zoomed down the candy aisle. To weather this storm, we'd at least need some Charleston Chews and Snickers. A few moments later, food staples in hand and enough water to irrigate a small drought-ridden farm, I headed towards the empty registers.

Millie smiled at my endless parade of canned fruit and vegetables. "You're crazy for staying."

16

I heaved the cases of water bottles onto the sliding shelf. "I won't leave them. You know that. Besides, when have you ever known me to back down from a threat like this, huh? I weathered Hurricane Harriet a couple of years ago, remember?"

"The weatherman didn't forecast that one to wipe out the town." She peered up at me, her eyes furrowed towards the bridge of her nose. "You should rent a box truck, pile all of those dogs, cats, and whatever other animals you've got there at the shelter, and get the hell out of town. You still have time."

"If only that option existed." I flipped through my wallet and handed her my credit card.

"You're going to be all alone."

"Trevor, Natalie, and Melanie are hanging back with me."

"You guys are all crazy, then. When they say mandatory evacuation, I listen."

"Well, none of us at the shelter takes orders easily. So, we'll just have to take our chances."

Millie scanned my items and within a few minutes gripped the sales slip with two arthritic fingers, and I signed it. "Please take care, okay?" Her wrinkles dug deep into her forehead and the corners of her eyes.

I patted her hand. "I promise I won't do anything crazy like peek outside for a view." I smiled and pushed off, steadying my galloping heart for a crazy few days ahead. I sure hoped my roof wouldn't collapse.

God help us.

~ ~

I drove down Elmwood Drive towards the shelter. Cape Cod-style houses lined both sides of the two-lane road, all of them boarded up and braced for the storm. Weathermen forecasted this one to hit us straight on as a category three or four. The

17

flooding would be the real issue for many of these homes in the low-lying valley of Elkwood. Thankfully, the shelter sat on a hill.

I arrived back at the shelter and Natalie, Trevor, and Melanie had dismantled the front showcase of literature, removing the pamphlets with loving, precious faces of dogs and cats looking for good homes.

"I've got a ton of supplies in my truck," I said to them. They dropped everything from their arms and rushed to my aid. We piled pounds and pounds of kibble and treats in the front waiting area. "If things get bad enough, these can serve as sandbags."

No one laughed.

"I'm kidding," I said.

"We're going to need a lot of sage to get through this storm," Melanie, my best friend and reiki master, said. "When things aren't so pressing, I'm going to help you come up with a plan B for these types of events." She dropped a case of water on the counter and looked up at me with panic in her eyes. Melanie, the queen of bliss and tranquility, never panicked. That's what I loved most about her. She leveled my moods with her reiki, candles, sage, and balanced emotions.

I fiddled with the Snickers and canned peaches, lining them up on the front desk like a well-executed team of soldiers preparing for battle. "You're more than welcome to leave before the storm hits. No one is forcing you to be here."

She balanced her hands on her hips and inhaled, then released it with ease, never taking her kind eyes off of me. "I'm not going anywhere."

"Thank you," I said, rounding the front desk. "How about if we walk the dogs before we can't anymore?" I walked past my dear friend, the same friend who swore she'd only succumb to yelling and freaking out if I ever dangled her out of ten-story building. Miss Master of Healing and everything yin and yang didn't fall

18

under the pressures that would crush the average person. But even though she relaxed into her breaths and draped her hands on her waist as if ready to lunge into a peaceful walk on the beach, I sensed her fear. "I'll take Trooper, Tucker, and Snowball," I said to Trevor and Natalie as I rushed past them towards the kennels. They trailed behind me, keeping up with my pace. Melanie stayed in the front.

"Olivia, I think we might need to board up the front windows," Trevor said. "My dad called me and said the storm had slammed through his bay window. The storm is only a category two for them."

"No need to panic," I said to him.

"Right," he said. His face turned white and he looked about ready to throw up.

Trevor, eager with a boyish, gingery grin, always looked out for me. Once he even passed up a spring break trip to Cozumel because three of the volunteers stopped coming suddenly. He loved the dogs and couldn't bear to think of them cooped up without proper exercise and socialization. So, he canceled his trip and waited to go until I had secured and trained more volunteers. He actually made out in that deal, because on that very trip he met his boyfriend, Michael. They had signed up for the same booze cruise and hit it off so instantly that Michael moved up from Florida the very next month.

"Let's try to get in all the walks first, and then we'll secure the windows."

"Right, boss," he said. "I'll take the big guy here." He referred to Max, our resident Rottweiler who would rather cuddle up to one of us than eat. Anyone who wanted a hundred-pound laptop would be thrilled to be his companion. Unfortunately, no one had come through the shelter seeking such love in the two months that Max had been abandoned at the shelter's front door. Typical cowardly drop-off method. Of course Natalie often argued that this method trumped ditching the poor, defenseless animals on the side of the interstate. Natalie, my exuberant and

19

upbeat assistant, always pointed out the bright side of any dirty coin. She could make trash look good by citing the value in composting. She could bring out the beauty in a dishrag by remarking on the brainpower it required to build a machine brilliant enough to manufacture it. Natalie, different in a theatrical way, could drive a person crazy after a small fraction of time. Her voice climbed just as high as any gifted soprano when greeting visitors to the shelter or perking up a depressed pet. Her bouncy spirit could get under my skin, but she livened up the shelter to a level more akin to a newborn nursery than to the place families came to dump off their pets.

"Olivia," Natalie said. "I don't think Snowball is going to make it out for a walk today." She looped a leash around her shoulders and headed over to Snowball's kennel. "She's been throwing up all morning and is looking like she lost her best friend."

"She didn't eat today," Trevor added. "She wouldn't even look at the treats, either."

Snowball had arrived at the shelter in a wire crate a few days ago. Someone had dropped her off outside the door with a note saying she had grown too large. Indicated by her matted white fur, earfuls of mites, and half-inch too long nails, the poor girl had been neglected for far too long. I named her Snowball because I couldn't bear to call her by the ill-conceived name referenced on the note. What sane person would ever imagine that a purebred Siberian husky would ever remain small enough to be called Tiny?

"Maybe the pig's ear I fed her isn't agreeing with her," Natalie said.

"You brought in pig's ears again?" I asked.

"They love them." Natalie's voice morphed into its unnatural, animated tone.

I stopped in front of Snowball's kennel, and she didn't jump to her feet to greet me. Instead, her eyes crawled up to meet mine, and then lowered again. Tears stained the fur beneath her eyes a dark brown. The three of us stood in silence watching her. "Maybe she senses the storm," Trevor said.

I'd seen too many cases like Snowball's in my time working at Shubert's Animal Hospital to understand that the poor little girl sensed little at the moment. "We need to get her into the isolation kennel."

Natalie looked about ready to burst into tears. Trevor sighed, wiping his strained eyes with the back of his hands. "I'll get her kennel ready," Natalie said before heading off to the lonely kennel reserved for those doggies with a possible communicable disease. No doubt, Natalie would be placing the flowery blanket on top of the sick bed for her.

"What do you think it is?" Trevor asked.

"Parvo." I spun around to get my medical bag. "I'll need to start an IV on her and pump her with some antibiotics, vitamins, sugar, and potassium. Can you start the walks while I get her settled?"

He nodded and headed back to Max's kennel.

~ ~

The lights zapped off. Natalie screamed and Trevor jumped off the stool.

"The worst hasn't even begun and you're already falling apart?" I turned on the flashlight. Fright hung on their faces.

The wind whipped and howled, pitching higher than the dogs' whimpers and howls. I reached out for Melanie's hand and squeezed it. She squeezed mine back and steadied her trembling body against mine. "You're not supposed to panic," I said to her.

21

"I'm a human being." She wrapped a sheath of her salt and pepper hair in front of her eyes. "I'm allowed to panic."

I shuddered. I should've planned this better. I should've rented a box truck like Millie said and trekked out of this vulnerable matchstick building and into a stronger shelter. Melanie never caved. Not even the time when a couple of ski-masked thugs mugged us one night. She didn't even blink when she surrendered her purse to the bulkier of the two and told them to have a nice life. When I rear-ended a police car one snowy night, instead of mirroring my panic, she sat submerged in a sea of tranquility, patting my hand.

This night, though, sitting in the dark recesses of the pharmacy room, huddled up against the unforgiving cabinets, she moaned with every creak as if the world threatened to cave in on all of us.

I couldn't have her break down.

"You think it's going to hold up?" she asked with a touch of timidity clinging to her voice.

"The roof?" I asked

"The building."

I lost my breath on that one.

Chapter Three

Chloe

Since leaving Elkwood thirteen years ago, I'd learned some things. One, never trust my gut instincts. Two, consequences sucked. Three, perfect moments didn't exist. Before I learned these things, my life had spiraled out of control. I was eighteen-years-old, pregnant, and alone.

The one and only time I ever considered tossing my sorry self over the St. Mary's River bridge was right after I walked out of the Sisterhood Clinic. I sunk into misery, stepping out of their double glass doors and into the cloudy, fall day, ambivalent over the news. How could an eighteen-year-old have a baby and survive in the world? I had barely crossed the stage of my high school auditorium, had barely placed the tassel from left to right, had barely a chance to embrace the new freedom of the open road to a hopeful, fruitful future before my boobs had started aching and morning sickness took a front row seat to life.

The baby's father stammered, "I'm not ready to be a dad. I'm going to college. I've got plans for my life. I don't want a kid."

"Well, what am I supposed to do? Get an abortion?"

"Well, yeah. You're eighteen. That's what I say you do."

I walked away numb, harboring our secret, assuring him I wouldn't bother him again with this.

Thankfully, my Aunt Marie, my only blood relative still sane and competent, answered my cry for help. My age number still ended in the word teen, my belly swelled, the girl I loved hated me, and my maturity didn't add up to absorb any of this mess. Aunt Marie, who lived only thirty minutes from town, drove up to get me on a rainy, freezing Saturday morning. I had returned Olivia's winter jacket to her already, and so, I huddled under four sweatshirts waiting for my aunt to arrive at the bench on Mulberry Avenue. She pulled up honking her Buick LeSabre's horn, waving as if hyped up on too many candy bars and skidding her tires into the curb. I climbed into her car, frozen and scared, foaming over in tears from the mess I'd stirred into my already screwed up life. As she hugged her steering wheel with crochet-mittened hands and drove down Mulberry Street, past the small chapel that Olivia and I would go into from time to time, no option compared. I had to ditch my mess and leave town.

I'd leave for a while, have the baby, and when I could secure an adoption, I'd return and piece my life back together again. My gut instinct cheered me towards this brilliant plan that surely would not result in consequences, and would land me back in the pocket of perfect moments.

My aunt set me up in her spare bedroom. I entered the cheerful room, blossoming with a canopy bed complete with a pink and white flower bedspread, and adorned with fancy round and oblong pillows. A gray cat with eyes as black as coal spread across the bed like a king. His name was Oony Gato, and according to my aunt, he coveted the supreme role as keeper of the house. She and I just borrowed some of his space.

My aunt and I shared Earl Grey tea and biscuits by the fire in her den that first afternoon. Amidst the crackling of wood and the smell of a cold winter's night, she asked about my mother, first. I reported what I could recall. Guards, locks, nauseating green metal doors scrambled in my memory. Compassion dripped off the cheeks of mental health staff ushering me in to the community area where people talked out loud to no one, yelling and screaming at them as if being attacked, chastised. It pained me too much to drum up the details of walking up to a lady knotting her stringy black hair and realizing that lady was my mom. I didn't want to remember the stale smell of cafeteria food, or the squeak of the orange cushion as I sat on the couch next to her. I didn't want to remember the hollow fright in her eyes as I called her mom and reached out for her hand. I didn't want to remember the kicking, crying, screaming as the guard shuffled her back to the safety of her room, away from me.

Instead I told Aunt Marie my mother thrived in her new home, a place that served her scrumptious cucumber and avocado sandwiches for lunch, punch in the afternoon under a maple tree, and long walks at dinner to ease her into the sweet lullaby of a long night's sleep. I added how she enjoyed watching reruns of *Happy Days* on the flat screen TV in the pretty community area that had tables filled with daisies that smiled at us as we sat hand-in-hand laughing as Fonzie stuck his two thumbs up in the air at the end of a good scene before a commercial break. My aunt smiled and patted my hand, happy to hear the nice report. I knew Aunt Marie didn't buy an ounce of that story.

Then, she asked about my stepfather. I lied and told her he encouraged me to leave town to deal with the baby situation. I couldn't bear to go into detail about how he tried to kill Josh with a baseball bat that night we returned the ring. I certainly didn't want to let on that I spent two years sneaking into my girlfriend's

25

bedroom for a safe place to sleep. She would've been hurt that I hadn't turned to her first.

I didn't want to spend my high school years with my aunt a whole thirty minutes away. I wanted Olivia.

So, coming as no surprise, sitting there in her living room drinking tea like an old lady, I sunk into a mellow funk. "I'm not cut out to be a mother," I said to her.

"Of course you're not, sweetheart. That's why we'll do the right thing and find the right parents for your baby."

I didn't want to be pregnant. I didn't want to push out a baby. I didn't want to live for the next seven months with a constant reminder of all that I'd just destroyed. What an idiot I had been, all pumped-up and emotional, falling into that stupid guy's arms and allowing him a quick, sufficient release. A clumsy act performed and swept away in a riptide of a cruel miracle.

I placed my hand on my belly and imagined cells bursting into life, forming organs and fingers and toes, a face, eyes, ears, and a cute little nose. "You'll help me?" I asked my aunt.

She looked up from her teacup with the kind of gentle smile I had prayed to see since my mother first went crazy. "I'll keep you safe." She patted my knee. "Now, drink your tea before it gets cold and yucky."

Aunt Marie never judged me, even when I told her the truth finally that night about my being in love with Olivia, and my falling victim to happenstance. She simply urged me take good care of my nutrition and fed me smoothies with blueberries, bananas, wheat grass, and fennel seeds. I hated it, and pinched my nose every time just to get it past my lips.

I grew enormous fairly quickly. Around the middle of my second trimester, I stopped digging my friends back in town for info on Olivia. Dread crawled up my back whenever I'd hear about how they'd seen her out sharing coffee with new college friends or how she'd just won a community award for her work with shelter animals. She grabbed onto life and ran with it, without me.

I couldn't call her. She despised me. I couldn't explain the real reason I had disappeared. I'd have to lie more. I wouldn't pile on more lies. I would wait.

I figured, after I placed my baby in the loving arms of adoring adoptive parents I could ease back into her life with love as my tool. I'd sweep the guilt away and eventually get past the lies I dealt her. Of course, at holidays I could just picture circumventing the truth, hiding my secret under cinnamon, Christmas carols, and Yuletide gifts, smiling for the sake of covering up the biggest lie I'd ever tell.

About the close of my second trimester, I decided to focus on having this baby and finding the perfect parents. We met with some beautiful people with tragic stories of how they couldn't have children because of a childhood disease or injury, and we met some who already had children and wanted to adopt a baby in need.

My baby was a baby in need. This phrase ran through my head night after night. My choice would change a couple's life and place them on a trajectory far different than the one they traveled at that point. My baby harnessed that power and she hadn't even been born, yet. Imagine the possibilities when she actually learned to breathe the air, focus her eyes, wriggle her toes? Pride shot through me, hitching a ride on my nerves and splashing me with all sorts of mommy jubilee. Whenever this happened, I'd further punish myself with countless hours in a baby boutique, perusing over baby bottles, pastel diaper bags, soft blankets decorated with sheep and ducks, and baby carriages that looked comfortable enough to sleep in myself. I'd leave gooey and confused.

Aunt Marie came to every counseling meeting with me and after each session, she'd talk me through my fears and apprehensions of the whole adoption process, helping me to decide if I wanted an open or closed adoption. She eventually helped me select a nice couple of Hispanic descent to be the adoptive parents. We talked endlessly over milkshakes about what life would be like for my baby growing up in a house with two capable parents, one a lawyer, one a doctor. They planned to hire a nanny and teach the baby Spanish and Mandarin before the age of five when the ability to learn new languages started to fall off, as they explained to me in hushed, soothing voices. The child would go to the same private school they both attended, where they both met. He or she—the sex didn't matter, they said—would attend summer enrichment camps and participate in school music and sports, whichever the child preferred. I imagined my baby growing into a beautiful, bright, well-respected young adult, surrounded by grand pianos, recitals, and fine people who could carry on conversations with others around the globe, accentuating dialects with an expert tongue. Who knew, maybe my baby would grow up to be president of the United States, or a world class tennis star, or the creator of the next big technological device capable of changing the world as we all knew it. Maybe, just maybe, my baby would invent a transportation device that would allow us to beam ourselves from China to The Keys faster than we could blink.

Aside from all of these wonderful benefits my baby would acquire, I couldn't help but worry if the child would be loved enough. Would she sit and worry about how others viewed her? Would she stumble over insecurities of not being loved enough because her mommy shipped her off to strangers? Would she recognize me one day, twenty years or so into the future, when we reunited with the help of a good lawyer? Would she hate me for sending her off into the arms of people who wanted a prize baby they could show off to their rich friends?

When that sunny Monday morning of my baby's birthday arrived and I stood in a puddle of my fluids, my aunt shuffled me to the car. She drove like a mad woman, weaving around buses, cars, pedestrians to get me to the hospital. She stood by my side, covering my hand with hers, blanketing my forehead in wet towels, urging me to push and breathe. Five hours later, when I pushed my baby out into the world into the arms of a waiting doctor, I cried. I already missed her.

I feared for her life without me.

I wailed when the doctor handed her to me all slick and innocent. I kissed her slippery face and smoothed her dark hair, loving her before the nagging moment when the joy of this precious baby would be sucked from my life forever. My aunt wept along with me, stroking my hair and cradling me as I stared into those unfocused eyes and fell in love with my baby girl. Aunt Marie and I cradled her tiny fingers. She wriggled. Our souls connected.

I prayed that God would help ease the blow for the couple waiting on their new baby because no way in hell was I handing her over to anyone.

My life corkscrewed out in front of me, going off in a tangent far removed from the life I envisioned I'd be living with Olivia one day. I kept telling myself as the weeks turned into months and then finally into a year when my daughter, Ayla, blew out her first birthday candle, that one day I'd get back to her and confess the whole messed up story. I'd tell her everything because time healed all wounds, even ones created out of dark secrets.

I'd introduce my baby to her father and he'd rescind on his idea that aborting her would've been the best choice for us. He would take one look at his beautiful girl and hug her and cry for time wasted. He'd blame me and forget he ever told me to abort her. He'd fault me for keeping such a gift from him that whole time.

I'd take the blow for Ayla.

As the years passed, I could only assume that Olivia probably hated me for not attempting to contact her. I prayed that she didn't view me as a spoiled brat starring in off-Broadway plays and allowing money and fame to consume my every waking moment. I hoped that she didn't envision my life to be one filled with caviar, fine champagne, a dazzling beauty nestled into the crook of my arm, attending one lavish party after another, ending the day spread eagle in a pile of my money, laughing, giddy with selfish pride over my artistic luck.

How surprised she'd be to see me changing shitty diapers and playing with My Little Pony.

My sacrifice.

When Facebook arrived, I signed up and waited patiently for Olivia to catch on and sign up, too. When she did, I pored over her profile day after day, studying pictures of her working with a variety of dogs, cats, horses, even turtles. Her bio stated she attended college and was studying to become a vet. One day, she'd like to open a shelter, "one that didn't kill animals." I could picture her pounding the keys on that note.

Ayla loved animals, too. She and I rescued several cats from our local shelter, giving Oony Gato even more of an air of authority. Ayla would giggle at them, pointing, screaming, and blowing bubbles as they walked past her.

When Ayla turned five, she managed to somehow get all the cats to sleep together in her bed. They purred to her, the cat whisperer. One night, when I tucked her into bed, she grabbed Marmalade, an orange Tabby cat, and placed her on her back, paws up in the air as if dangling. Over her loud purring, Ayla asked me the question I'd dreaded since she first said "Da Da." "How come I don't have a daddy?"

How do you tell a five-year-old that she doesn't have a daddy because her mommy failed to face the truth? "Some kids just don't. You have a favorite Auntie Marie instead."

She rolled over with Marmalade and giggled. That answer fit just fine with her.

"Ayla asked about her daddy last night," I said to my aunt the next afternoon while we sat in the backyard watching Ayla take Oony Gato on a walk around the fence. "I'm not sure how much longer she'll accept my pathetic answers."

"The questions will only get harder."

I pictured a wiser, older Ayla confronting me, her terrible mother, for not blessing her with the freedom to meet her father and to decide for herself whether she wanted this man in her life or not.

Ayla galloped alongside Oony, giggling at the grass that tickled her calves.

~ ~

I looked up Ayla's father on Facebook. His arm caressed the shoulder of a pretty brunette with a cropped, smart hairstyle. She smiled wide at the camera and swaddled a baby in her arms. I scanned his albums, and in most every picture, he carried his baby, smiling, the super dad of the year.

I flared.

Rage tore through me like a mad storm, kicking up all sorts of dusty anger. That could've been Ayla if he had owned up. He could've shielded the finger pointing, the upsets, by stepping up to the table and explaining that the sex meant nothing more than a release. Ayla could've grown up with a father who adored her as much as he adored his new baby.

My maternal instinct kicked into high gear. So much time had passed since I'd trudged away from Olivia with my dark secrets. My collection of time supported me, comforted me, and rivaled my inhibitions. Perhaps if she could accept the truth of what really happened, all of our lives would reshape to something more joyful.

I asked my aunt to watch Ayla and within minutes, I drove down the interstate en route to Elkwood in my beat-up Corolla with its muffler hanging on by a rope.

31

I braved my fear, running towards it and drove straight to Olivia's parents' house.

I pulled up in front of their white colonial with the pretty green shutters. A red pickup truck sat in the driveway. A Ford. Olivia's favorite color and model. I hopped out of my car and charged up the front walk before I could lose my nerve.

The time had arrived to face the facts. My daughter's future rested on my shedding the secrets and jumping into the frigid waters of truth. Perhaps Olivia would listen with an open heart, cushioned by the years, and convince me to introduce Ayla to her father. She'd wrap her protective arms around me and tell me she understood that I was young, impressionable, and vulnerable. She'd ask me all about the past five years and sink into every detail with focus, wanting to hear everything from her birth to her first steps, to her first word, to her love of animals. We'd enjoy tea parties and lazy days out in the park flinging Frisbees and barbequing burgers. She and I would drink wine under the umbrella of a cherry blossom tree while Ayla walked Oony Gato in circles.

I'd start with a visit and work up to the truth.

I braved a knock on her front door. A lady wearing curlers and a flannel nightgown answered. Cinnamon wafted from the foyer. A small Dachshund stood beside her barking and wagging his tail. He sported a leather collar with spikes. "I'm not interested in what you're selling, sweetie."

I scanned the foyer that used to house a bookshelf filled with classic, leather-bound novels. Nothing but an empty hall faced me now. "Does Olivia still live here?"

She lowered her shoulders and placed her hand on my wrist. "I'm afraid not. I bought the place a month ago."

"They sold the house?"

32

She cocked her head. "You don't know what happened, do you?"

My heart pounded, afraid to hear bad news. I shook my head.

"Olivia's parents died a few months ago. They were traveling up to New Hampshire for a family reunion, and they hit a moose head on. Olivia survived the crash with a broken finger. But, her parents didn't have a chance."

Shock vacuumed the air from my lungs. This woman who answered Olivia's door, the same door I had snuck in and out of for years, now owned the front door, the wooden staircase with the green paisley runner that I'd climbed, the bathroom I'd brushed my teeth in, and the bedroom that commemorated my early days as a liberated teenager in the arms of the one girl I loved.

The despair whipped through me, suffocating me, strangling me. I cried, and this stranger gathered me into her arms and let me sob.

After several gut wrenching minutes, the lady said to me, "She works part time at the Pet World right outside of town on route one if you want to see her. I'm sure she could use a friend."

"Thanks." I pulled away from her arms. "Maybe I'll stop by and see her one of these days."

"I know she's working now because Tuesday is always the day I bring Pepper in to get his nails trimmed. I only trust Olivia. Everyone else is too quick and stone-faced."

"I'll drop by one of these days."

"Give me your number in case you don't see her there. I'll give her the message that you stopped by."

"Sure. Why not?" I jotted down my number, then thanked the lady and drove off, heading back to where I belonged, back to my aunt's and out of the way of the Clarks' wrecked lives. If Olivia wanted to talk, I'd leave it up to her.

33

I no longer trusted my gut instinct. Consequences littered my life. And so much for perfect moments.

I drove south and before long saw the sign for the route one Pet World dancing ahead of me, beckoning me towards it. I could just pop in, say hi, and pay her my condolences.

Pulled towards the exit ramp like a magnet, I sped ahead towards the Pet World, figuring if I didn't stop in then, I never would.

I parked far off to the side of the building so my getaway, if it needed to be quick, would be less humiliating. A few people with dogs walked towards the building, some stopping to let their dogs soak up the attention from others, empty-handed of their own pets.

I applied some lip gloss, smoothed my hair and tightened up the string tie on my capris before stepping in front of the building. Then, I committed to my decision and braved the front door, waltzing in like I really belonged on Olivia's turf.

Shelves displaying dog biscuits in every brand imaginable lined the main aisle. Birds chirped to the left. Bright blue signs highlighting specials hung from the ceiling. Puppies, roped off in the center of the store, wagged their happy tails at their puppy class teacher. Puppies of all different sizes and breeds chased balls and ignored their masters' commands. The store buzzed with life and happy times.

I rounded the aquariums, and then I spotted her, looking every bit as confident, as lean, as pristine as she did years ago. An older man stole her attention, talking to her over by the dog food aisle.

I fell numb.

She laughed at something the man said. Her blonde ponytail still hung to the middle of her back, smooth and shiny and sun-kissed. She wore a white t-shirt with a bright blue vest and a pair of well-fitted blue jeans that hugged her slender athletic

34

frame just as I remembered. Her face lit up as the man shook her hand and walked off with a bag of kibble.

She smiled as she watched him walk away, and then she saw me. Her smile vanished. I huddled up by the fish tanks, clinging to my pocketbook when she locked her baby blue eyes on me, cocking her head slightly as if dazed from a hook punch.

I gathered up my nerve and approached her with a reserved wave powered by an out-of-control nervous system. My knees turned to noodles and my throat dried up. "Hi," I said, trying out a small smile.

She stared at me, pursed her lips together and blinked for an eternity. She opened her mouth to speak, and sealed her lips up tight again, shaking her head.

"I'm sorry. I shouldn't have just barged in here like this."

She sighed. Her chest rose and fell. She stared at a stuffed gorilla toy instead of me, digging her fingers into her biceps.

"Hey," I tugged at her sleeve.

She glanced down at my clutched fingers, then finally scrolled up to face me, guarded. "This is a surprise."

I caught my breath and exhaled in a shaky stream. "I stopped by your house a few minutes ago."

She swallowed and blinked away.

I moved in closer and caressed her arm. "I'm so sorry."

She nodded, leaning in to the arm I embraced. "Thanks."

I rubbed her arm. "Are you okay?"

Her chin quivered. She pulled in her bottom lip, squaring off against the pleasantries. "Yeah," she whispered, closing in on herself. Her body trembled and tears sputtered down her cheeks. She scoffed at them, wiping them away with the back of her hand. "Sorry, I don't mean to—"

I pulled her into my arms and hugged her close. Her heart pounded through her t-shirt, her breathing chopped. I led her down the aisle, away from the shoppers and the chaos of the puppies in training, massaging her back, caressing her ponytail. "I'm so sorry, babe."

She buried her face in my shoulder and wept. "It was the hardest thing I've ever had to deal with," she mumbled.

"I'm sure it was," I whispered into her ear.

We wept together for several minutes alongside bones and rawhides.

She pulled out of my embrace, hugging herself again, blinking away her tears. "I needed that." Her lips formed a tiny smile. My eyes landed on the corner of her upper lip, in the same spot I used to love kissing.

"It's good to see you, Olivia." I traced my finger down her bent arm. "It really is."

She considered my comment with a squint to her eye. "I thought if I ever saw you again I would hate you."

I circled her elbow with a lazy touch, hopeful that she didn't. "And?"

"I guess we were just really young." She bobbed her head, taking me in. "I did hate you for a long time. You actually fueled me to do something in life I wouldn't have done."

"Like?"

She inhaled, and her chest rose again. "Skydive, snorkel, run a marathon, oh and enroll in vet school."

"Puts my life to shame." I brushed away some hair from her cheek, lingering along her hairline.

"Good." She laughed.

"Good?"

She punched my side and tickled it. "Yes, good."

I wrestled out of the tickle, grabbing a hold of her hands. She gazed at me long and hard, a tease played in her eyes.

I latched onto this and reeled in. "Grab some coffee with me."

She stretched her gaze up to the clock, then back at me. "This is seriously the last thing I ever thought I'd be doing." She paused, pulled in her lower lip. "But, sure, I'd love to."

I leaned in and kissed her soft cheek. I couldn't help myself. "Great."

"I'll meet you out front in five minutes." She headed away from me towards the back of the store, looking back once and smiling.

I steadied my racing heart long enough to agree. "Perfect."

Several long minutes later, she walked out of the front door and towards me, carrying herself tall and strong. "I live right around the corner if you just want to grab a cup there? I have your favorite, chocolate hazelnut."

"Sounds good." I followed her, admiring the bounce in step.

"I'll drive," she said.

Within ten minutes, we sat on her couch nurturing a couple of oversized mugs and sipping chocolate hazelnut coffee, smiling and talking about the town as if we just picked right up from where we had left off years prior. When she spoke, I circled her face, taking her all in, the strength of her words, the magnetic quality of her energy, the sexy rasp to her voice. I forgot all about the secrets and just enjoyed the moment.

I loved being near her again. She laughed and her face radiated a beauty that had refined itself over the years. Untarnished by the bad circumstances of her past few months, she relaxed back against her couch and broke into my favorite lazy afternoon smile where her eyes closed slightly, her cheeks lounged against her pretty face, and her skin ripened to a healthy pink glow.

"You've gotten even more beautiful," I said, mirroring her position and lounging back against the couch, too.

She rubbed her lips against each other. "Thank you." She placed a lone finger to my lips and traced them. I closed my eyes sealing in her feathery touch. When I reopened them, she gazed at me with the same bedroom eyes that I had fallen in love with and could not erase.

"Those eyes," I said, running my fingers down the side of her face now. Her skin, smooth and soft, intoxicated me.

We inched closer, me waiting for her to strike first. She cradled my lips with her finger still, bringing in to light everything pure, blissful, and freeing. Our breaths danced, led by tantric heartbeats, unbridled passion, and a hungry desire to connect to that place of nirvana where only a hot hunger mattered.

She crawled up to me, cradled my face, and swept me away to a place I hadn't been to in years and frankly, never expected to be to again. Her lips pressed against mine, bathing me in sweet pleasure. She caressed my cheek, my neck, my shoulders with her soft tongue, running her fingers through my hair and then staring deeply into my eyes. A more mature, wiser Olivia set the course, traveling around my skin like a pioneer in search of treasure. In the rays of sunshine washing over us, we escaped into each other's arms, feeding our bodies with a kind of nourishment that breathed pure energy, pure bliss through our naked, pulsing bodies. Our skin touched, our bodies entwined, as we caved into each other's needs, releasing pleasure in wide, wonderful ripples that curled our toes, and bathed us in warm, delicious juices.

Wrapped up in each other's arms, we inhaled as one. I clung to her, not wanting to let this moment of innocence be trampled on by the truths that scratched at my back, reminding me of the façade behind the layer of purity. I tucked into the comfort of the façade anyway.

We hugged each other afterwards. Tears spilled down my face, and she wiped them with her healing touch. By the time the sun had circled up and around her roof and casted shadows on the wall nearest her clock, she moaned and climbed up and out of my arms.

"I'm really late for work," she said, standing to stretch, exposing her breasts, full and firm, nipples erect and every bit delicious looking as they tasted.

I stood and kissed her again, circling her nipple with the tip of my finger. She writhed under my touch, tilting her head back, exposing her neck. I traveled along her collarbone, up towards her jawline, stopping to graze along her upper lip. "You're already late. Just cancel the rest of the day."

She moaned, tickling my lips. "Have you forgotten who I am?"

"True," I pulled away, reluctant in lowering my hands.

A few minutes later, when she dropped me off at my car, she lingered on. "So?"

"So." Dread crawled up my spine, tapping me, reminding me of the secret that loomed, the one I had yet to dismantle.

"I'm not really sure what any of this means just yet."

"Yeah, me either." I cupped my hand over hers.

"I'm pretty busy with veterinary school and I'm sure you've got to get back to New York," she said, saddling me to her passenger seat with her smoky blue eyes. "How is New York?"

"Oh, you know, it's New York," I said, clunking out a vibe that sounded too bold for her small interior. A string of webs formed and spun itself around us, cocooning me to the lie I came here to end.

"Tell me about it." She squeezed my hand.

I fidgeted, uncomfortable with this buttery layering of lies piling up in the back of my throat. "New York isn't important."

"Oh come on. I want to hear about it," she said with a power in her voice I'd never heard before. "Tell me about some adventures."

"Adventures," I said, feeding my hot, stifled air to the car. "Let's see. I um, learned to sail." I really had learned.

"What else?" She searched me for more. "What about something New York-related? Did you ever, oh, I don't know…" she reached, that much I could tell, "…did you ever sneak into the front row at a Knicks game to get an autograph? Or sing on a crowded subway?"

I clenched my jaw. "No. None of the above."

"Ever charter a plane and head to Paris for lunch?"

I darted my eyes up to the sunny sky. "On what universe do you think I live?"

She inched closer. "Ever take a girl to sail down the Hudson with you?"

I gripped the clouds, hanging on for dear life, pulling in my lower lip and biting down on it. "Nope, can't say I did that, either."

"Ever have sex with a girl on the roof of a skyscraper?"

I swallowed hard and looked down at my legs. "There have been other girls, Olivia. I can't lie."

"So, yes to the skyscraper?"

I landed back on her and sighed, perhaps a little too aggressively. "I've lived a boring life since leaving here."

40

"So, if you didn't leave for excitement, then why did you?" Grit played on the edge of her words.

"Not now," I said, placing my finger to her lips. Another time. I wanted to drift home in a reverie, and fall asleep as the good girl for once.

"Was it worth it?"

I shook my head, shrugging off her line of questioning. "That's a complicated question."

"I see," she said. She pulled her hand back and gripped the steering wheel. "Would you do it all over again? Pack up and move to the big city in search of more fun, more adventure?"

I clung to my legs. "Come on, Olivia."

She pressed on, the pull of curiosity too great to fend off now. "I want to know about your life. I want to understand who you've become. I want to know how that grand city took you in and molded you into who you are today. What did you learn? Who did you meet? Tell me." Her knuckles whitened around the steering wheel, as if pleading with me to uncover the Chloe who used to need her to protect and guide. "Come on. Tell me. Does the city really smell like hotdogs and honey-roasted peanuts? Do people really sleep on park benches? Do people smile at each other on the street?"

I fiddled with my capris, realizing the moment to come clean and tell her the truth dropped in my lap and waited for me to act. "I don't know."

"How can you not know?"

Anguish crawled up the back of my throat. My secret trapped me. "It's just not my style."

"Then, why are you still there?"

"I don't want to talk about me right now."

41

"I really want to know." She touched my bare arm and I shook it off. I slipped away from her good graces like a ball descending a hill, losing my footing, and tumbling as I tried to catch myself before catapulting off a cliff.

"I packed a few bags, dated a few women, got drunk a few dozen times, danced naked in my apartment once or twice and spent my money on frivolous clothes and dinners. Not much more than that." *Stop! I yelled at myself. Stop the lies.*

I searched the parking lot for refuge from her questions.

Olivia sighed and sat up, paused, stared at my lips, then landed back on my eyes as if searching for a confession of murder, thievery, or something more than dancing naked in my New York City apartment. "I know you're hiding something." Her voice softened. "You don't have to."

I stared out of the window at the bright day. I wrestled with my lips to open and speak some honest sense. The safety ball rolled out of my reach, charging for a cliff to toss itself off so it could never be caught. I stopped, surveyed for a second, and let the ball roll without me.

Once I confessed to everything, we could deal with it all like two mature women who loved each other.

She smiled softly, waiting for me to unload. Just as I did years ago, I fell into her protective embrace and stepped up to the moment. "I've got so much to tell you."

"Tell me." She stared at me, waiting, hanging on my truth.

In a low crawl I said to her, "I've never even been to New York."

She looked down at my hand like I'd just branded her with it. "Um. Okay."

"I moved to my aunt's house thirty minutes away."

Her jaw hung open. "Wow. Okay." She backed up against her seat, her eyes still bearing down on my hand. "So, I'm guessing maybe there was someone else?"

I flushed. My cheeks burned under the pressure of her focused eyes on my hand. I drew it back, brushed some runaway hairs from my face and attempted to compose an honest answer. "I did leave because of someone else, yes."

She dropped her eyes to her lap. "I knew it."

"It's not what you think, though." I placed my hand on her elbow.

She shrugged it off. "It seldom is, isn't it?" She smirked through gritted teeth, still staring at her white knuckles. "I know I shouldn't be bothered after all these years, but I am. I feel like a fool."

Four words sat on the top of my tongue waiting for me to brave up and release them. I did everything to launch them, licked my lips, curled up my tongue, cleared my throat, even blew out whiffs of air. They toyed with me like an unruly child, punishing me with a prickly assault until finally I slapped my thighs and cried out, "I have a daughter."

Silence swarmed between us, thick as mud, powerful as quicksand. I couldn't look at her directly, so I stretched my eyes as far as they would move left and watched her chin quiver, her lips press into each other, tracks of tears roll down her face and onto her white strained knuckles.

She nodded. "Wow. A daughter."

"She's five-years-old."

She scoffed, bringing her clenched fist up under her nose. "Who was it? Was it that acting partner?"

I bit my lower lip, not sure what to say. I settled on, "It's not important, is it? The fact is I was young and stupid."

She hugged herself tight at this point. "So, you cheated on me."

The word "cheat" pricked me, seared me, nauseated me. "It just happened. I got caught up in a moment, and I'm not proud of myself for it."

She groaned and looked about ready to punch the steering wheel with her vulnerable fists. "Why couldn't you trust me enough to tell me?"

"It was complicated and I didn't want to hurt you."

"You should go."

"I'm so sorry. I never meant to hurt you."

She turned her head to her door again and waved me away. "I don't want to hear anymore."

What more could I say? I cheated. I hurt her. I lied to her. I still hadn't told her the complete ugly truth. I saw no point to it now. Why drag her into the worst of the truth when the result wouldn't be any different than the silent slap from betrayal I justifiably received?

Fuck my gut instincts. Fuck consequences. Fuck the idea of a perfect moment.

I slid out of the car in silence.

Half an hour later, I returned home, empty and unfulfilled. I drowned my misery in several glasses of rum and coke. How could she understand that I wanted no one else when I'd gone and hacked away at the trust she'd given me?

She hated me and had every right to.

A week later, I received a call from Ayla's father. "I heard you visited Olivia."

"How did you get my number?"

"I have my ways."

"So, why do you care?" I asked.

"You told her you have a daughter."

"Yes, *we* have a daughter."

"I'm not prepared to have a daughter."

"Well, that's okay because I'm not prepared for her to have a father."

"So, you're not going to tell her?"

"No," I whispered, unable to speak more words. I wiped my cheeks with the back of my hand, clearing the path for more. "It's best if I don't tell Ayla."

"I'm not a bad person. I just have a different life now," he said.

Five days later a twenty-thousand-dollar check arrived from him. "Trying to replenish some of the costs you had to shell out for the past five years of my daughter's life. I promise this won't be the last. I'll send along monthly checks until she's eighteen."

I deposited the twenty-grand into a joint savings account with Ayla. Then, I deposited check after check, month after month. When Ayla turned six, I enrolled her in a private elementary school that catered to gifted children. An intellectual whiz, she memorized the presidents in order of years-served, back-and-forth, by the end of her first year.

With Ayla in school full-time, I worked part-time at the library sorting books and videos so I'd be there to drop her off in the morning and home in time to get her off the school bus. I grew bored and restless with this. So, I applied for odd jobs at a nursing home, a breakfast restaurant, even a casino, only to be told I needed experience. For six years, I mothered after Ayla. I served as president of Ayla's life. Didn't that count?

I needed to do more. I needed to fill my mind with something than regret over Olivia Clark. She still swam in my mind and tangled around my heart. I imagined her in vet school, meeting someone wonderful, someone trustworthy, someone lesbian.

So, one day, while moping at the counter of a café, I answered an ad from Ayla's school magazine about a seminar to get motivated. The next week I sat in the middle of a crowded auditorium listening to successful self-made millionaires talk about how I could be just like them. I spent the twenty-thousand-dollars Ayla's dad sent to me on a series of investment classes. I needed to take charge of my future and of Ayla's. This would be the best use for Ayla's money.

I enrolled in stock investing classes, real estate investing, and then learned all about tax liens and deeds. Within six months, I purchased my first mobile home trailer with seven-hundred-dollars.

One trailer turned into many.

Within two years, I rolled in money. I funded a non-profit organization dedicated to helping pregnant teens get through the tough process of pregnancy. The organization sheltered many teens who would come to the house by their third month and have a safe place to live while they nurtured their bodies and protected their unborn babies from the maladies of malnutrition, judgments, and bodily harm. Many adopted their babies out, some like me, kept them. I enjoyed investing in this organization so much so that I invested in many non-profit startups with the purpose to protect and provide for those less fortunate.

Soon, I learned how to set up charitable trusts with all the cash I earned from my mobile home parks and trailers, trusts that would outlive me if properly managed. My mom's trust tickled my core the most. I purchased an estate house, turned it into a residential home for adults with mental health disorder, and placed her in it. Gone were the institutional hallways, smells, food, and shared bedrooms with twin mattresses rats wouldn't even want to sleep on. A beautiful home replaced this. I decorated it as I would my home, with hand-crocheted blankets, tailored window treatments, luxurious sofas, daily flower deliveries, and oil paintings of cottages and beach scenes. I wanted to envelop her in love. A musician performed for them every night in the grand room around the piano. A chef prepared gourmet meals and snacks for them every day. A staff of caring health professionals catered to their needs twenty-four hours a day. I had settled that part of my life finally, the

46

day I visited her and she managed to hug me. In those few moments when her arms wrapped around me, the needless, pointless insanity that usually engulfed her had vanished, replaced by a woman with a smile and a happy heart. I wished I could've created this piece of paradise for her sooner.

I purchased a bigger house for Ayla, my aunt, and myself, taking much of the pressure off of my aunt. She retired shortly after and cared for her cats, crocheted, and watched soap operas. I'd never seen her so relaxed.

When Ayla turned eight-and-a-half, I bought her a horse farm so she could learn how to care for her horse, Trixie. Every day she'd beg me to bring her to Trixie so she could brush her. And, I did. We'd buckle up and drive along the country roads all the way to Ashland Farms where Trixie rested comfortably in a grand stable across from her best friend, Boomer, a magnificent horse with an uncanny ability to neigh as soon as we entered their courtyard, as Ayla liked to call it. Ayla and I would spend the morning grooming our horses and talking about fun things like alphabet soup, friendship bracelets, and braids. She never brought up questions about her father, about her grandparents, about her life outside the stables. That came later on, when she turned twelve and befriended the daughter of a guy I had been dating. Her friend's name was Alexia. She asked me as we licked ice cream cones at Cool Licks down on Main Street one blistering hot summer day. "Where's Ayla's dad?"

"I don't know," I said mid-lick, searching for something in the chaos around us to draw their attention. I landed on a boy kicking a soccer ball to no one. "Hey, you two should join him. Poor kid needs someone to field the ball."

Ayla eyed me like I'd just asked her to march in a marching band at prom. "Mom, just answer the question."

Her mature words knocked me back. Her years had caught up with her and now she faced me with a look one couldn't walk away from with much ease. "Shouldn't we talk about this when we're alone?"

She blinked. "No."

My boyfriend's daughter scooted closer. "Spill it. Who is he, and why has Ayla never met him?"

My ice cream dribbled down my hands, my wrist and onto my bare legs. Ayla handed me a napkin. "We can talk about it later, Mom."

~ ~

Later on that evening, my boyfriend, Scott, handed me the *Wall Street Journal* and a glass of wine. "I'm thinking grilled salmon for dinner. How about you?"

I had Olivia on my mind again thanks to his daughter's prying. Who needed food? "Sure."

"I'll fire up the grill in a few minutes." He sat down across from me, sipped at his Merlot and opened up his version of the *Wall Street Journal*. A true sweetheart, Scott cornered the market on kind, intelligent, and overall guy-next-door appeal. He'd be perfect for one of those Old Navy commercials. "The stocks rallied high today. I'm going to pull out of some of my put trades." He peeked over the corner of his paper at me. "What do you think?"

I needed a sounding board. "I haven't taken a look at the markets today." *My daughter wants her daddy*, I wanted to scream.

"Maybe I'll go long on some SWFT stock right now. The candlestick pattern on it is confirming."

How did I land in this place sitting across from a man discussing candlestick patterns and bullish markets? "Fascinating," I said, burying behind the newspaper. *What does a mother do when the father of her child doesn't want anything to do*

48

with being in her life? "You know, I'm not all that hungry." I folded the paper and placed it down on the braided tablemat. "I'll just grab a bowl of cereal later."

He peeked over the paper at me again. "That actually sounds good." He returned to his paper.

I wanted to say to him, *I need to be alone. Could you go home, please?* "I'm really tired. I might just go to bed."

He dropped the paper again. "It's six o'clock."

I rounded the table and offered him a quick peck on the top of his thick dark waves. "It's been a long one."

"I'll leave." He stood up, straightened his paper. "You get some rest."

He left without prying.

A few minutes later, I sat Ayla down on her bed, grabbed onto both of her skinny shoulders, and squared into a big fat lie for the sake of her sanity and emotional well-being for the years and decades that would follow. "Sweetheart, do you really want to know who your father is?"

She nodded, her face stoic and strong.

"The truth is," I tightened my grip, prepping for the launch, "You're a test tube baby."

She stared off to the side, contemplating my words and probably assessing how this should weigh on her. She stretched her eyes back to me; squinted and said in pure Ayla fashion, "Don't lie to me. I'm not fragile. I can handle the truth."

I had a choice. My girl's brain operated at a higher level than most fifty-year-olds I knew. I could save her from a lifetime of pain and insecurity by standing firm to my lie. She'd never wrestle with the inadequacies of abandonment carved out of being unwanted by someone in this world. On the flip side, didn't she deserve to know? Maybe one day, her father would come around and want to meet her. Then she'd know I lied to her, and she'd hate me. I couldn't have her not trust me, too. I owed her at least a partial truth. "He's a boy I used to hang out with in high school." *Oh yeah, and he saved my life so I repaid him by fucking him. So pretty much, you're the result of a traumatic situation that we'd both rather forget ever happened. I love you so much, though, sweetheart.* Me, the good mother, would spare my little girl the sad details of the moment I conceived her. "He's a very nice guy who helped me through a rough time." Some things were better left unstated. *You are not the product of a debt collection.*

"We were both so young," I continued. "He had plans to go away to college." *He chose a football, uniform and a fraternity over you.* "He wanted to help. I told him to go study at college." I wanted to spare her the unnecessary pain of being unwanted. I'd take this brunt for her sake.

"Has he ever tried to contact you about me?"

"We lost touch." Another lie. I pouted along with her, two souls caught up in a riptide of uncontrollable mishaps.

"Was he a nice person?"

I smiled at my twelve-year-old daughter. "Very nice. And, smart. And handsome."

Chapter Four

Olivia

I loved working with dogs, especially Snowball. My heart always melted at that moment when her eyes locked on mine, reaching out to me, friend-to-friend. I opened her kennel and sat beside her on her bed. Her tail wagged and she bowed her head in reverence, and then climbed onto my lap. She curled into a ball, shutting the rest of the world out. Cocooned in my breathing pattern, she relaxed into a zone where all her pain and suffering melted away. I petted her soft fur and she snuggled up closer, this time burying her nose under her paw.

I could sit for hours soothing her spirit, taking on her burden, and snuffing out its power. She snored like a baby. I liked to think that her big heart, weak from the strains of parvovirus, swelled with gratitude for this sliver of time where safety and comfort enveloped her and allowed her to drift off to sweet dreams.

I fought back anguish, not wanting to concern her with my fears. The tears rolled down my cheeks anyway. I wanted to take Snowball on a walk and let her run freely in the park behind Wilbur Road where dandelions bloomed and butterflies flew. I wanted her to frolic amongst the long grass and roll around on her back, all fours up in the air, dancing with the sweet meadow breeze. Most of all, I wanted to see her play with other dogs, yipping and yapping, jumping and running.

"All in good time. I promise, little girl." I kissed her fluffy head and she looked up at me with eyes that told me she would not disappoint.

When I opened the Clark Family Shelter three years ago, I funded it with my inheritance. I had just enough cash flow to sustain the shelter with its food, medical supplies, staff payroll, and basic operating expenses for roughly a year. I also received monthly donations that helped take the edge off when unexpected things crept up like repairs and special foods for special needs animals. The past two years, I spent raising funds from local businesses, events, and door-to-door campaigns. This consumed about thirty-percent of my time, time I wished I could've been working the shelter instead.

Natalie earned the title of fundraising hero. She consistently converted naysayers into donors by pulling at their heartstrings. Sometimes I wondered if all that magic derived from pure passion for the animals or from survival. She loved working for the shelter and constantly echoed how she would just die if I ever came to her one day and told her I didn't have the money to keep her employed. She could work at any vet office and earn more money than I could afford to pay her, yet she remained loyal to me. I assumed her loyalty stemmed entirely out of the purpose behind the work we did. Then, about a year ago, when I overheard her talking with Trevor in the back, I heard a different tale, one that caused me to blush and hide in the kennels for the rest of the day.

Apparently, my prized employee had a crush on me, and sought counsel in Trevor one day when she heard me agree to a date with one of our food suppliers, Corrine. I had broken Natalie's heart without even realizing it. She had misread my friendly winks and nudges as signs all along that I reciprocated the chemistry.

So, I spent hours sitting on oversized pillows with affectionate dogs who took up refuge in my confused and numb state. Natalie, only three years out of high school, was my friend. How I handled the delicate situation would chart the course for smooth sailing or rough seas. I needed Natalie and her inflated joy. She tended to the shelter like a talented sailor tended to the open water. Without her, I'd list heavily in the wrong direction. Her efforts kept this place afloat, and provided safety, security, and love to hundreds of abandoned pets each year.

So, that same night I overheard this conversation, I took action. I decided to invite her in to one of the kennels and help me coax our newest shelter member to allow me to trim his nails. She sat next to me, wrapping her secret up in a smile. Her eyes sparkled and her lips quivered as she moved in closer to clutch the hound's paw. "I wanted to ask you about something," I said, ready to reveal what I overheard and how we needed to define the boundaries so things didn't get weird.

Her tanned skin deepened. "Oh?" Her eyes darted from me to the paw a few too many times. She struggled to inhale. I'd never seen her so shaken and at a loss for words. "Did I do something to upset you? I'm so sorry if I did." She pulled in her lower lip, clenching it as if bracing for ridicule or reprimand.

I couldn't risk doing either to her. "No." I blinked her comment away. "Of course not." I laughed a little and she welcomed the relief with a sharp exhale and her signature goofy laugh.

"I just wanted to ask you if you've heard back from Della Range on whether they have any foster homes available?"

"Not a word, Olivia. Not a word." She directed her full attention to the needy one in the kennel. Suddenly, teamed-up, she armed to assist me, waiting for the right moment to unleash the pressure for the pretty hound with claws too mighty for kennel life.

I decided to just let things slide. I went on that date and raved about it, even though it sucked. I even lied about a second and third time, just to ensure we still stood tight together, animal protector to fellow animal protector. She never asked about the fourth date, and I didn't throw her any additional lies. We just worked our butts off protecting the safe world for our beloved guests with event after event to raise funds. Everyone loved our cause. The donations funneled in from the poorest parts of town to the richest.

Now with the storm, though, the donations dried up.

I kissed Snowball's warm nose before jumping to my feet and dealing with the mess at hand.

A while later, as I stood staring out of the front window at the ravaged town, I wondered how the flooding would affect shelter life. Now that the town needed money to rebuild their houses, their cars, their businesses, where would the shelter get theirs?

Melanie rounded the corner wearing an apron and wielding a wet mop. "You're lucky. You only had a little water get in through the back wall and the side exam room. The kennels all look dry. Snowball is resting just fine on her new fluffy bed in isolation. The rest of the dogs, on the other hand, they look like they could use a break."

"I'm going to go see what we can do about at least getting them into the yard to play around a bit." I pushed through the double doors and into the kennel area. The room smelled like gasoline from the generator. I rushed to the back door and pushed it open. Trevor stood on the patio smoking a cigarette and singing. His bleached hair poked out in all directions. The generator cranked a few daring feet from him.

"I'm going to close this door tighter," I yelled out to him. "All I smell is your cigarette. The dogs aren't happy with you right now."

Trevor tossed his cigarette to the ground, crushed it out and scooped it back up in his hand without my having to ask. "Sorry about that, boss. I've been waiting hours. You're at least a little proud of me, right?" He broadened his smile and opened his arms up wide.

"I'm closing it." I shut the door with an extra strong tug.

He stepped back into the kennel room and shut the door behind him. "Thank God the smell is all we've got to worry about. The scene is unbelievable out there. I walked down to the edge of the grounds and looked down into the valley. Rooftops are floating."

Our view of the colorful town from atop the hill on Mulberry Street could usually put a Thomas Kincaid painting to shame. I couldn't bring myself to look out into the valley just yet. Instead I walked back out to the waiting room where Melanie had just powered up the television, thanks to Trevor's bravado with the generator.

"The town is a mess. Main Street is underwater. The schools have all but drowned. There's not a utility pole for miles that's standing." She pointed to the television screen. "Look, that's St. Michael's steeple."

We huddled around the twenty-inch flat screen. Our faces hung in horror at the scenes of what used to be the town center. Muddy water now covered what used to be a beautiful park touting the prettiest birch trees. A few stranded people stood on their rooftops waving at the news helicopter.

Natalie bit her nails. "Oh my goodness, look at that lady."

A middle-aged lady wearing a drenched t-shirt cradled her cat under the crook of her arm and waved with her free arm to the helicopter.

Thank goodness the cat could snuggle up to its owner, despite her being drenched and scared to the core. "I imagine there's a whole town full of abandoned pets right now panicking on top of soaked couches and beds." I walked away shaking my head unable to fathom the horror.

~ ~

Right out of veterinary school, I worked at one of those national chain pet store hospitals where every second of the business day I cared for every imaginable breed of dog. Some would end up waiting for hours to be seen because we worked primarily on a walk-in basis. Only surgeries took precedence over the appointment book. Right out of school, and with a white lab coat starched and pristine, I had much to learn about handling pets, especially the ones that launched full force at me the moment I entered the examination room. Some days I'd leave the hospital in tears, embarrassed that I couldn't deal with the stress, beating myself up for not deserving to wear a white lab coat with doctor inscribed in front of my name.

Some of my former classmates called me crazy for working in such duress. I began to think so, too, until I met Melanie. Her aura soothed me. She walked in one day, long feathery peppered hair swinging around her, with the prettiest green Conure bird. She found Lucky while out on a walk with her dog that afternoon. Lucky evidently escaped from his home, got injured, and fell sick. No one wanted to deal with her bird. Lucky intrigued me. So, I offered. I learned about birds a little in school, but not nearly enough to diagnose the problem. Nonetheless, I offered to hydrate Lucky and clip her wings. Melanie thanked me a day later with a gift certificate to Outback Steakhouse and a sweet thank you card. I helped her pick out Lucky's new bird cage, a wall-length, mammoth one complete with swings, toys, birdbaths, and all the seeds imaginable.

A month later, she returned with Lucky to ask for my help with clipping her wings again. The hospital didn't want to start treating Conures, and so the boss reprimanded me for surrendering to Melanie's plea. So, I offered to come out to her house to clip her wings and nails the next time.

On my first visit, she confessed that she had taken Lucky to three different hospitals that first afternoon and no one showed an ounce of compassion, except for me. This floored me, because I didn't understand how a doctor who dedicated her life to caring for animals wouldn't step back for a moment, see the big picture of a sick bird in dire need of water and care, and not step up to the plate and drive home the needed solution.

By my fifth visit, she had counseled me on everything from breathing correctly to transferring the right energy to my pet patients. She was a reiki master, and this intrigued me almost as much as surgery did. I trusted her. She, as well as Lucky, changed the course of my life. Within a blink, I had secured the building and resources to reopen the old town shelter and outfitted it with a medical facility on site to care for all domesticated animals, regardless of if they grew feathers or fur.

Twenty-five years my senior, Melanie became that person I relied on to check myself, to keep me focused, to stay centered. She also came in to my life at just the right time, when I needed someone to trust, three years after my parents both died in a car accident. Melanie swooped in and cradled my broken soul with her wide expanse of spirit and knack for healing. I learned to trust again. In return, I clipped Lucky's wings, supplied her with every imaginable delicacy any fine Conure could ever want, and an endless supply of referrals for her reiki business, both in adopted pets and parents.

We were two friends in perfect control over our lives, deterred by no one, especially romantic partners. Well, I was more in control in that department than Melanie. She dabbled in a date here and there with mysterious women and boring men, but always backed off just when things steamed up a bit too much for her.

Many years before, she had married her mechanic, Henry, who drove her crazy with his rants about how unlucky they were to be stuck in the small town. They met when her sixty-nine Ford Mustang lost its muffler on the side of the interstate one rainy Saturday afternoon. He drove up in a tow truck and in less than one year, they married under the gazebo at Huntington State Park with two strangers they plucked up from the side of the fishing pond to serve as witnesses. They enjoyed about two years of honeymoon bliss before Henry started hiding out in his garage, eating breakfast, lunch, and dinner out there and replacing his joy for sexual romps in bed with his new wife with used car parts and a lady named Bethany who constantly needed her oil changed. Bethany had wrapped her pretty little arms around more than just Henry. Melanie confessed to me that she enjoyed Bethany even more than Henry did. The end came when Henry popped home for lunch only to find Melanie and Bethany hot and bothered on their bed getting off on each other under the covers. Later, Henry and Melanie both admitted their love had fizzled and probably had seen its finest days in the first sixty days of marriage back before Melanie realized how much she hated the smell of grease and hand cleaner and Henry hated the smell of sage. The two split, remained friendly, and still each enjoyed their fair share of sexual pleasure from Bethany before she ran off with a wealthy banker from Pennsylvania. Soon after that, Henry had failed to secure the lift before getting under it to fix his Buick, and the car fell on him, crushing him to death.

Melanie told me time and again how much she preferred living alone. Being tied down to one person when you're a bisexual is nearly impossible," she said on more than one occasion. "It's like being told you have to choose between shelter and food. How can I survive with only one of those?"

I knew this to be true from Chloe who always tested her eyes on guys. "That's why I'd never get tangled up with a bisexual ever again. I'd always have to worry if the girl wished I had a penis to help rock her world."

"For me, I like my freedom to choose. We're all free spirits who thrive on special moments. I like to keep my options open. I don't want to be boxed in. I enjoy my privacy and would never want to depend on another human being to fulfill me in ways I couldn't fulfill myself."

I agreed.

I never wanted a Henry in my life.

I couldn't be bothered. No one could be trusted with my heart. I'd dated over the years, but never committed. I refused to be that lesbian who pulled up in a U-Haul on the second date.

Fuck love. I'd take freedom and guilt-free sex over the drama of a relationship any day.

~ ~

Now that the town languished under a pool of water and threatened my shelter, I needed to focus more than ever on things I could control. After shaking off the sad sights of the television, I decided to call my friend Phil at the county jail and tell him to bring me the weakest and most vulnerable pets. I'd figure something out.

The shelter, consisting of twenty dog kennels, a free roaming cat room with carpeted nooks and crannies, another room with various finches, parakeets, gerbils, ferrets and even a tarantula, buckled with the addition of new animals. Over the course of two days, Phil had brought in four more dogs and ten cats.

He arrived around four o'clock that afternoon with our fifth dog in need of rehab. I placed her in the kennel closest to the isolation ward, to where Snowball struggled for her life. She snuggled up and pointed her big doe eyes at me. "You'll be okay now, little girl." I blew her a kiss and closed the gate. "I'll be back to check on you in a few minutes." Her concerned eyes followed me until I rounded the corner to where Phil stood staring at a chart describing dog breeds.

"How many more do you think are out there?" I asked.

He turned to me. "How many more can you take?"

"Well, maybe if I get some temporary large crates, we can take on a few more."

"Olivia," he cocked his head and adjusted his pants, which dragged down by the enormous gun holstered to his belt. "This could stretch on for longer than temporary."

"I'll figure something out. It's better than having them drown or starve."

"I've got an idea," he said. He bit his lower lip and walked around back to the kennels. The dogs howled and barked. Some just stared at his burly figure, too scared to move. He counted the kennels. "Ben at the hardware store waited out the storm, too. I'm sure he's got some fencing or plywood he wouldn't mind donating. We could rig all of these kennels and double your capacity."

I pulled on his arm. "Would you talk to him for me?"

"I'm on it." He scanned the door leading to the isolation room. "Do you mind if I say hello?"

I waved him to the door and he led the way.

He walked up to Snowball's kennel and stuck his finger through the bars. "Hey, little girl." She rose, stretched and wobbled over to him, still sleepy from her meds. She licked his fingers and he scratched behind her ears.

I opened the gate. "Go ahead. I know you want to snuggle."

He walked into her kennel and knelt down and Snowball hung her head low. He petted her between her ears and she relaxed into his touch. "Is she getting better?"

"She's coming along. It's still too early to tell if she's responding fully to the meds, though. Unfortunately, parvovirus digs its ugly fangs too deeply and can take over."

He cooed and hugged her. "You're going to survive this. And when you get better and are ready for your first walk outside, Ms. Olivia is going to let me be the one to take you."

"You might have to fight Melanie on that one."

"Or maybe I'll finally charm my way into her day and talk her into letting me come along." He looked up at me and winked.

He had a better chance of skyrocketing to the moon with an air compressor attached to his back. "Yeah, maybe."

Phil hinted often. Melanie pretended not to notice.

"Listen, if no one comes for her, I want to adopt her." He scratched behind her ears and she leaned into his touch more.

"She certainly hopes so." *And*, I wanted to add, *Melanie just might consider a date with you after all, considering this new turn in Snowball's future.*

He turned to me. "Take extra good care of her, okay?"

I nodded, concerned for her health and for his premature emotional attachment to her.

~ ~

In the weeks that followed the storm, the town started to rebuild. Cars started to drive down the street again. Joggers ran past the shelter again. Moms with small children and dogs walked past. Even Snowball bounced back after a series of successful rounds on strong meds. Everything started to spring back to life, all except the leaky roof, the cracked concrete in the kennel walls, the overcrowded double kennels, and of course the absence of many donation checks.

We arranged a pancake breakfast, complete with a volunteer from K-9 Trainers and the usual hundred-person crowd we attracted didn't come. Sadly, only two families showed for it and donated twenty dollars each. Worse, they didn't bother to visit with the adoptable pets. We were used to adopting out several and cashing in several hundred from this type of event. We dumped a lot of pancake batter down the drain that day.

We arranged a dog wash day another day. I purchased some donuts, coffee, and juice and waited for people to flow through the door to wash their doggies in our oversized sinks with the nifty ramp. The fifty or so people I usually got to attend that type of event didn't show. I tossed out a few dozen donuts that day.

"I don't know what to do," I said to Melanie one afternoon while she sat in Snowball's kennel and channeled her energy to the sick dog. "The town is unresponsive."

"I can offer some reiki treatments if it'll help. We'll ask for a donation that is half the usual treatment price I charge at my studio."

"Can you afford to do that? Didn't you lose a lot of clients this month?"

"That's why I'm here in the middle of the day." She rubbed her hands together forming the energy ball and targeted it over Snowball's tummy. "I'd rather be doing something productive than sitting around twiddling my thumbs."

"I'm afraid people aren't even going to be willing to pay half price for reiki treatments. Everyone is strapped waiting on help from the government."

The end of the month raced towards us and I had no extra funding after paying the overhead bills to fix the structural problems in the shelter. I had to cancel our usual spot in the *Valley Breeze Community Newspaper* because I needed the cash to cover the extra kibble needed to feed double the hungry mouths. So, I relied on my website to pique the interest of potential adopters.

"Give it time," Melanie said, stretching her hands the full length of Snowball. "Everything will come back around."

The townspeople strained to dig up money to fund their own rehabilitation projects. I needed help sooner than later. "It'll be months before any of us see funding to get us the repairs we all need."

"You're killing my energy here," she said, stopping.

"I'm sorry. I'll let you be." I backed away and she returned her focus to Snowball.

I walked down the kennel aisle and looked into the hopeful eyes of dog after dog. They relied on me, and I needed to step up to the challenge. I needed to look beyond the town and somehow get outsiders to understand our plight. I knew just who to turn to.

When Josh answered, sounding rushed and surely on his way out the door to one of his son's many baseball practices, I cut right to it. "I need your help with getting someone up here to interview me."

He cleared his throat. "I'm a production assistant, not the general manager of the network."

"Do what you can, please."

"Is it that bad?"

"Worse," I said.

"I'd loan you some, but I'm barely able to pay my mortgage each month."

"I just need a reporter, cameraman, and some coverage outside the scope of Elkwood."

"I'll see what I can do. It'll cost you a night of babysitting your nephew if I succeed."

"Done."

"Fine," he said. "Oh, and," he blew out a breath, "I read something troubling last week."

"Hint, please."

"Did you know Melanie's house is in foreclosure?"

"That's absurd. She and Henry inherited that house from his parents like twenty years ago."

"Well, I went there for a treatment the other day and when she went to the bathroom, I went to get myself a glass of water and the notice was on the counter, opened. Maybe after Henry died, she took out an equity line of credit."

After Henry died and she moved back in to the house, she gutted out the living room and turned it into a reiki studio. She also bought a new four-wheel drive truck and took a vacation to Spain for two months. "Anything's possible." Her clutter entered my mind, and I dreaded the day she'd ask for help in clearing it out. I couldn't deal with one more thing on my plate. "I'm not going to bring it up. So, you don't either, okay?"

"I'm heading over there for a reiki treatment tomorrow. I'll do my best."

"I'll babysit for you if you can manage an interview," I said.

"Done."

~ ~

Working in a shelter required lots of patience and emotional control. Some of the pets had been abused, malnourished, unloved for years. Many arrived wagging their tails anticipating a fun field trip with their owners only to be discarded at our front desk with a pat on the head and a shrug. *He's too much work. She pees in the house. He sheds too much. He barks all the time. She's just too big.* As a responsible guard of animal welfare, a shelter worker simply thanked the person for not abandoning their pet on the side of the road. Lecture these people and they'd do that next time, for sure.

So, we'd take the animals back, and I'd examine their shaky bodies as they stressed over when their master would return for them and bring them back home to where they belonged. My heart broke every time I had to place them in a kennel all alone without a window to gaze out, without a couch to climb up on, without a master to please.

I wanted to take them all home with me. I wanted to cook them homemade chicken and rice with a dash of pumpkin and cuddle up with them on the couch and watch *American Idol.* I wanted to dress them up in cute clothes and take them on long runs through the park. I wanted to spend time sitting on a park bench, reading a book, and glancing up from time to time to catch them smiling and wagging their tails as they scoped out squirrels hoarding acorns.

Unfortunately my dreams for this happy-go-lucky life never panned out quite like I'd wished. I could only sit with them for minutes at a time, clip their nails, bathe them in soothing warm water, feed them beef and chicken cookies, and comfy up their kennels with blankets, bed pillows, and fun toys. I fostered several cats, but I couldn't foster the dogs as easily because of my crazy schedule. I spent more time at the shelter than I did at my apartment.

Natalie, equally as sensitive to shelter life as I was, would spend hours cuddled up in kennels, petting, nurturing and talking with the dogs. She'd move in to the shelter if I let her.

That afternoon, Natalie choked back tears when I looked in on her and our newest arrival. "He won't let me put a leash around him. He needs to pee. It's been hours. He won't pee in his kennel."

I stood beside Natalie in front of the scared dog's kennel. He avoided us from the back of it, whimpering. I'd seen this too many times before to understand only a good dose of respect and love would work to gain his trust.

I showed him a cookie and he sniffed the air, refusing to meet my eye.

I waited.

After ten minutes, I knelt down beside his kennel, bowing my head, sending him love and energy the way Melanie had taught me to do. Natalie took a seat on a stool several feet away, out of his sight.

Every few minutes, he crept a little closer to me. I imagined us sitting together on a grassy hill overlooking a clean, fresh lake. My arm draped around his neck, his mouth opened slightly to enjoy the cool breeze. I'd hug him and he'd lean into my safety and love. Stoic and strong he'd relax as we watched birds fly overhead and listen to cicadas chirp a lovely song.

I imagined all of this with my head bowed. I didn't look at him. I simply sat still, breathing, meditating, and sending vibes of safety and love to him. Close to fifteen minutes later, he crept over to me, slowly, steadily, his head bowed, his tail tucked between his legs, a whimper here and there.

I inched my eyes up to meet him. "Come on, boy. It's okay. You're safe here."

He stretched his neck as far as it would allow and sniffed the cookie. He froze, staring at the cookie, no doubt contemplating his craving.

"Here," I placed the cookie down in front of me. "Come get it."

He stared at it. Drool fell to the cement. His head hung to the same level as his belly, low, barely half a foot from the floor. I scooted backwards, allowing him the freedom to get his prize. He sauntered a few more feet and when close enough, he snatched it up into his hungry mouth. He dared to look up at me once he swallowed. He sniffed some more. I offered another cookie. "Come on. You know you want it."

He inched towards me. Finally, as gentle as a summer breeze, he opened his mouth just wide enough to snag the cookie from my fingers. "That a boy."

I savored the tender moment.

He circled in closer and smelled my hand, snuggling up to the scent left behind by the cookies. I stroked his neck and he licked my hand. I rose to my feet and he didn't budge. I dropped another cookie to his left, just far enough away so I wouldn't frighten him when I stepped inside his domain. He gobbled the cookie and watched me step inside. I offered one more treat in the palm of my hand, and when he licked it from my open palm, I looped the leash around his neck and petted him. He allowed me to pet him without whimpering. I looked over at Natalie. She wiped a trail of tears from her cheeks. "You're amazing."

I accepted the compliment with a smile and led him out of the kennel and towards the back door to the fenced open area. "I can't imagine doing anything else with my life."

Natalie trailed behind. "We are not letting a few lost dollars close this place. My uncle will help find someone to repair the roof and put this place back together again."

I watched my new furry friend walk with his head high. He stopped near a bush and peed like he'd been saving it his whole life. "I don't care if I have to stand on the interstate wearing flashing lights and a string bikini to gather attention, we're going to find help."

Natalie blushed and kicked the ground. "Well, alleluia, then."

Chapter Five

Transparency between best friends should be natural law. The principle of the universe that binds atoms and molecules together, ensuring they all activate in a timely efficient manner, should surely be at play with this critical component of human interaction. Best friend trust perched high up on the list of necessities to keep the flow smooth, right alongside the rising and setting of the sun, the ebb and flow of the tide, the rotation of the earth on its axis.

That afternoon, as I prepped for my news interview, I asked Melanie how life was treating her and she smiled. Not a big, stretched out, exaggerated smile, the likes you'd expect from someone harboring a secret as big as being kicked to the curb at fifty years of age. Nope, her smile mirrored her genuine and pleasant spirit, sitting on her face like a pretty daisy in full bloom, radiating everything peaceful and right in the world.

As the girl from the evening news smoothed a thick creamy foundation all over my virgin skin, Melanie showered me with smiles, coaching me not to stress over the interview – even though she and I both knew that forty dogs, several dozen cats, and many other beautiful animals counted on this interview to keep a roof over their heads and food in their bellies.

"We need this to work," I said to her.

"Relax." She gripped my shoulder. "Everything always works out. You're not going to lose the place because several million raindrops toppled the town. People will pull together. You watch and see."

"I'm dreading this. I'm always the one who provides the help, never the one in need."

"Breathe," she said.

"You never lose control. Nothing ever seems to rattle you." I eyed her carefully, allowing her a few precious seconds to ponder her words and segue into a conversation about her home. Nothing. Just that motherly, guiding smile she always displayed in the wake of wise words.

The girl brushed my face with a powder, applied some mascara and lipstick and held up a mirror for me to see her hard work. A stranger with rosy cheeks, sparkling eyes, and full lips stared back at me. I looked more ready to give an interview on a red carpet than break out a heart-wrenching story about poor, helpless animals in dire need of supplies and donations. I rubbed my cheeks, and blotted my lips with a napkin. I hated wearing makeup, just like I hated wearing dresses and carrying pocketbooks. Give me a wallet, a pair of jeans and a set of sneakers any day.

"Too much?" the girl with overdone eyes asked.

"A bit." I stood up from the stool and ruined the smoothing blowout she did by pulling my hair back into its usual knot at the nape of my neck. I headed over to the reporter, a primped brunette with flipped layers resting nicely at her shoulders and dewy skin. She looked the type who ran marathons, snacked on carrot sticks and apples and blanketed her skin in expensive moisturizers. She didn't smile, though. She wore a blank face even when Natalie tripped over a cord snaking around the desk.

"I'm ready," I said.

"Okay," she said, looking like she had to be coaxed into a happy mood. She pointed to a lock of my hair that escaped my knot. "Hmm, you have a little bit of hair hanging."

"Does it really matter?" I asked.

She fixated on it. So, I tore out my knot and rebuilt it. I didn't need her screwing up this opportunity by focusing on my hair instead of the camera. "There, better?"

"Much," she said. "Okay, Fred, let's have you swing over here near this wall with the pretty portraits. I'd like to have them right behind us." On command, Fred carried himself and the enormous camera over to us. "Just follow my lead," she said to me.

"I just want to make sure we're on the same page. I really want to focus on the welfare of the animals and the influx of new ones being dropped off after being rescued. We need people to come out and adopt."

She tilted her head to the side as if studying me. "Sure. I get it."

Fred steadied himself in front of us, and when cued, the reporter dove into the segment like a well-trained national correspondent, precise and on-point with her words, her inflections, her timing. She summarized the last month and the financial distress of the town and how this distress negatively affected the flow of donations into the shelter. She briefed the audience on the struggles of non-profits when faced with disasters such as the hurricane and how it's critical more than ever to get involved.

"What's your biggest need right now?" The reporter asked, pointing the microphone at my mouth.

"Well, we've had an influx of animals come into the shelter, so we need blankets, food, beds, pillows. Any of that would help." *Ask for money!* "Toys even."

Natalie and Trevor zeroed in on me, as if pleading with me to get out of my humble state and cut to the chase. "And people to consider fostering or adopting."

The reporter smirked. "Okay, well, besides all of that, I also understand that your building is one of the few that has weathered the storm in this immediate area."

"Yes, thankfully. We've had some damage, though."

"Yes, of course," she said. She looked around as if the thought had just caught up to her that she probably should have set up the shot to be in front of something other than Melanie's pretty artistic wall display of beautiful pet portraits. "Tell us about that."

"We've lost part of our roof, a wall is ready to collapse in the kennel area, and some of the grounds have washed away towards the back of the kennel runs." *We need money for repairs, money we normally needed to keep the place up and running.* "We're slowly trying to get it all worked out."

"Any plans to relocate at this point?"

"Relocate?" What a dumb question. I briefed her on my needs and never did I mention relocating. *Why was she not leading me where we needed to go?* "We have a great spot here. It's all fixable. Unfortunately, everyone else in town is going through much of the same and—" I paused to gather up the momentum I'd need to overcome this stupid need to stay humble. I looked over at my staff who urged me with a nod, with intent eyes, to carry onward with our plight. *Our plight, not mine.* "—the funding we rely on has stopped because everyone else is funneling it to rebuilding their homes and businesses. Because we're double over our capacity, we're low on supplies and food." I smiled at the camera. *I'm irresponsible. I know. I should've set up a trust fund like Josh advised me to do. Save for a rainy day and plan for the worse to happen.* "We need help."

72

"I also heard that you've had to turn away animals because you're over capacity."

In what universe? My face flushed. I would knock on every door and beg for foster help before I turned away an animal. Outrage seeped from my pores. "You heard wrong."

She bypassed my answer. "And, I hear you're getting requests from other neighboring counties to take on rehabilitation of more strays they're finding."

I snapped my eyes at her. "I'm not sure where you're getting your information."

She pressed on. "I understand that you are considering expanding the shelter if the funds can be secured. That would really be a win for the animal community. You had mentioned possibly sixty kennels in total?"

I tripped and stumbled over her lies. "Um."

"So, what you really need are cash donations?"

She fed me with lies, lies that could help our cause, nonetheless. "That would be helpful, yes."

"I know there are so many people affected financially by this disaster, and you're worried to ask for their help. Is that right?" She pointed the microphone at me again.

"We'll make due," I said looking over at my trio who stared back at me with jaws dropped, weary frown lines on their foreheads. I turned back to her. "I know it's not an easy time for the community right now."

"It's a beautiful thing you're doing here. And, I'm sure I'm speaking for a lot of people when I say thank you." She finally smiled.

I just nodded, lost for the right words.

The reporter stared into the camera and spoke like a fine-tuned instrument. "If you'd like to donate and help the Clark Family Shelter's continued efforts to caring for defenseless, homeless animals, please visit our website to find out how. Stan, back to you."

The cameraman backed away from his tripod. "That's a wrap."

I stood with my arms crossed, stunned. "What was that all about?" I asked her.

"I'm not here to waste my time," she said, looping the extension cord around her thin arms. "Your story needs an emotional plea." She turned to the cameraman. "Fred, I'll need you to take some stills of the staff interacting with the dogs, cats, and any other animals you can find back there. Look for the most pathetic ones." She turned to me. "You're not done, yet. We've got to create a story worthy of landing a spot on the evening news." She pointed to Fred. "Follow him."

Thirty minutes later, and at least one hundred pictures snapped of all of us cuddling up to the animals, the reporter handed the extension cord to Fred, gathered her pocketbook and notepad from the counter, and headed out of the door. "You can thank me later when the donations start pouring in faster than you can blink." She stopped midway through the front door. "Oh, and you can tell your brother that I said you're welcome. Call me when you get some puppies. I get first dibs. Josh has my number." She winked and walked away.

74

Chapter Six

Chloe

I listened to Olivia deliver a plea that wrapped around my heart and twisted it up into a knot. The anxiety in her tone, the desperate panic in her eyes, the twist of her mouth, all blended together, sweeping me up in a windstorm of emotions and blowing me off balance. My heart pounded as she submitted to the financial distress of her shelter. *Her* shelter. Pride swelled in me. She rose up to a grand and selfless pathway. Her eyes flickered whenever she addressed the reporter. I recognized the unease in the slight stretch to her upper lip. The reporter led her, taunted her to admit vulnerability. Olivia Clark did not beg.

She angled her eyes at the camera and spoke cautious words. Her lips, still pouty and bright, drew me in. Her cheeks still chiseled, shined under the camera's light. Her hair still highlighted blonde and stretched back into a low ponytail, gleamed. A veil of worry shadowing her face marked the only difference since the last time I'd set eyes on her. She resisted the reporter's aggressive questions, and turned them in her favor by remarking on the plights of others during such distressing times, on how others competed for basic necessities.

Olivia circled around her own troubles, disguising a loss of control with strength and a determined spirit.

After the report, they cut to a video montage of the staff adoring dogs, cats and even a pretty bird. Their hearts reached out through the camera and attached to mine. Olivia showed off a bulldog, lifting him in the air and kissing the tip of his nose. A young guy, with blonde spikey hair, traipsed alongside a fence with a Saint Bernard, stopping to pet the top of his head. A pretty, heavy-set black girl with a pile of curls on top of her head, admired a beautiful yellow and green bird as it perched on her finger. The soft piano music combined with the emotional plea mesmerized me. Even after several days, I found myself sneaking into the living room to watch the news clip over and over again.

"You're going to wear that segment right out," Aunt Marie said, walking past me with a basket of laundry. She scooped down to pick up a sock that had fallen out.

"I want to help her," I said.

She placed the basket down on the couch next to me and plopped down, too. "You really think she'll let you?"

I looked back at the television, to Olivia's blushed cheeks. I paused the recording on a shot of her sweeping a piece of her hair behind her ear and narrowing her eyes at the reporter. "Maybe enough time has passed."

She stole the remote from my hand and pointed it at the television. "I'm going to erase it."

"No," I screamed knocking the remote from her hand.

We stared at the remote on the tiled floor. The battery popped out and landed a few inches away from it. The television screen, still paused on Olivia's narrowed eyes, casted a crude reminder that Olivia had moved on with her life and forgotten all about me.

76

I plopped down on the couch, tossed my head in my hands and screamed. "I just wish things were different."

Aunt Marie sat down and hugged me. I pulled away. She pulled me back and squeezed me to her. I wrestled. She wrestled. Finally I conceded and cried into the crocheted flower resting on the lapel of her cardigan sweater. "I still can't get her out of my mind after all of this time."

"You're driving yourself crazy," she said rocking me back and forth. "You really should erase the segment."

"She needs help."

"And people will come to her aid."

They would come to her aid just like they did when I left her, when her childhood dog Floppy died, when her parents died, whenever some dramatic piece of life caught up to her. "I want to come to her aid."

Aunt Marie patted my back. "What's your plan? Go into town bearing envelopes stuffed with hundred bills and maybe a friendly dinner?"

"Something like that, yes." I pulled back, kicked up my feet and reclined back against the leather. "If I don't help her, I'll be wasting my last chance to wipe the slate clean."

Aunt Marie kicked up her feet, too, and lounged back. "What about Scott?"

I stared up at the chandelier. Dust grazed its brass and cobwebs formed a bridge between the arms. "We're just dating."

"He has a drawer in your bedroom."

"I'm a liberated woman, Auntie."

"I don't get your generation."

"This is my chance to do something good and balance things out."

"I don't think she's going to be open to receiving your help, sweetheart."

77

I rested my head on her shoulder and sighed. "You're probably right."

~ ~

People assumed because I earned a lot of money, my life was one big happy hoorah. I enjoyed money for the freedom it offered me, but it didn't protect me from lonely nights. My happiness bloomed the most before the money, before my life tangled up into a big messy wad of lies and people tossing their flirty eyes and accolades at me like I had actually deserved them.

Before Ayla arrived in my life, I viewed myself as a decent human being with a shot at a good life if I had played my cards correctly. I never set out to hurt anyone. I never wanted to be that girl who blocked out everyone else but herself. I wanted to be far different than my mother, and in a different solar system altogether from my stepfather.

I had promised myself a long time ago, that I, Chloe Homestead, would always do my part in paying back those who served me in my time of need. I would one day go off to college, earn a degree, get a well-paying job, and pay back Olivia for all those times she raised me up to the level of a queen.

Broken promises looked an awful lot like litter. They repulsed, antagonized, and left a trail of ugliness too real to deny. To clean up the mess required getting down on the ground and plucking up one shattered piece at a time. Controlling damage this way would take forever, though. Thankfully, money offered me a shortcut. Because I invested in a shitload of mobile parks, I could pay to clean up the mess a whole lot quicker and without getting my hands and knees all scuffed and dirty.

I watched as my daughter shoveled Honey Bunches of Oats into her mouth. She sensed no clue of the sacrifices I'd endured to get her to this point in her life – a beautiful teenager with lots of cool friends, trendy clothes, and a stable, loving family that only a fool would run from. No messed up mother who would rather smoke cigarettes and walk in circles talking to herself on the terrace of a mental institution; no stepfather who would sneak into her room at night and try to fondle her; no excuses to fabricate so friends wouldn't be annoyed at her for not reciprocating an invite to sleepover. No searching for love in the eyes of a stranger who only served to please him or herself by getting her to spread her legs and remedy a serious case of horniness.

No, Ayla would never go through any of this because Aunt Marie and I loved her, respected her, and molded her into a young lady who knew she deserved exactly what she put out into the world. Thankfully, Ayla wielded more sense than I did when it came to measuring choices. She analyzed the world through lenses more magnified than I ever did at her age. When she didn't want something, she walked. When she did want something, she focused on it until it became hers. Thankfully, she also understood the concept of cause and effect. What she contributed, she received back a million times over. She offered to rake leaves for our neighbors for free and in return they set her up with beautiful saddles and delicious homemade cherry pies. She baked her friends cookies for no reason, and in return they never overlooked her in the school cafeteria or on carnation day. She served others and received blessings back in the way of friendship and goodwill. People naturally gravitated towards her because she brought out the best in them. She never faked. She'd never live a lonely day. I wished I'd have understood that at her early age.

I had no doubt that if genuine love presented itself to her, she would never disregard for the sake of conformity or weakness. Nope, my daughter would extend her delicate hands, take that love in and honor it. She'd never shit all over it like I did. She would've thanked the guy who risked his life for her with a dinner instead of a fuck.

"I'm taking a trip to my old hometown this weekend."

"You're not coming camping with us?" she asked.

"No." I shook my head, and then sipped my coffee. Camping with Scott, his friends, and a bunch of teenagers didn't sit at the top of my ideal list of things to do.

"Was that her on the news report?"

I placed my mug down. "Her?"

"The girl you loved," she said without any judgment.

"That's her, yes." I didn't keep my bisexuality a secret. I told her all about Olivia and my love for her. I only lied about how I left her. Instead of messing her up with the ugly truth, I buried my dark secret and told Ayla that we both just needed to go our separate ways.

"You're going to see her, aren't you?"

I exhaled. "Yeah."

"Do you think you'll get to kiss her?"

"I'm not going there to try and kiss her, Ayla. I'm going there to help her out with her shelter."

"And what about my father?"

My skin fizzled in a moment of ridiculous panic over the impossible. "What about him?"

"Will you try to find him?"

"Not this time around."

"When will it be time?"

"I'm not sure, sweetheart."

She bit her lower lip. "I don't feel like camping anymore."

"Your friends are counting on you."

"I wish my father would want to know me like Scott likes to know Alexia."

I wanted to hug her, protect her. She rarely allowed me to console her on this subject. I searched my mind for the proper words that would comfort her and make her feel less like an unwanted old dog and more like an irresistible puppy. I had nothing. I just gripped her wrist and squeezed, offering her a knowing smile. "I love you, sweetie."

"I know." She spooned in another mouthful of cereal. "I'll go camping."

"You'll have fun. Just don't let any anyone talk you into sneaking off on a walk in the dark. That never ends well. I always got bitten by a million mosquitoes and had nightmares for weeks that someone would grab my leg from under a bush and pull me into it."

She placed the bowl up to her face and drank the remaining milk. She emptied the bowl and sighed. "You are so weird, mom."

I pinched her side. "It's true." She trusted people too much, and I worried that one day that nightmare would become a reality.

"I'll bring a boy along if I decide to go for a walk." She peered up at me with a smirk.

"You love me too much to put me through this kind of worry already."

"Yes," she said. "Yes, I do." She hopped off the stool and swung around the counter to the sink. Her long, golden curls flitted around her, reminding me of her little girl days when she enjoyed spinning around in circles with arms outstretched, chasing the elusive wind. "I'm going to tag along with you someday up there, and I'll be old enough where you won't be able to say no."

"All in good time," I said.

"Yep, all in good time," she echoed our usual phrase, ending on a wink.

Chapter Seven

Olivia

When Tucker, a handsome Golden Retriever mix, had first arrived at the shelter a few weeks before the storm had hit, he had collapsed in a seizure right there on the waiting room floor. The owner had already cleared the parking lot. A little girl and her father stood in horror as I knelt beside the big guy and pressed against him until his body stopped twitching and the fear vanished from his big brown eyes.

"Daddy," the little girl trembled, "I don't want that one."

The daddy cradled his little girl, smoothing her hair and asked me, "Is he going to be alright?"

I smoothed Tucker's fur with a reassuring hand. He raised his head up to my lap and laid it down, peeking up at me with his beautiful soft eyes. "I'm going to take good care of him. He'll be alright."

And that's what I did. I took in pets that owners didn't want anymore and cared for them, rehabilitated them and prayed someone kind would come in and adopt them instead of going to shop at one of the many puppy mill supporting pet stores. "Go on back to the kennels," I had urged the father. "There are lots of beautiful dogs in all different sizes and shapes that would love to meet you both."

"This has been traumatic enough for her," he said motioning to his daughter. "Maybe we'll come back another day."

I nodded. "Please do."

They left, surely never to return again, with the same faulty notion many regarded about shelter animals, that all of them had something wrong with them. Why else would no one want them?

Despite my terrible public speaking skills, I stood in front of classrooms, mall crowds, and auditoriums and did my best to dispel the myth that shelter pets were leftovers, discarded because they were aggressive, ugly, or unloving. I educated crowds on the love, health, and care of shelter pets, and how they ended up there not because of who they were, but because of who their owners were – people who didn't contemplate their adoption or purchase well-enough. I lectured to these crowds that pets should never be on trial. "Pets are family members," I would repeat, my voice reverberating against walls. "They aren't beings to discard because they soiled carpeting or refused to stop barking. They need training and love just as children do." Then, I'd get carried away and start jumping into stats that I hoped would wake up potential pet owners to a sad reality. "In America, only about twenty percent of pets are adopted. The rest come into a family through breeders and other sources. If we can push that twenty percent up just a few points, experts say the large number of adoptable pets being euthanized could drop significantly."

I had hated that this father and daughter had to witness Tucker's seizure, and as a result would most likely run directly to the nearest puppy mill supporter to purchase a supposedly healthy puppy.

Soon after I had examined Tucker, ensuring no obvious medical conditions, I had called Melanie. Over the course of his first two weeks, he had collapsed into several seizures. Melanie had worked with him daily. Since then, he'd been seizure-free and a happy-go-lucky tail wagging golden mound of fur who wanted to walk and play catch every second of the day.

Fully accustomed to shelter life now, I lathered him up in the doggie sink. Earlier that day, he had skidded into some mud while chasing a tennis ball in the fenced yard. I created a sink full of bubbles as I scrubbed his belly, laying the suds on thickly. He stood proud, relaxed, happy as ever to be loved. He'd be a great friend, and I prayed he could prove it to someone worthy. I scrubbed his back, splashing suds all over the place and he shook them, soaking me in bubbles from my head down to my ankles.

Natalie bounded towards me from the reception doorway. "You've got a visitor, Olivia."

"Is it the insurance adjuster?"

"She doesn't look like an insurance adjuster."

"She?" I backed away from Tucker, sudsy and wet. "Can you take over?"

A moment later, while tidying my ponytail and looking down at my sudsy apron, I opened the door to the waiting area. I looked up from my suds and locked eyes with Chloe. My breath stopped midway up my throat.

I'd played this scene a million times in my head since the last time we saw each other, but never did I imagine it with my face flushing and my heart racing and my throat getting dry and chalky all over again. Somehow, she still managed to tie my heart up into a knot and squeeze it just hard enough to take my breath away.

Chloe Homestead looked every bit as stunning as she did the last time I saw her. She shined with her black hair, slicked back into a tight, short ponytail, her lips glossed with the color of a red delicious apple, her hips curved in just the right places, accentuating her taut waist and her grapefruit-sized breasts. She smiled and her whole face lit up. I hated that she looked so hot.

85

She opened her arms and I just stood staring at her, shocked to be locking eyes with the girl I promised myself to never see again. "I'm sorry to just show up here like this." She moved in closer, placing her warm hand on my arm. "I saw you on the news."

The room hazed. My fingers and toes tingled. The protective barrier I'd built so carefully over the years melted within seconds, exposing me to familiar tummy rolls and flutters. Her eyes, soft and concerned, pulled me in. Her hand hot against my skin, dizzied me. "You didn't have to come down here."

"I want to help."

The room narrowed and vanished into a steamy mist. Chloe always managed to sweep in and chase away reason. She could incapacitate me with a wink or a curve of her lip. "I don't have time for this right now."

She dropped her hand and fidgeted with her oversized Coach bag. "I just want to help."

The dogs barked above our silence as I faced off to her. She cheated on me. She hurt me. She toyed with me. She broke our trust. "We're fine. The shelter's fine." She smelled like a tender bouquet of lilies and marigolds. I inhaled deeply to steady the spinning and to calm my pounding heart.

She nodded and looked down at her sandals and red toenails before meeting my eyes again. "I saw the segment, and you're not fine." She inched in, sharing my air, my space.

I tore away from her gaze and cringed at my baggy cargo pants and muddy sneakers. Of all days for her to march in to my shelter acting like my savoir, toying with my emotions. I exhaled and reminded myself that I stood at a much better place now, a place where pretty girls with flippant ideals could no longer numb my brain in sensory overload and control my life, my destiny, my purpose.

86

I was strong. I was successful. I was not Olivia with the senseless need to toss aside my own goals to catch a ride on the air of lust and orgasms. Too many people and animals depended on me now. I couldn't afford to play this schoolgirl game. I faced her, looking beyond the concern in her eyes by pretending she had just dumped her pet off to me. "Why are you here, really?"

She didn't break the stare. "Because I can help you."

I crossed my arms over my sudsy apron, clutching tight, angry at the wetness that pooled between my legs. I searched her face desperate to uncover that selfish girl who stomped on lives and expected people to fold up in her lap like obedient Pomeranians. She hid that girl behind a thick layer of peace.

I snapped away. I was stronger now. I didn't need her. I'd built this shelter from scratch, and I would build it back up with bloody, bare hands if I had to. I raised my head up higher and peered down on her. She spoke to me without words, reassuring me she intended harmony. *Those eyes.* "Why do you want to help me?"

She turned and eyed the paw-printed cardboard donation box that Natalie had crafted. She walked over to it, traced her manicured fingers along the cute red bows and black paw pads. "Have coffee with me, and I'll explain," she said. Her finger, long and slender, circled the words 'donations appreciated.' My spine tingled imagining that same finger circling my nipple as it had so many times before.

The dogs continued their howling and barking in between my palpitations. Her bag slipped down her shoulder, teetering on the edge of her pretty blue scalloped t-shirt. She waltzed in there expecting me to drop everything, to ignore the dogs barking wildly, to forget the piles of paperwork on the desk. She powered the situation and expected me to follow like a lost soul. "No," I said. "I really don't have the time."

Her eyes flew open wide. "You don't have half an hour?" A chuckle rested on the edge of words.

I lost important ground. I gripped my conscience, but slid down a hill anyway, clinging to weeds and branches and roots to stabilize me. I wrapped my arms tighter around my chest. "I'm just busy."

She pouted and my stomach flipped.

Control yourself. "I appreciate that you want to help. But, we're managing fine."

Curling her lips up and dousing me in her sexy vibe, she tilted her head and shrugged. "Okay, I'm not going to beg you. If you want my help, you got it." She reached into her bag and handed me a business card. "Call me anytime."

I put the card in my apron pocket without glancing at it. I needed her to leave. "I'm sorry. I have to go." I inched away from her and headed over to the kennel area door, glancing back at her. I caught her arched eye, judging me as if I was the bad person here. "You don't get to do this," I said, flinging open the door. "You don't get to just barge in here with this notion that somehow you get to save the day after all of this time. Friends do that. Family sometimes, even. Not an ex."

Her forehead creased. She backed away towards the front door. "I'm sorry. I just wanted to help." Suddenly, she appeared naked and exposed, fumbling for cover against her vulnerable state. Regret steamed across her face, leaving in its wake a tuft of desperate anguish, the likes of which could only be erased with reprieve. If I let her walk out of the door with me being the bitch, then she'd win. The world would tilt and nothing would taste right or come easy. I wouldn't let her unravel what I'd spent thirteen years building up. I needed to control this.

"I appreciate your offer. I'll keep your number in case I need your help."

"Okay, then." She smiled and pulled in her fleshy bottom lip the way she used to do when I'd bring her breakfast in bed or massage her feet at the end of a tough cheerleader practice. "Please do."

The dog barking heightened. "I've got to go." I turned and closed her off, promising myself to never cave and call her. I would figure something less desperate out. I walked back to Natalie half mad and half elated that my stomach fluttered out of control.

~ ~

"Chloe popped into the shelter today," I said to Josh.

He stopped pouring wine and angled towards me. "Why?"

"Said she saw me on the evening news and wanted to help."

Just then, Thomas came running out from the hallway wearing superman pajamas and flinging an airplane. "Buddy, please go fly that down in your room for a few minutes."

"But, it's boring down there. I want to play in here." He skirted around the couch and leaned onto his dad's shoulders. Josh softened and squeezed his son's scrawny fingers. "Bridget," he yelled out. My sister-in-law emerged from the kitchen with a polka dotted apron and a mixing bowl in her hand. "Can Thomas help you?"

"Thomas, come in here and help me bake this cake," she said, opening her free arm for him.

He launched himself over the couch and landed at his dad's feet. "Can you help us, too?"

"I have to talk to your auntie right now."

He looked up at me and shrugged. "You can help, too."

89

A miniature Josh stared up at me, only a much sweeter version than his father at that age. "I'd love to. I just need a few minutes to talk with your dad."

"Fine." Thomas stomped off to greet his mother. "Can I lick the bowl?"

She wrapped him in her arm and carried him off into the kitchen. "Of course."

Josh poured the half-filled glass of wine in his mouth and resumed pouring. "So she just popped into the shelter?"

"Pretty much." I reached out for the wine. I skipped the glass and gulped it from the bottle. "That girl still gets my stomach all in jumbles." I emptied a great deal of the wine down my throat.

He took the wine from me and followed suit. He exhaled after finishing the bottle, dropped down in his chair and said, "Don't get involved."

"I don't plan on it."

"Are you sure?"

"No, I'm not sure." I sighed, shedding my weakness at my twin brother's feet. "She said she can help me. I certainly could use some help. With the overflow of animals, I don't have time to fundraise." I exhaled and sank. "It's hard, you know. On one hand I hate her for leaving me, for lying about why she left, for coming back to tell me years later she's got a daughter. And on the other hand," I stopped, reflected on the empty wine bottle.

"There is no other hand, Olivia. You don't need that in your life right now."

I depended on Josh to guide me. Ever since our parents died, he'd been my rock. I had spent many nights zonked out on his couch after watching movies with him and Bridget and little Thomas. They invited me over constantly and watched over me. They protected me from all those empty nights at first that used to crawl up and attack me, paralyzing me in a deep sadness that only a twin could understand. Being around him and his family brought me comfort and brought me back from the initial shock.

"My wise, twin brother. You're right. I don't have the time or the energy to deal with any woman right now." I lounged back. "I wonder what she really wants?"

"To get in your pants."

"She's not like that."

"Why do you care?" He punched my knee. "Hmm?"

It shouldn't have mattered what she wanted. I didn't have time for her to come in and start messing with my emotions. "I really don't."

"Bullshit." He punched me harder, this time on my arm.

I did care. Since she came in to the shelter earlier that day, I couldn't stop fantasizing about her. I saw her pretty face everywhere. Those hazelnut eyes pulled me into her, dancing on my heart, pounding their power into me, rendering me incapable of focusing on much of anything else. I could even smell her delicate fragrance still, lilies and marigolds rolled into one intoxicating scent purposed to mess with my head. Flashbacks of her caressing me in my apartment that day beckoned me to replay the waves of pleasure over and over again. Funny how those were the things I embraced, washing right over the cheating, the kid, and the abandonment.

I popped up. "I seriously don't care."

"Let it be. She'll burn you all over again."

Josh got me. He knew just what to say when someone pissed me off. He knew how to make me laugh after a bad day. He knew how to pick me up from the heartache I suffered when I realized again and again that my parents were dead and never coming back. He just got me.

91

"I'll figure something out."

"I'll help you. I'll ask around and see if anyone's willing to help out."

"By the way, that reporter was a total bitch."

"She said you were cute." He winked.

That did not excite me. "I'd rather roll around in a pool of snakes."

He laughed. "She's a bit over the top. You still have to call me if you get a litter of puppies, though."

"I don't think I trust her with puppies." I plucked at the knitted wool blanket on his couch.

"You don't trust anyone."

"Do you blame me?"

He tossed a pillow at me. "Get over yourself."

I whacked him with the pillow and he squirmed like a little girl, kicking his feet up in the air, screaming.

"You're pathetic." I threw the pillow down beside him.

"You won't think so when I get you the help you need."

He intended to provide hands-on support, but seldom followed through on things that required action. He got the procrastination gene. When Josh offered to help me put in the dog wash, I waited a month and figured it out myself through watching a YouTube video. When he promised to swing by the shelter and feed the dogs the night I attended Melanie's sister's wedding, I arrived to find he had forgotten to refill the water bowls. "Well, see what you can do." I said this even though I knew no one had spare time to just come and help some girl fix a leaky roof when houses were flooded out and disintegrating before their eyes.

He rose. "We need more wine." He headed for the wine holder on the dining room hutch. "Red or white?"

92

"Whatever's strongest," I said, wishing my brother could dole out some advice I could actually follow instead of numbing my mind with cheap wine.

~ ~

I decided after waking up on my brother's couch with a hangover that I would avoid two things. One, I'd never drink wine straight from a bottle ever again. Well, at least not three bottles. Two, I would throw away Chloe's business card. I needed to focus, and I couldn't with her card calling out to me in the deep, lonely pockets of the night. I couldn't become that helpless fool who fell for some pretty girl's charm a third time around.

~ ~

The news report went viral a few days after Chloe showed up at the shelter, thanks to Josh. He called me all proud. "I worked my magic and got everyone I know to share it on Facebook, Twitter, and YouTube. You're famous."

"I'm shocked."

"You shouldn't be. The segment sold itself."

"Of course it did," I said, deciding not to bring up that my shock had little to do with the appeal of the news clip and everything to do with him never following through with anything this important.

Within a week, over ten thousand dollars of donations poured in along with encouraging notes and cards. Many people within our geographic region even volunteered to foster some of the dogs and cats until suitable homes could be secured. We weren't out of the dark in terms of financial distress. We still needed a lot of money to cover the repairs and supplies. But, the donations certainly gifted us with a month or two of wiggle room.

We celebrated with an Italian feast at Melanie's house. Melanie even invited Phil. I walked in on them giggling. Phil wrapped his arms around her waist from behind and tickled her neck with his lips.

I coughed when I entered the kitchen and Phil jumped back a few feet. "We were just goofing around," he said, scratching at his neck, then disappearing into the dining room where Trevor, his boyfriend Michael, and Natalie were debating over the correct position for the fork and spoon.

Melanie relaxed with a hand on her wide hip.

"Phil?" I whispered, eyeing her. "Seriously?"

She shushed me with a finger to her mouth. "He can hear you."

I placed the jug of sangria and a loaf of Italian bread that I brought with me onto her breakfast bar. "I never know with you. One day it's a gorgeous redhead, the next a burly sheriff."

She turned to her stovetop, to the tall stainless steel crock. "Keeps me young." She lifted the glass lid and a wave of delicious steam wafted out spreading tomato, basil and garlic through the kitchen. "Do me a favor, sweetheart, and take out the bag of mussels from the top shelf in the fridge." She continued to stir the sauce.

I opened her fridge and scanned her shelves. Organic yogurt, milk, juice, and veggies blanketed them. The bag sat behind the organic creamer. The mussels smelled like the bay on a humid summer day, salty and fishy. I plopped them in the sink and ran cold water over them. I scanned her countertops, her refrigerator walls, and her corkboard for signs of foreclosure. Nothing but photos of dogs and cats adorned her kitchen. I decided on a tactic. "I was reading the *Baltimore Sun* the other day and came across an article about the housing market and how so many people are being foreclosed on."

She closed the lid and then reached for another stainless steel pot. "Sometimes that kind of news can shake people up in a good way, get them out of their comfort zones to see the world from a different perspective." She nudged me away from the sink and placed the pot under the faucet.

She then continued with a story about how the other day she set her curtains on fire while cleansing her treatment room with a sage stick. She cracked herself up, bellowing out laughter. I stole glances around her kitchen looking for any kind of clue that she'd be moving. Not a packing box or a missing figurine. Nothing.

I interrupted her mid cackle. "How can you still laugh with all you have going on?"

She halted, inhaled deeply and released the breath as if smoking a good cigarette. "Sorry?" Her voice rang higher than normal, and the four stopped talking in the dining room. Trevor left Natalie, Michael, and Phil to the silverware debacle and entered the kitchen on a skid.

"Are you two okay in here?"

I pressed forward, tired of the secret ballooning between my best friend and me. "Enough already. Just tell me what I can do to help you save this place."

Melanie pushed back against the counter and scooted up tall. "How did you find out?"

"Josh saw the letter on your table."

She paused, shifted her gaze between the two of us. "Well, it's true. But, don't worry. The world isn't ending. I've still got health. I've got my cats. I've got great friends. All is good."

I pointed my eyes at her, unwilling to let go of the opening I just created. "How bad is it?"

"It's not death." She waved us away. "It's just a house."

"It's your home." I scooted up to her, leaving the mussels in the sink.

"Honestly," she said placing a strong hand on my shoulder. "I am not heartbroken over this. The less baggage in life, the freer I am."

"We've got to be able to help," Trevor said.

"There's nothing you can do," she said smiling at Phil and Natalie now as they entered the kitchen and listened with quiet mouths. Michael stayed put in the dining room, petting one of the cats. "I'm behind on my mortgage and taxes. Everyone's in the same boat these days." She folded her hands in front of her. "It happens."

"I'm sure I've got some wiggle room on my credit card," I said. "I can do a cash advance and you can pay me back when you're able to."

"Olivia," Natalie said, wincing. "I just paid the credit card yesterday and you don't have much wiggle room."

"I've got a little I can lend you," Phil offered, standing on a slant with his hands tucked deep inside the front pockets of his jeans.

"I'm not taking anyone's money." Melanie returned to her pot, to her source for balance and control. "Now everyone lighten up. We're here to celebrate the shelter. That's far more important than this old house."

"Can't you just repay them in installments? Work out a deal?" I asked, desperate to help her.

"I don't even like this big place anyway. It's drafty, half of the windows don't open, the carpeting is tattered, and it's just too big for me."

"Where are you going to go?" I asked.

Phil stepped forward. "I've got the entire bottom half of my raised ranch available. It's got two bedrooms, a living room, a kitchen and an oversized office area that would work fine as your treatment room."

Melanie flushed. I'd never seen her turn red before. "Oh Phil," she said, squeezing his cheek between her stubby fingers. "Phil, Phil, Phil."

"It's empty and I'd love to have someone in there I can trust."

She stood on her tiptoes and kissed the tip of his nose and smacked his ass. "I might take you up on that for a while."

Phil turned red. "Cool."

Natalie reached for the wine glasses.

I reached for the jug of sangria.

Trevor reached for his pack of cigarettes.

Melanie shifted towards the mussels. "Show's over. Now, everyone out of the kitchen. I need space."

None of us budged. "Hang on," I said. I don't understand how this all happened. How did this fabulous house end up in foreclosure?"

"Olivia, my friend," Melanie said. "We're gathering here tonight to celebrate the good nature and generosity of strangers pooling together for the common good of those lovely animals in need. No polluting the night with talk of anything that is not on the same level as that generosity." She tapped my ass this time.

Natalie giggled.

"People sure are generous," Trevor said, twirling his unlit cigarette between his fingers. "We still received the monthly check from our anonymous donor today."

Every month since I had opened the shelter I received a check from a generous donor. This check had sustained the shelter over the years by providing a consistent cash flow to cover many of the operating costs. "Thank God for that donor, right?"

"That's the spirit," Melanie said before waving us out of the kitchen again with her ladle.

"Times like this are making me realize that I shouldn't let that one monthly check serve as the bridge to our survival." I pointed my eyes at Trevor's cigarette, then back up at him.

"Oh come on," he said. "Ease up on yourself. You're a nonprofit relying on the generosity of others. Without that check we'd probably never get paid."

"Our salaries are covered by the veterinary services," I said. "Unless people all of a sudden stop taking their dogs to get their discount routine shots, we've at least got that covered."

He shrugged. "Clinic visits have been down since the storm."

Natalie stepped up. "Things are stressful for everyone. We'd all be lying if we didn't admit to being a little concerned. I've got a car payment due and I just started this whole series of karate classes."

"How about applying for a grant?" Phil asked.

"I heard about one called the Meacham Foundation Memorial Grant," Natalie said. "It's for funding of building improvements and equipment purchases that directly affect the welfare of animals in shelters."

"I'm sure the Humane Society must have some grants, too," Trevor said placing his cigarette back in its pack.

I had applied to the Meacham one four days ago. "All those grants take time," I said.

"Well, surely the two grand you get from this donor every month will continue to see you through?" Melanie asked.

Shock waved through me.

I never shared donation amounts with anyone other than Trevor, my resident bookkeeper and assistant. "Trevor?" I asked without taking my eyes off of my friend, closing in on a suspicion I prayed wasn't true. "Did you tell Melanie how much was in that check?"

"Nope. I'd never ramble on about the business figures to anyone."

Melanie's knuckles whitened around the ladle. "Enough of this stress," she said. "My shoulders are starting to hunch and the wrinkles are setting in deeper by the minute with all the toxicity in this air. Everyone get out of the kitchen and let me cook in peace."

I pointed to Natalie, Trevor, and Phil to leave. They obeyed like three well-trained professionals would. "It's you," I said to her after they cleared the room. "You're the monthly donor."

"Rubbish." She wouldn't look at me. She placed the ladle back in the pot and stirred it with a vengeance. I stepped in and tore it away from her.

"Really?" I asked. "This is why you're losing your home?"

She wrestled with her face, stretching it into a smile so plastered it could crack if she coughed. "Just leave it alone, will you?"

"Leave it alone?" I cornered her between the sink and the stovetop. "Are you crazy? Losing your home because of me?"

She danced over to the sink, flapping her long skirt. "I did this because I wanted to. I sent you the checks anonymously because I knew you'd be too proud to take them from me. This offered me a chance to do something worthwhile, a chance to better the lives of countless animals losing their chances at a decent life."

I stared her down. Arguments rolled around in my head like a bowling ball, hightailing their way from left to right searching for reason.

"I can't accept any more from you now." My emotions tangled. In one moment anger flooded in, and in another gratitude. Blown away, a bitter fight ensued and tangled me into a fit. Tears sprang from my eyes, leaping from me as if afraid to wait around for the grand finale. "I could've arranged for different funding. I could've organized more bake sales, more charity walks, more family photograph sessions, damn it." I flung my hands up in the air, devastated by what this news meant to both of us. "How am I supposed to sleep at night knowing you lost your house over me and my venture?"

She grasped my arms and spoke in a whisper. "Stop this."

My pulse raced. Tears continued to roll in waves. I blubbered, pitying myself, her, Trevor, and Natalie. "What am I supposed to do? How am I supposed to fix this?"

Melanie opened up her arms and I sank into them. "You don't have to fix things. You have everything you need. Good fortune is all around you. You just have to open up your eyes and see the beauty of it all."

I pulled away. "I don't know what lens you are looking through, but for me, things are looking gloomy."

Melanie rubbed her two hands together and pulled them apart slowly. "Do it."

"I'm not in the mood for this positive energy crap."

She grabbed my hands and forced them together. "Rub until I tell you to stop."

I exhaled and followed her command, rubbing my hands together like some sort of Neanderthal attempting to create fire. Heat mounted, friction built and finally Melanie released me with a simple tug to my wrist. The energy ball rested between my hands, pulling them slightly apart, relaxing my arms and tickling my skin.

"If that little motion can move your hands," she paused waiting for me to complete the sentence.

"Yeah, yeah, yeah. Imagine what else it is capable of doing." I hated that her philosophy proved so spot-on all the time, especially when I wanted to be mad.

"So see, I imagined all along that my situation would turn out just fine in the end. Phil offered me a place to rest for a while, and he's kind of a cutie, so who knows, right?"

I nudged her. "You're considering it?" I loved Phil. I loved the idea of her being happy with someone as genuine and loving as Phil.

"Just for the time being, sure." She shrugged and opened her face into a huge smile. "See, the world always gives me what I need, when I need it. And, it'll do the same for you."

~ ~

Maybe Melanie's positive vibes really did work. She encouraged me to start out my day doing the energy ball thing so I could focus in on the fact that we're all energy and energy can be positive if we direct it. So, I worked on directing it towards my shelter, my dogs, my cats, my ferrets, and my birds and within a few days, the good fortune of the donations that had poured in started to really impact us in a great way.

I purchased enough medical and food supplies to last three months, and I paid the electric and utility bills in advance. Additionally, Phil, that sweetheart of a sheriff and also Melanie's new boyfriend who spoiled her with all sorts of lavish dinners and praise, had managed to talk his brother-in-law into fixing the roof and foundation for cost. In return, his brother-in-law would receive lifetime free vaccines, wellness visits and minor surgeries at cost for all three of his Great Danes. He would swing by when time permitted.

I waited in limbo for several weeks for his paid clients to stop calling him with request after request that would put actual food on his table. Meanwhile, Phil helped us deal with the leaky roof with some sturdy pails, and the cracked foundation with a mixture of this goopy tar stuff from the hardware store. Phil even equipped us with new leashes and collars he picked up at a flea market that he and Melanie went to one sunny Sunday afternoon. They came back laughing, holding hands and looking very much like a couple in love.

When I teased Melanie about this she said his love for Snowball won over her heart. She adored that he loved Snowball. So, not only did Snowball get a great home, but the shelter also got some great repairs, Phil's brother-in-law's dogs got vaccines for life, and my best friend got some much-needed happiness back in her life. Soon, she'd be collecting her belongings and moving them into his raised ranch. Time would tell whether she'd be moving into his bedroom or not. I surmised from the way he cradled her hand that the bottom level would be reserved entirely for a new treatment facility.

~ ~

I focused all of my attention on business as usual. The others followed suit, even volunteering to stay later and come in earlier so we could properly care for the full house. Trevor and Natalie loved these animals just as much as I did. One day, I'd repay them for the hundreds of hours over the past three years during which they sacrificed time with their families and friends to care after our sick and injured, our lonely and scared, our matted and dirty furry friends.

"It's an honor," Melanie would say over and over again through the years. Since opening, Melanie volunteered her reiki services for almost every animal at the shelter. For the ones who were most needy, she'd perform her techniques until positive healing results surfaced. "Animals are my best patients," she'd say. "They don't fight the energy flow. They ease into it. That's when the real progress happens." She'd direct this to me with a smirk because I always resisted her treatments. If my neck ached, she'd get me to lie down and she'd start by waving her silly sage stick around my body, and then instruct me to breathe and enjoy the

102

energy flow. I'd always end on a laugh too deep to contain. How could I take her seriously?

Eventually I did. My doctor ordered me an ultrasound and mammogram because she discovered a mass under my left breast.

With four weeks until my scheduled testing, Melanie had cleared her calendar every morning at six thirty for an hour to work on the area with me. Too scared to laugh anymore, I simply closed my eyes, inhaled the mint and sage, and let her do her magic. At some point, I even joined in, visualizing the pink and healthy breast cells dismantling the mass. I wouldn't admit it at the time, but one day my skin twitched and contracted at the mass site. Two days later, I arrived to the appointment, stuck my boob in the machine and sucked in my breath while they took digital images. And, later, when they had smeared warm jelly on my left breast and swirled that ultrasound wand round and round, clicking, beeping in the area of my mass, I imagined only pink, vibrant breast tissue. Sure enough, the radiologist later revealed I had a set of healthy breasts with no signs of the mass as reported by my doctor.

I trusted Melanie and relied heavily on her gift to heal precious animals who took up residence in my shelter waiting for their new families to meet them and bring them home. She explained to me that all living beings had life energy flowing through them and when life energy rose high, health and balance did, too. When life energy sunk to negative levels, stress barreled down on us and brought on illness.

Melanie never said no when Natalie, or Trevor, or I asked for help. So, when she called us to ask if we could help her pack up her house, we dropped everything else and lent a hand. She divvied days up between us. I arrived at her house first one Sunday mid-morning, leaving the shelter in the capable hands of Trevor and Michael.

I pulled into Melanie's driveway and admired the single room attic that sat on her Victorian house like a top hat. I imagined in the early nineteen hundreds an author up there with her typewriter punching out the words of a fabulous novel. I pictured the sun beaming in on her through the wall of windows, shrouding her in a veil of comfort and light as she wrote scenes wrought with relentless conflict.

I climbed out of my car bearing two cups of coffee and a bag of bagels.

She answered wearing a colorful green and purple sari wrapped around her waist and the other end draped over her shoulder. She swept me in to her foyer and I cried out at the boxes she had piled up at the foot of the staircase. "So many."

"I figure, we'll start up in the attic and I'll work my way down to the basement eventually."

I handed her a coffee and I followed her lead through the front foyer, which bore the heavy scent of sage. "Recent treatment?"

"On myself."

I pictured her waving her sage stick, chanting some mantra about peace and love and slipping into a meditative stance, drawing the negative out and welcoming in the positive with grand waving. I loved my friend and all her hippy, flower-child innocence.

She pulled out the steps from the ceiling and we ascended into the depths of her spooky attic, complete with cobwebs laced around objects like white veils. The space smelled sheltered, like a wet towel that hadn't quite dried enough.

Each step creaked, sounding as if the floor would cave in. I feared I'd fall through and land two floors down in a pile of towels in the kitchen's pantry. Boxes were piled up everywhere, zigzagged with no purpose, no sense of order, just haphazard afterthoughts to a move that had gone unplanned. Melanie led me over to the right hand corner nearest the window. I peeked out on the old maple and smiled at the song of birds chirping their joy in the branches. The perfect backdrop to an afternoon sifting through my friend's belongings.

We explored box after box. Each one she refused to trash. *This one is from my grandma. This one is from kindergarten.* About two hours into the ordeal she tore open the lid to a box stuffed in between a rocking horse statue and a scary life-sized doll she called Beth. "Oh, this box is going to bring in some provocative memories." I peeked over her shoulder and surveyed a pretty lacy towel. She plucked it up. It smelled like an antique shop. I burrowed in closer to get a better look and discovered piles and piles of letters addressed to Melanie from a Ms. Jacqueline LaFleur from Hershey, Pennsylvania. "I loved this girl."

I picked up a stack of letters and thumbed through the envelopes that contained beautiful handwriting, pretty flower stamps, colorful envelopes with smiley faces and hearts. "What happened?"

"NOH8 didn't exist back in the seventies, that's what happened."

"So you just walked away from each other?"

"Haven't spoken to her since she walked out of my life many years ago. I did learn she married some dweeb who went to our high school. He used to stroll around like a king in charge of the social landscape of the school, robbing everyone of happiness with his stuck-up attitude and bulging muscles. I don't hate too many people. I hated him."

"How did you find out she married?"

"My sister styled her hair on the most perfect summer day in June 1986. I spent the day bawling at the park."

"Why didn't you just tell her how you felt?"

"Oh, she knew, sweetheart. She loved me, too. But, back then society shunned homosexuality, and both of our parents forbade us to be together. Being of strict

105

Catholic backgrounds, the two of us complied with their wishes. So she married the captain of the football team and from what I understand gave birth to a set of twins, and I married Henry."

"Can I read one?"

"Be my guest."

I read letter after letter and each one carried the weight of two broken hearts who lost out on love because of other people's phobias and close-mindedness. Jacqueline revealed her ups and her downs, her anguish and suffering at the hands of a marriage she didn't want to be in, her disappointment in caving in to others who had no clue about true love.

"We listened to our parents condemn our love, and we ran away from it instead of facing it like two brave women in love should've done. I didn't trust in the love. It scared me. People's judgment scared me. I was pathetic. I'd never let someone talk me out of something I wanted now."

"People must have said some pretty bad things to you for you to just walk away from each other."

"I regret that I listened to them. I pretty much drove her into the arms of her husband."

"I take it you don't still write to each other?"

"Once she had her children, the letters stopped."

"That must have torn you up, huh?"

"I broke it off. I wanted her to embrace her motherhood without me standing in the way. Besides I had started learning about reiki and the importance of channeling positive energy. Sneaking love letters to a married woman didn't exactly follow the proper reiki methods."

"Have you thought about reconnecting?"

106

She traced a letter with her finger. "It's been over twenty years."

"Times have changed."

"We've changed. I'm sure she's got a giant family now and would in no way want me barging back into her life."

I flipped through to another letter, swelling at the sweetness of her words. "She's the one who got away from you."

"We all have one of those."

I shrugged.

"She wrote a novel you know," Melanie said.

"Oh? A seedy romance novel?"

"She wrote our story." Melanie dug to the bottom of the box and pulled out a book called *Soul Mates*. The cover bore an image of two hands entwined. "She mailed this to me."

I took the book from her and opened it. "Dear Melanie, may you enjoy reading this as much as I enjoyed writing it."

"Written by J.L.," I said, running my fingers over the cover again. "Wow, she wrote a book for you."

"Not too many people can claim that." She stared at the cover with pride, a sense of peace emitting from her.

"How did it end?"

"Idealistically."

I opened to the last page and read the last sentence. *She whispered into her ear, "I won't ever say goodbye. So, my love, until we meet again." Then, she turned to her husband and two children and walked towards them, fulfilling her commitment to them as a wife and a mother.*

"We should Google her," I said.

"I'm not reopening the past."

"But what if she's divorced and single? You can still have your life together."

"I'm not interested in that anymore. I like to come and go as I please. I like to eat tuna fish out of a can when I don't feel like cooking. I like leaving my bed ruffled after waking. I like treating reiki patients whenever I please. I like the option of meditating in the middle of the day. I like being free."

"Aren't you at least a little curious?"

She placed the book back in its nest under the pile of letters, and then closed the lid. "Fuck yeah." She smiled sweetly, stood up and strolled away, calm and demure. "Let's go eat our bagels before we tackle this place any further."

I followed her across the creaky floorboards and down the skinny, steep staircase. "Let me Google her for you."

"I don't live in the past. I live in the here and now." She walked past the dining room and into her kitchen where we dug out our bagels.

I blocked her from picking up the cutting board. "Well, in the here and the now we have Google." I wanted nothing to get in the way of this conversation.

She turned to face me. Her cheeks flushed. "Of course I wonder. She crosses my mind all the time, still. Not a day goes by that I don't see her handsome face. Sometimes, I laugh out loud at the wacky things she used to say and do."

"It'll take two seconds," I pleaded, wanting to learn all about this girl who possessed Melanie's heart.

She twitched her mouth to the side, biting her inside cheek. "I'm not interested." She opened up a drawer and pulled out two knives. "Now, be quiet and butter your bagel."

I reached out for my knife. "Fine."

"And, don't you dare come by later and tell me you Googled her," she said, pointing her knife up in the air.

"You've got no sense of adventure."

"You're lowering my energy level."

Chapter Eight

My energy level dropped drastically a few weeks after rummaging through Melanie's attic. Natalie and I were enjoying a bowl of chicken soup that she had cooked that morning when Trevor came out from the back and told me the bad news from the day before. "I ran into Howie, the handler at the Clyde's City Shelter. He told me that they turned away a litter of kittens the other day because of overcrowding."

I dropped my spoon in the soup, which then splattered all over the paperwork I had started for a modification loan to the shelter building. "Why didn't they call us?"

He rounded the corner and patted my shoulder. "They figured we didn't have any room, either."

"We'd never turn any animals away." I wiped my spilt soup. "We need to get out there and educate more people about spaying and neutering."

"We really don't have much space in the cat room, Olivia," Natalie said.

I thought about the kittens surviving alone in the woods, curled up to one another, hungry and unable to satisfy their basic needs. My shelter would never become one that turned desperate animals away. We needed more room.

111

I called Melanie to see if she could ask Phil to rig up something.

"I have no idea where he is," Melanie said.

"Can you have him call me when you see him?"

"He just left here a couple of hours ago and said he's heading to his mother's for a couple of weeks. I guess she's sick with her heart valve. I've already started on remote therapy for her."

Of course she had. "How's the packing?"

"I'm not making much of a dent. I'm looking after Snowball for him, and that little girl is keeping me on edge with all of her barking. She barks at leaves, you know. She is going to give my kitties heart attacks. I'm about to dive into a treatment with her."

"Pet her for me."

"I will. She's a great companion, even with all of her barking. This morning as I reread those letters again, she snuggled up to me and buried that cute little nose of hers in my tummy. She's wonderful."

"You were reading the letters again?"

"Yeah."

"That's it? Yeah?"

"They bring back some good feelings. Right now, I need them."

Melanie never lacked good feeling. "Are you okay?"

"Yeah, of course." Long pause. "Olivia, sweetheart, you should ask someone other than Phil to take care of the work at the shelter."

"Will he be gone longer?"

"Once he comes back, I'm going to hand over a much more balanced Snowball and I'm going to go my own way."

"Why?"

"He's already talking marriage."

She feared dependency more than I feared dying. I pictured her sleeping on a cart in the shelter's backroom, fixing her meals on a hot plate. "Where are you going to live?"

"Don't worry about me. I never lack for a solution."

"But, he was your solution."

"Your solution," she said. "He was never my solution."

I rubbed my eyes with my fist, warding off the beginning pangs of a headache. "You seemed so happy together."

"Phil is traditional. He'll never understand how I work."

I didn't understand how she worked. "You're a complicated woman."

"I guess that's why we get along so well."

"I can't argue with you on that one," I said. "Can't you just tell him you're not interested in anything more than being roommates?"

"Men like Phil aren't interested in being roomies. I don't want to bother him with my independence."

Sometimes her 'independence' served as a good excuse to fold in on herself. The moment any of us did too many nice things for her, she stepped back for several weeks and came back revitalized, more free-spirited, and stronger. She hated being the taker. Now that she no longer could give how she wanted, she crumpled under the weight of guilt, of sadness, of weakness. Melanie didn't understand how to be vulnerable.

"Don't decide just yet," I urged her. "Just wait out the few weeks he's away and see if you feel the same way when he returns. If you're in his way, you can come stay with me. I've got the sofa bed in the living room. We can flip a coin and see who lands on it."

113

"Don't worry about me. This will all work out."

I hung up and worried. She would be kicked out of her home, reduced of her treatment center all because of me and my dependence on the good fortune of others instead of figuring out how to effectively fund the shelter in a financially responsible way. Without her consistent donation money, the shelter could fold.

I turned to my bank statement and cringed. How would I be in a position to serve the needs of animals in a town financially and physically ravaged with only three hundred and thirty-five dollars in the bank? I'd be homeless along with Melanie. The two of us would be circling around the kennels, sniffing out an appropriate spot to rest our tired, poor bodies.

I turned to some wine, and before long found myself desperately seeking out Chloe's business card that I hid in my sock drawer. I fired up my Mac and landed on her website, Homestead Capital Ventures. The site, colored in blue and white, communicated loyalty. She invested in a host of organizations. A quote sat front and center on her homepage: "We're proud of our projects, the experience of our team, and the breadth of our network – let's talk about how we can put these resources to work for you."

A knot pressed into my gut, fisting its way up the back of my throat. I read all about how she earned her first million investing in mobile home trailers. I could see her studying by a dim light in a public library, hungry for a sense of ownership over her life, transfixed on providing for a child and being the stand-up parent hers never were. I imagined her wearing business suits, talking with company heads, negotiating business deals. She always captivated, always persuaded. I even envisioned her team—a group of seasoned steel-headed men who smoked cigars and sipped brandy, circled around a boardroom table listening to Chloe dictate which companies they funded.

Her success intrigued me, tickled me, and drove me to drink a bottle of sangria as I sat staring at a picture of her looking every bit the part of a Wall Street whiz.

My mental footing slipped. I'd always been the one in control, the one she looked up to and relied on to protect and guide her in this world of money, danger, and abusers like her stepdad. I always assumed we'd get married, and I'd be the one supporting and protecting her, buying her Coach bags and taking her on expensive getaways. She'd look up to me as her mentor, and ask me questions all night long, a curious soul intent on one day rising to that occasion. I never imagined her alone in this world, running a successful venture capital company, being the one who controlled money flow and success. I never saw myself as the one who would crawl to her and beg her for help, for guidance, for protection against all the world had thrown at me. I never saw myself slipping, gripping a skinny rope for dear life, crying out for saving. I stood at the helm of fate, releasing my best friend into the wild without a morsel and failing to pay her back for her sacrifices, failing to provide my trusted assistants with a viable place of employment, and dishonoring the lives of countless animals in need because of stupid pride.

Pride eroded things. It corroded friendships, gutted businesses, murdered families, and worst of all, served as a stake nailing bad fortune into place for decades. I couldn't let any of this happen. People relied on me. Animals relied on me. Melanie's good vibes relied on my balancing things out in the universe. Natalie and Trevor's livelihoods and senses of purpose relied on me to get my act together, to swallow my useless pride, and to just ask the freaking girl for some financial help.

By ten o'clock that night, ignoring the pull on my chest, the lack of air in my lungs, I caved and finally called her.

~ ~

She agreed to meet me down the road at the only working diner in town. As I entered, I reminded myself that the shelter needed her, Melanie needed her, Natalie and Trevor needed her, the animals needed her. I did not need her, at least in any other way than her money.

I entered and waved at Rick, the owner and cook. The fifties-style diner smelled like percolated coffee and pancakes. Elvis blared over the mini jukeboxes. Silverware and plates clanked. Light chatter filled the small space. Only four other tables brimmed with customers, a sad reality since the storm. No one spent their money on anything other than hammers, nails, sheet rock, and new carpeting. Pancakes, Belgian waffles, and maple syrup were not necessities.

Chloe sat in the same booth we used to occupy over a decade earlier as horny, innocent fools. She greeted me with her sweet smile. I strolled over to her, mindful of her new side-swept bangs and her cleavage poking out of her fitted scoop-neck t-shirt.

She stood when I arrived at the table and drew me into her arms, patting my back. Her soft black layers tickled my cheek.

I pulled back. "Thanks for meeting me."

Her glossy lips curved up and a tiny flirt rested in her eyes. "I'm happy you called me."

We both slid into our respective seats. An espresso sat in front of her, a remnant of her fabricated New York City life. "I'm surprised they knew how to make one of those here."

"Oh, I instructed the man behind the counter a bit." She leaned into the table, spreading her presence wide so that it filled the space. She circled her lips up to the brim of the delicate white mug and sipped.

116

Sally, an older lady with a one-inch band of silver at her roots, arrived at our table with a sunny smile. "Hey, doll. Espresso for you, too?"

"Since when do I drink espresso?"

She chuckled, stuck her pen above her ear, and strolled away leaving the two of us alone in our little pocket of air. I folded my hands and sat tall, leaning slightly forward. She rested back against the booth with ease playing on her face, looping those eyes around that part of me that melted with her single tug.

I plucked up the menu and dove into it for escape.

She followed my lead. "Everything looks so delicious."

I scanned the pictures of a mushroom omelet dripping in butter, a three-inch stack of blueberry pancakes drowning in maple syrup, and golden hash browns sprinkled in salt crystals. I always ordered two eggs over medium and a side of hash browns. Yet, I dissected each picture afraid to get lost in Chloe's soft glance. I zeroed in on that menu until Sally returned with my steaming mug of coffee.

"The usual?" she asked me.

I handed her the menu. "I'll just have a couple of eggs and a side of hash browns."

"You got it." She jotted this down as if I'd just tossed her a complicated new order.

"Can I get oatmeal, plain, and three scrambled egg whites with some salsa?" Chloe asked.

Sally jotted this down, too. "Healthy and boring. You got it, sweetie." She grabbed her menu.

Chloe slipped me a glance that sent me spinning. I escaped to the saltshaker this time, twirling it around my fingers and examining the rice grains at the bottom.

"How's Josh these days?" she asked.

117

"Josh is Josh." I passed the shaker back and forth between my fingers. "He's married and has a son named Thomas. Cute kid."

She nodded. "Whatever happened to that football career he bragged about?"

"He played for two seasons in college but then hurt his knee. He fell madly in love with his physical therapist and married her."

"I never pictured Josh to be a family man." Her tone tightened. "He struck me as a lifelong bachelor who would travel and flirt his way through life."

"He's a good dad," I said, defending him. "He hangs out with Thomas as much as possible. He's his coach and fix-it buddy. He reminds me of my dad."

She forced a smile this time. "Your dad. Now he was a great man."

"He was."

Chloe sank into the moment with me, tilting her head and nodding. "He was my father figure."

I couldn't imagine my childhood without a dad who loved me. I lowered my guard to comfort her on this. "He cared about you, you know."

She pursed her lips and grabbed the peppershaker, fiddling with something now, too. "If only he knew I snuck in every night. Not sure he would've taken me under his wing all those times he tried showing me how to fix motors in the garage."

"Better you than me." I hated fiddling with tools and engines. "Josh and I will be eternally grateful to you for sparing us from his mechanic lessons."

She stopped twirling her shaker and reached out for my hands. "Those were good times."

I pulled back. "All good things end." I still cried into my pillow some nights over the void.

She spun the peppershaker in her hands again, and I reciprocated with my saltshaker. Thirteen years of separation from those good times and we had turned into a couple of condiment majorettes.

"So," I said, deciding for us both that one of us needed to take the reins on this visit.

"So." She looked up and caught my eye. "The shelter's in trouble?"

I sat back and released the shaker. What an understatement. "We're having a few small issues, yes." I saw her investor mission statement in my mind: "Serving your needs, so you can get back to serving others."

"I want to help."

I folded my hands under my legs, contemplating her motive. "Why do you want to help me?"

"It's the right thing to do," she shrugged.

I gripped the seat. "You don't owe me if that's what this is about."

She leaned in. The lights bounced off the gloss on her lips. "Maybe I just want to be generous."

I tore away from her moist lips and down to her slender fingers. "Well, you're certainly in a position to be." Where her bio failed to explain, I wanted her to pick up the pieces. I wanted to learn how she went from poor kid without a family to a smashing success. "How did you earn all of your money with everything you had to deal with? Did you win the lottery or something?"

She backed against the booth with a trail of hurt on her face. "I'm a capable person."

I fled to her rescue. "I'm sorry. That sounded wrong."

She cushioned me against the booth seat with her downy eyes. "You've always pitied me."

119

"No," I stammered, locking eyes with her.

A sparkle rested on the strong spokes of her eyes. "Yes, you did. That's okay. In your defense, I did spend my high school years sneaking into your room, because I had no room of my own. I was homeless at sixteen. I wore your clothes and shoes. I ate dinner with your family. I hung out with your dad in his garage on the weekends."

I hated the garage and had avoided it every chance I could. My dad always raked her in every Saturday morning when she'd pass him by on her fake walk up the front driveway. Little did my dad know that she had just climbed down the tree from my bedroom and circled around the front of the house. "I hated that garage."

"I loved it. Your dad taught me a lot. I wanted to learn how to fix things in case one day I had to actually fend for myself."

I always assumed she relied on me back then to be her savior, to be the one to rescue her from her hardships. "I never knew you worried about that."

"Not an easy thing to admit." She gazed into my eyes. "Just like it's not easy for you to take help from me, is it?" She smiled and eased into her espresso.

I spent too many years rebuilding myself for her to waltz into my life and act like she had an edge over me. She'd have to fight me for the upper hand with more than a pretty set of eyes. "I don't understand your motive."

"Motive?" She placed her mug down.

"You feel guilty and you shouldn't. We needed to go through the fun just like we needed to go through the breakup. You needed to cheat on me. I needed to be cheated on. You gave birth to a baby. That baby is alive because she is supposed to be. What we went through needed to happen. I don't hold any grudges. Your actions are just that, your actions. So, if you're coming here to settle some guilty part of your conscience, you don't need to. I'm fine with how everything went down. I haven't given it a second thought in years."

She blinked and her eyes watered. "You still hate me."

"No," I slapped the table. "Didn't you hear anything I just said?"

"You're angry still."

She stole my grounding again, rendering me incapable of standing tall and prominent against her shortcomings. "I'm not angry," I said in a whisper. "I have no reason to be."

She exhaled. "I want to help as a friend, as a concerned fellow animal protector and lover. I see value in your work. After your segment aired I researched nonprofit, no-kill shelters to learn more about how they can operate under such hopeful guidelines and my heart started breaking. I read stories about how other shelters operated and determined which dogs and cats got euthanized and about the sad statistics of how many animals get dumped off each year compared to how many pets are bought at puppy mill supporting pet stores. We can do better than that."

She pinched the edges of a story I lived and worried about daily. "I wish I could save them all," I said. "I wish I could educate more people. I wish puppy mills didn't exist. I wish pets were spayed and neutered. I wish people would wake up and realize pets are not disposable. They're family members with as much of a right to exist as their human counterparts."

"If your shelter goes out of business, all of those poor babies could be killed. That tears me up. I can't let that happen to them."

I adored how she referred to them as babies.

I never considered Chloe to be anything more than a pretty cheerleader concerned with doing proper cartwheels and jumps. I never realized she loved animals as much as I did. However, she always did brush Floppy while we watched episodes of *90210,* and Floppy cuddled up to her in the middle of the night instead of me. Whenever we'd go on long walks past the baseball fields, she never failed to stop and pay attention to a dog barking for her, begging for her to pet him and toss a ball. "The way a person treats an animal says a lot about her character."

She nodded, even blushed, catching the compliment.

I got lost in her smile. Before I knew it, she had reached into her oversized bag and slid an envelope under my fingertips. "I don't know how much you need. It's just enough to cover some expenses for now."

I studied the envelope. "So, how does this work, exactly? Do we agree on an amount and then I pay you back in installments? How long do I get to pay you back? At what interest rate? Are there alternative ways to do these types of transactions like maybe instead of a set amount, you get a percentage of revenue from the clinic visits?"

"No," she said. "This has nothing to do with my company. This is a personal donation."

I eyed it, lured by its possibilities. "I can't accept this. Not from you. It feels like payback and it doesn't feel right."

"This isn't for you." She punctuated her words. "It's for all of those adorable babies." She inched up closer to me, "Besides, it's a tax write-off for me." She pushed the envelope into my reluctant fingers.

"So what you're saying is, I'm really doing you a favor by accepting?" My voice had more flirt to it than I wanted.

"If that's how you need to look at it, then, sure." Her fingers lounged a mere inch from mine.

Lured in by what the money could do, I gripped it and sealed my eyes shut in surrender. "Thank you."

Firm and resolved, she patted my hands. "That's just to get you started."

I managed a weak smile to mirror her bright one, feeling a little too much like I had just offered my soul to her for a while. "I appreciate it. I'll put it to good use, I promise."

"So, I'm curious how you get funding to keep the doors open."

"Ah, that's always a challenge. We're a small, dedicated team who work our asses off. We don't take days off. We work constantly. If we're not treating animals in the walk-in clinic, we're grooming, socializing, training, or cleaning." I paused, considering explaining the truth behind my new desperate position. "In the spirit of full disclosure, I was getting a monthly donation check and that stopped. I learned my friend was the donor and she is now losing her house because of her generosity." I sidestepped Chloe's large eyes and continued. "Then, there's the whole fundraising piece. We spend a lot of time organizing events to draw attention to the animals up for adoption and to the shelter's needs for basic necessities and cash donations. Ideally, I'd love to have more time to educate proactively about adopting shelter dogs, about training so people can learn to handle difficult situations with their pets, and about basic health concerns that are easily treatable. I want to do so much, but I have so little time."

"And resources," Chloe finished the sentence for me.

"To say the least."

"Why do you do all of this? I mean you could be working as a vet, earning a better living. Why take all of this on yourself?"

"Same reason as why you're here right now. If I relied on others to do this here, some of the greatest animals you could ever meet would've never had the chance to play fetch, to go for a run, to brighten up a sick person, the list goes on. We're the keeper of the keys to their happy lives. It's a no-brainer for me. I can't imagine serving in any other capacity. These pets need me. They need my assistants. They need my best friend. They need this shelter and the compassion of others."

Chloe's eyes filled. She pulled in her bottom lip, but her chin still trembled. She shook her head. "Wow. You really struck a chord. I mean, what purpose you have in this world. We should all be so fortunate."

"I do feel blessed by it. Even though it's tough financially, it's worth it."

"It doesn't have to be so tough financially."

Always so ideal. "Orphanages have difficult times raising funds."

She cradled her mug. "Tell you what. I'd like to sit down another time with you and discuss more ways I can help."

The lid to all I had closed off slowly started to unseal. She reeled me in so easily. "We'll see."

"Okay," she smiled, accepting my reluctance. "Aren't you even curious how much is in there?"

I wanted to rip it open, but would wait until I privately tucked into my truck. "Any amount is going to be helpful."

"You mentioned on the news segment that you want to expand?"

"The reporter tossed that in my mouth. That kind of expansion requires more staff, more resources, more funding that's just not readily available right now. The community is torn up. They're focusing their money on themselves right now. Justifiably."

"One of the things I could do is start a charitable trust fund." Her eyes danced, brimming with shine and life. "The Clark Family Shelter could become a model for a no-kill shelter success, offering education, compassion, and rehabilitation."

I pictured shiny new kennels, a series of private adoption meet and greet rooms, an expanded medical facility with an additional room for surgeries and a separate one for examinations. I envisioned a classroom for training. My legs bounced. My eyes opened to the bubbly possibilities. I wouldn't have to stress every month waiting for donations to pour in. I wouldn't have to charge the electricity bill to the credit card on those months that only had four weeks to them. "Another tax write-off?"

"I'd rather the animals benefit than anyone else."

I sprang to life, erasing bad memories with endless possibilities.

Chloe's eyes danced wildly and mine joined in, whipping this way and that, weaving up and down, tangling into a primal beat that revived old memories and sparked new ones. *Why did she have to look so damn sexy?*

Accepting that offer would mean she'd own a part of me and we'd forever be cemented together. The void left years ago filled with hope, while my hesitation fought to temper that filling. "I have a lot to consider."

"Then, let's start considering," she said.

I sipped my coffee and tried my best not to appear too committed or too concerned with all of the time we'd have to spend together planning this thing out. She rubbed her hands together like she used to do when ready to tackle something really big, like tell off her stepfather or when she would rally the cheerleaders together to show off to the opposing team. Suddenly, I was transported back to the time when I first learned that simple will alone would not protect me from her power to seduce and stir me.

"How did you get so—" I searched for the right words.

"Wealthy?"

I nodded.

"I didn't like being a victim or interpreting life through only one lens," she said, her cheeks, nectarous and full, angled with her words. "So, I opened my eyes

125

widely and latched onto gaining knowledge about the one thing I lacked and that had kept me from being free all along. I studied money."

I rested on her words, and when Sally delivered our steaming breakfasts, I devoured mine, escaping into the heaps of golden hash browns and gooey egg yolks. "You're a survivor," I said, finally breaking my silence.

She wagged her head up and down. "I've got a daughter who's twelve going on twenty. I need to be."

"Does she look like you?"

"Not at all. She's way prettier."

Time was a funny thing. It erased things—things that used to get me up in the middle of the night to throw up, things that caused me to break out into convulsive cries without notice, things that made me state such declarations as 'never again' and 'over my dead body.' Sitting across from the girl who shoveled dirt onto my life and buried my soul, I realized that I no longer felt pain or revenge for these things. Now, excitement burst in me, excitement for times to come, feelings to explore, and buried moments to dig up. Time glossed over the bad and paved a path for future travel. My hard exterior disintegrated. Now, I sat spooning eggs into my mouth, a naked spirit waiting to be lifted to that level where my toes curled and my heart galloped.

"Is she a cheerleader?"

"Gosh, no." Chloe laughed. "I'm lucky if I can get her to wear sandals with her school skirts. She's all about hammering nails into tree houses and building bonfires."

"I'm happy for you," I said, lifting the hook off the door to my heart, freeing her from my rage, my confusion, and my hardened spirit.

"Thank you," she said, stirring her oatmeal. "I just want to forget about the hard feelings if we can and start fresh. I hope you'll let me to help you."

I needed her, and this reliance placed me in a strange position far outside comfort. "Under one condition."

She spooned some oatmeal between her moist lips, the same lips I nibbled on countless times. She wiped her mouth, then asked, "Condition?" She laughed. "Okay, let's hear it."

"We treat this only as it is."

She cocked her head. "What is it exactly?"

I rose and tossed a twenty down on the table. "Business."

I left her to her half-eaten bowl of oatmeal and the playful smile resting on her lips. I walked out of the door and to my pickup truck across the street, stepping out strong, confident, and in control of this new situation, and more than a little excited at the prospect of getting to know this new Chloe.

I turned the key and the engine rolled, refusing to turn over fully. I tried again. After five attempts, gasoline stunk up the inside. Chloe turned in my direction, staring straight on. I counted to twenty and tried again. More angst from the tired engine. The truck did this to me every once in a while. My mechanic couldn't figure out why. Each time it happened, I'd climb out, open the hood, stick a screwdriver in the choke, and start her. I sat for several long minutes pretending to text. Chloe chatted with Sally, sipped more espresso, jotted something down, looked in my direction, and finally got up and headed to the bathroom.

When she disappeared, I jumped out of my truck, screwdriver in hand, and got to work on getting Big Red out of her slump. When I sat back in the driver's seat and turned the key, she still refused to turn over.

Chloe showed up at my side not long after, strutting her long legs under a short skirt. "Want a lift?"

"I don't need a lift," I said. "I climbed out of the seat again and walked back to the hood. I readjusted the screwdriver.

When I came back up, Chloe swayed that sexy look my way, the one where her eyes lowered and her lips curved into a half smile. She moved in closer to me, and with her thumb, rubbed my cheek, not hiding the sultry chuckle playing around inside. "You've got some black stuff on your face."

She smelled like I'd remembered, like fresh flowers on a spring day. She wiped, and I looked down, down past her neckline to the soft curve of her breasts, a view accentuated by her revealing scoop t-shirt. She pulled away. "All gone."

"Thank you."

I lingered, allowing the moment to breathe, allowing my senses a chance to catch up with me. I focused back on the problem. "I flooded the fuel injectors and I'll just have to wait until they've dried out."

"If you've got a lighter and something I can take the sparkplug out with, I can show you a neat trick."

"Something you picked up from my dad?"

We laughed over this.

Sure enough, within ten minutes, burning up the soaked spark plugs with the hungry flame from a simple lighter, Big Red turned over her engine and cooperated. Chloe tapped her hood and dashed off to her Land Rover offering up a wave and a promise to be in touch. As I followed a few car paces behind, I tried feverishly to erase the view of her leaning over the hood of my truck with those long legs and her toned ass, flinging tools around like a girl who knew how to handle a shot of whiskey, a big cigar, and a ratchet wrench, and all while wearing a skirt and heels.

128

Chapter Nine

Chloe

My secret had marinated for so long that it turned sour. It had grown into a life form all its own, cutting off circulation to neighboring principles, logic, and dignity. At first, the idea of hiding Ayla's father's identity from Olivia protected me from having to face the consequences. Slide the secret under the rug, out of sight, out of mind and deal with it later. Of course, when later arrived, this secret had grown too large to bring into the light of day and to smooth over its nutty appearance enough that she wouldn't be totally shocked. So why not place ourselves somewhere else, in another town altogether?

Coming clean about him could actually affect more than just Olivia now. I could hide for a bit longer or just come out with it and deal with the consequences.

Consequences scared me the way a black hole scared explorers. It was much simpler to evade it, circle around for light years if that's what it took, and arrive safely, intact on the opposite side of it. Unfortunately, what I needed existed only in that black hole. I'd either have to jump in or evade it altogether. I'd have to surrender to move forward.

Giving up had never been an easy thing for me to do. I didn't surrender. I pushed on. I dug deep. I survived. I didn't quit. I hated to lose. When I set my eyes and heart on something, I needed to call it into being. If I wanted a car, I earned a car. If I wanted a summer cottage, I earned a summer cottage. If I wanted my daughter to grow up around horses, I earned her a horse farm. Well, how could I earn her a daddy when he asked me not to uncover our secret? If I couldn't disclose the truth, how could I help Olivia? If I couldn't help Olivia, how would I ever earn back her friendship and respect? I needed that from her. Sitting across from her at the diner, I realized more than ever that her trust was the missing piece that blocked me from living my life out loud.

I wanted Olivia. I couldn't summon her love and respect, demanding her from the universe as I would a car, a summer cottage, or a horse farm. For as long as I harbored this dark secret from her, I'd be circling her for eons, instead of jumping into that mysterious black hole and gambling that she'd be there to catch me with willing arms.

Ayla and Aunt Marie were riding the afternoon I got back from handing over the check to Olivia. The sun glimmered through the windows on the enclosed sundeck, so I decided to call Ayla's father from the lounger near my favorite hydrangea plant in the corner of the room next to the pool table.

He needed to be on board and willing to take this plunge, too.

As I waited for him to pick up my call, the years unraveled before me. All the years we'd protected our secret in hopes of sparing pain from the last person on this earth either one of us wanted to hurt. A freak night, a tangle of emotions, and over a decade of secrecy needed to break out of hiding so it could be swallowed, digested and hopefully forgiven.

Olivia needed to learn the truth. She needed to know that my daughter was someone intimately connected to her.

He answered after four rings. "It's Chloe."

"I expected you to call at some point."

"So you talked to Olivia?"

"She nearly passed out when she read the total on your check. Thirty thousand? Really?"

"The shelter needs it."

"It does. I'm just shocked at the amount of it. When you stopped cashing my checks, I figured you either moved or you struck it rich. I guess I know which one."

"Well, the climb has been slow and steady. I'm just glad I could help."

"So you just want to help her?"

I paused, wondering how to broach the question. "I want to be honest with her about everything."

"You can't," he said firmly. "I've got a family. I thought we were clear on this?" Fear burned on the edge of his words.

"Aren't you curious to meet Ayla?"

He cleared his throat. "I can't meet her. Not now." I could picture him rubbing the top of his head, pacing the floor.

"Have you told your wife about Ayla?"

He exhaled. "Why do you have to keep mentioning her name?"

"Would you rather me refer to her as 'it'?"

"Fuck, Chloe," he said. "I'm not an asshole. I'm just a fucked up guy who wants to keep my life simple."

I paused. Keeping his life simple meant continuing to complicate mine, further weaving my lies until it created a web so thick I'd never reach her. "I need to come clean."

He took a deep breath.

"Olivia will hate me for not telling her sooner. I'd have to be transparent about it all. About wanting my own daughter aborted. About refusing to see her. About sending her money all of these years. About it all. How will Olivia ever trust me again after I kept all of that from her? I know you don't care about me in this dilemma, but think about Olivia and what it would do to her. She doesn't trust people now, imagine if she learned all of this?"

He panicked at that prospect of revealing Ayla after all of this time. He was right. This news would destroy her.

"Fine, I won't say anything." I hung up and pressed the cell to my chin, contemplating this secret and how I could possibly get around it and still live the life I wanted, a life where Olivia respected me, a life where I could prove my valor to her. I simply wouldn't talk about Ayla's father. If she asked, I'd shrug off the question and toss her a white lie about it not really mattering.

I would never, ever reveal that the father of my baby was her own twin brother.

~ ~

I stoked the fire, and didn't care about the consequences. I showed up to the shelter one bright sunny day. A lanky guy named Trevor led me out back to Olivia. We passed rows of kennels where adorable dogs stared up at me with longing, probably hoping I'd come to take them home. The kennel room smelled just like Floppy used to smell after she'd get loose and run into the river behind Olivia's house. Barks echoed off the cinder block walls, breaking my heart. We headed for a windowed door where I could see Olivia, her blonde ponytail flipping side to side as she tossed a ball and waved her arms above her head. As we got closer, I noticed the hole in her jeans right below her back pocket and teetering quite close to the curve in her butt.

Aunt Marie's concern barreled around my head. *Don't do it. Just walk away from this like you did before. The more you go, the harder it is.*

I didn't care. I wanted to be a part of this.

"She's right through here," Trevor said opening the door with a push from his skinny butt. The warm breeze welcomed us in to this dog's paradise, a parcel of green grass and yards of running space. Tennis balls dotted the field, as did a handful of large dogs all wagging their tails and skipping along as if life had just handed them the golden ticket to happiness.

Trevor whistled and Olivia turned to us. Her eyes flew open and a smile burst on her face. "Hey you." She strode up to us, her arms swinging high with her steps. She approached, breathless and smelling every bit as fresh as the green grass. "What are you doing here?" She brushed away some flyaways from her cheek. Her eyes twinkled in the sunlight. I wanted to wrap my arms around her and swing her.

"I was just in the neighborhood and figured I'd stop by and see how everything is going."

"I'll leave you two ladies to chat. I've got to feed the cats." Trevor waved off and left us to fend for ourselves.

A retriever ran up to us and barked. Olivia bent down, picked up a tennis ball and flung it far out into the field. The retriever ran after it as if his life depended on capturing it. "That's Tucker. He's my boy." She crossed her arms over her chest and stared out at him. A motherly love danced on her face.

"I remember coming to this place as a kid," I said. "My mother wanted a cat. She picked out an orange one. She let me name him, so I called him Orange."

"Got to give you props for originality."

Her eyes traced my profile. "The place is much nicer than I remember it."

"I hope so. We've worked hard on it, and thanks to your donation, we were able to repair a couple of faulty lights, get the roof and wall repaired and we even had some left over to get new beds for all the dogs and cats."

I reached out for her hand. "I want a tour."

She blushed and squeezed my hand. "I thought you'd never ask."

~ ~

I called my lawyer the second I plopped into my car after leaving Tucker, Max, and the rest of the furry gang. I loved the shelter. I loved the animals. I loved brushing up against Olivia to sneak peeks into the cat room, into kennels, into the tarantula aquarium. I needed to belong to this project.

I instructed my lawyer to draw up the charitable trust paperwork and told him I'd be at his office that very next day to sign them. I didn't stop to analyze the books, the industry, the building, or the workers. I charged forward eager to push the momentum of this project full steam ahead.

I surprised Olivia with the paperwork the very next day. I invited her to celebrate at a pub, and she asked if we could also invite the rest of the gang, Trevor, Natalie, and Melanie. The five of us ate lunch at McBride's Irish Pub. Lively music blared over the speakers begging our legs to bounce to the beat. I loved the gang before I finished drinking my first beer.

Natalie, sugary and adorable, smiled and sucked on her sweet tea, and Trevor lost himself in his flaky shepherd's pie masterpiece. I sat across from Melanie, introduced to me by Natalie as "Olivia's very best friend." She stoked the friendly conversation with interesting facts about everything from the history of the pub to the reason vinegar, with all its magnificent qualities, served as nature's miracle for both body and house. We shared a guacamole dip and she offered the celery stalks to me. I hated celery but sank my teeth into them with fervor anyway. Olivia sat

134

next to me and listened. At one point, I shifted and my leg brushed up against hers. I didn't move it away, and she didn't either.

The music grew louder as the afternoon coursed on and created a backdrop for us to sink into a relaxed moment, discouraging any and all conversation. Instead, we chewed our food, smiling, enjoying this get-to-know-you-better lunch meeting. I didn't want them viewing me as an outsider who threatened their utopia of loving animals and surviving on a smile and IOUs. I didn't want my money to frighten them. I didn't want them to fear that I would swoop in and turn their little empire into some money-making, for-profit pet sale venue where people could pre-order their puppies from a predetermined puppy mill.

When we said goodbye, I hugged them all, landing in Olivia's arms last. "I'm really happy to be on board," I whispered into her ear. She squeezed me a little tighter and then unleashed me into the misty fog for the thirty-minute drive back home.

~ ~

Typically, when I invested in a project, I stepped back with hands off. I allowed the management team to deal with everything from finding the contractors, to cementing the plans, to planning the strategies, to opening the doors. With Olivia, I not only wanted to be involved because she had no desire to hire the contractors, to execute the plan, to write the business model, to manage the process, but also because I wanted her to see my passion for her cause, and that I could be a good person, despite my character weaknesses along the years. I needed redemption, and money so far had been my only ticket down that road.

In the weeks that followed, I wanted everyone to see how much I really cared by volunteering. They trained me to work the front desk. They had a few volunteers who would stagger their hours, but at times the volunteers had to tend to other commitments. So where they lacked, I jumped in to help. Olivia would pass me like a whisper, sweeping in and out of clinic visits and meetings with adopters. She remained elusive and guarded mostly, but every once in a while, she'd sneak me one of her pouty smiles and I'd respond with a tug on her white lab coat and a wink. She'd blush and travel onward past the desk and onto her work.

Natalie worked with me at the front desk quite a bit. When she discovered I had a twelve-year-old daughter she lit up and begged me to bring her in sometime so she could show her around. Trevor later disclosed that Natalie ran the youth education program and dedicated her free time to teaching the young about the responsibilities of pet ownership.

I promised to consider it.

As the weeks passed, and I tucked into a comfort zone, I started to plan ways to pump some fun into the place. I showed up every week wearing jeans and a white t-shirt as instructed. How boring. I noted to hire a designer and get some fun t-shirts designed to elicit some extra zing. If people came here to embrace the spirit and joy of adopting, then we needed to liven the place up to those happy standards. I would also hire someone to wire for stereo speakers so light, relaxing music could play day and night for the animals. I had so many ideas.

One Saturday, I focused in on fixing a broken hinge on a kennel gate. Tiger, a somewhat feisty little dog with thick straw-like fur poking out of him, kept a firm eye on me as I knelt down beside his kennel gate and went to work. He stared at me from his pillow bed. Every time I swung the door to see if I fixed the problem, he sprung to life from the back of the run, bolting towards me, pouncing his front paws against the gate. He slapped it over and over again with his right paw, cocking his head, urging me on.

"Aw, he wants to play." Melanie came up from behind me. She handed Tiger a bone.

"Or kill me," I said, half joking, half not. At eight-years-old, a neighborhood dog attacked me on my walk home from school. I strolled past his yard and out he ran, this little guy no bigger than a medium-sized cat. He chased me around in circles, and his master screamed out from the third story deck of an apartment. He wanted a bite off my ankles. He had pulled his lips back so his teeth appeared large for his little mouth. The lady screamed at me to stop running in circles. So, I did and just balled up to the ground crying. Before long, the scary little dog turned into a pile of giddiness as he pounced around me, wagging his tail, barking for me to pay attention to him. That's exactly what I hoped Tiger wanted—a simple, good old-fashioned dose of love.

Tiger chewed on the bone, shaking his head side-to-side and grunting. Then, he ran up to the gate and pawed at me again.

"Looks like you've got a determined little guy there. He's not going to give up until he's gotten what he wants."

I put down my screwdriver and grabbed his front paw on his latest snap. "Ah ha, now what are you going to do?" I asked him. He pounced back, rubber bone still sandwiched in between his canines. He lifted his butt in the air and lowered his front to me. Then, in a mighty return, he pounced with both paws once again. I grabbed his right paw again and he once again recanted. We continued this until his tail stopped wagging and his eyes latched onto a new adventure happening at the rear end of his kennel run. The Schnauzer-mix next door began chasing a tennis ball around, and apparently this piqued Tiger's interest more than a human being trying really hard to prove her caring intent true and worthy. So, off he trotted.

I stood up and stretched out a kink in my neck.

137

Melanie, wearing a flowery skirt that stretched past her knees, cascaded over to me in a breeze and studied my neck. "I can fix that for you."

"It's killing me. I can barely move my head to the right."

"If you're interested, I can schedule a reiki session for you later this afternoon after we've finished here. I only live a few miles away."

"Perfect," I said, stretching it again. I had never heard of reiki. Olivia had mentioned her friend performed it on some of the animals, but at the time I didn't care to talk about anyone else but her. I wondered if Melanie was the donor friend who was losing her house. "Your house survived the storm?"

She smiled and her spirit echoed a delighted ripple. Even her salt-and-peppered flyaway hair bloomed in the swell of her reassurance. "It sure did. It's set up on a hill just like this shelter. You'll see for yourself. I'll leave the address for you." She patted my back, and flowed off to the reception door. "I'm going to see where Trevor is. He's supposed to show you more of the ropes this morning."

"Okay," I called after her. "I'll just wait here, then."

Within two minutes, Trevor pushed through the door and the dogs went wild, barking, howling, whining, and all vying for his attention. He smiled like a celebrity, opening his arms up widely. "Doesn't get any better than this."

He carried that large smile throughout the entire day as he trained me on how to properly open a kennel gate and loop a leash around a dog's neck, how to walk with the eager ones, how to clean up their messes, how to read their charts so I could properly educate potential adopters on each dog's habits, likes, dislikes, and history. Trevor got choked up when he told me the story behind a handsome, white boxer named General who was about twenty pounds overweight, deaf, and a gentle giant. We entered General's kennel and sat with him on his bed pillow. He placed a paw on my leg and licked my face with gentle, loving, gritty licks. He latched onto me like I was the most important person in the world. "The sheriffs picked him up after the storm. Apparently, the owners evacuated and left him tied to a bedpost on the top floor of their house. Who does that?"

He petted General with a loving hand, squeezing his neck and back. General loved this. His eyes closed, and I could actually hear him moan.

"He's precious."

"He was so scared, dehydrated, hungry, and shaky when he first came in here. I spent the first three nights in the kennel with him. We all slept here comforting the dogs."

"The owner never came looking for him?"

"No. Can you believe that?"

General stared into my eyes as he continued to lick my face. "How come no one has adopted him?" I cradled his face in my hands. "He's perfect."

"People read that he's deaf and they turn away."

Ayla would adore him.

~ ~

Melanie's reiki studio smelled like a garden salad, fresh and summerlike. She dressed up the room with chocolate suede curtains draping the walls and ceilings and plaid pillows to match. Romantic guitar instrumental music added to the atmosphere. Her table sat off to the side of the room near the potted hydrangea, leaving the center of the room open. "I feel alive in here," I said to her. "The energy flows nicely." I traced my finger along the corduroy wallpaper. "It's the perfect oasis for relaxation."

She draped her flowing orange sari around her shoulders. "Olivia didn't want to join us?"

"She's much too distracted. I just let her do her thing and tried to stay out of her way."

"I wanted to give her some of my canned tomatoes. I'm trying to clean up the clutter around this place."

"You've got a beautiful spot here. I actually grew up a block over in that ranch on the corner of Whispering Pines and Meadow Acres."

Her eyes grew larger. "March and Diane are your parents?"

"Diane is my mother. March, hell no. He's just the bastard who sucked the life out of my teenage years."

"Well, I'm sorry you had to go through life with that jackass. He used to flip me off anytime he stood on his porch smoking, because I once accidentally ran over one of his bushes when it snowed."

"His bush? God help you woman." I laughed. "I remember that day. He came inside the house, covered in snow, flames blazing out of his ears. I just remember being really happy that someone pissed him off so badly."

Melanie touched my arm. "I like you." She paused, stared into my eyes as if searching for something I didn't even know existed. "Forgive me for sounding so bold, but I must." She cleared her throat, softened her stare. "You seem like a genuine person, but I can't help speculating that I'm missing something. Your showing up like this and solving all of her money issues with the shelter is sweet. This shelter means everything to her."

"I wouldn't hurt her."

"Again?"

I stopped my argument. "I was young and very stupid."

"That's just an excuse, isn't it?"

I cross-examined her intent, searching her eyes for some sign of reprieve. "You're right. No excuses. I regret how things ended between us back then."

"You still care for her a great deal, don't you?" Her voice rang out delicately, like a wind chime.

"It's not like that with us."

"No?" She tilted her head. "I think it is."

This woman guarded Olivia with vibrant flowers and sweet fruits instead of pointed daggers and guns. She stood at the front gate, master of the vibe, healer of the pain, assuager of the wronged, pacifying those who entered with her gift to read signals and toy with auras. She, being the priest in the confessional, asked for truth.

I confessed. "I do care for her. When I saw her on the news, I got excited. I saw an opportunity to sneak through the opening to right a wrong, to prove to her that I'm not a bad person, and that I really always did care about her."

"Olivia is a strong girl. She would cringe at what you just said."

I swallowed hard, wishing I could take it back.

"Want some friendly advice?"

I nodded.

"Don't ever tell her any of that. She'll shut you out and never let you back in."

"I'm not looking to get back into a romantic relationship with her." I couldn't, unless I told her the truth about Ayla, and I couldn't do that because of Josh. My feet sunk into purgatory's grip where I teetered between renewed ecstasy and loneliness.

"I don't buy that and she won't either."

I wanted her respect, this master of reiki, of soul, of peace. "It's true. I'm here in friendship."

She arched her eye.

"Honestly. I have a boyfriend."

Melanie turned to a table and picked up a bristly stick. "Ah, a boyfriend. Well, that explains a lot."

"Like?"

She lit the stick and waved its smoke around in small circles. "Explains why you're being so defensive about still being in love with Olivia." Charm and play danced in her eyes.

"I'm not."

She sauntered towards me, circling the smoke around. "You are, too. If you want to be with her, you might not want to even mention the boyfriend thing."

"So, you're proposing I lie to her?"

"Do you disagree?" She toyed with the smoke, looping it around me, she the master, me the tiger under her spell, calmed by her command.

"I don't deceive."

She agreed with a thoughtful sigh. "Good answer." She moved with the citrus smoke, centered by its power to soothe. "This is sage, and it filters out the negativity."

I laughed.

She didn't. She continued walking around the room waving it.

"So, how does this work?" I asked, satisfied that I passed her initiation. "Is there another space for me to undress or maybe one of those freestanding tri-folds to stand behind?"

"No changing rooms are needed here."

"So, do I just drop my shorts here and scuttle under the blankets?"

"I won't be touching you." She looked up at me, carving a smile. "Touch isn't necessary with reiki. It's more about energy flow."

142

"I see." I must've overlooked that tidbit online when I researched it earlier.

When she returned the stick to the table, her face softened, probably taking pity on my ignorance. She flagged me over to the white vinyl table. "Come this way. Mount the table, darling. Let me show you."

I walked over to her reiki table, breathing in the soothing ambiance, the warm tones, the clove scent. The room hugged me. Past the hard part, I relaxed at the hands of a woman who would keep me on the up-and-up with Olivia, no doubt protecting me from skidding off the high road.

My body rested and an overwhelming sense of radiance flowed through me and surrounded me in a bubble. Carried away by the soft music and the deep breathing, I let go of all tension, anxiety, and fears I'd carried in with me. Filled with peace, I floated like a leaf in a gentle breeze. I peeked up at Melanie at one point, and I could swear I saw a glowing band around her entire being as she channeled energy into me. When she finished, I felt so refreshed, like I'd just taken a bath in a garden in paradise. When I breathed, air entered and left without a kink. It flowed in and out with purpose, cleansing and purifying my soul.

"That was amazing."

"Take your time in rising. You might be dizzy."

Melanie braced a hand on my arm and smiled like an angel, no judgment present. "You're a good person, Chloe. I just wanted to make sure."

I teared up at this sweet gesture. No one besides Olivia and Aunt Marie had ever called me a good person. I wanted to live up to this. I wanted to be a good person. I wanted to rise above the threshold of a selfish girl who ravaged lives for her own goodwill. Despite my punches, my kicks, my focus, I couldn't break through the strength of this threshold. I was selfish. I wanted Olivia back. I wanted to come out looking like a hero. I wanted everyone to like me. None of this could

143

happen if I approached it with any other intention than to be a genuinely good-hearted person putting others above myself.

I wanted to jump right back into a life where Olivia stared past my sour and guilt and saw only sweetness and innocence.

I might not have been able to be innocent again, but I could be a good friend and help her out without having to meddle in the peace between her and Josh. I just wanted her in my life.

"Thank you," I said to Melanie. "I'm trying."

~ ~

Josh called me and asked me to meet him. He wanted to talk about Ayla. His hair had thinned. He sat next to me on the park bench and stared straight out at the pond where a family of geese paddled across riding on the coattails of each other. I told him about my plans to help Olivia and reassured him of my pure intent – to help with a critical cause close to his twin sister's heart.

"You're saving that place." He rested his hand on my knee. "Thank you."

I cupped my hand over his. "You're welcome."

"Can we talk about what happened that night?"

"Of course," I took back my hand.

"I never should've taken advantage of you the way I did."

"You saved my life. My heart raced. Adrenaline stoked. It happened."

He nodded. "I just don't want that night to be a bad memory for you because I'd hate for Ayla to think her life started out of a mistake. I just hope you don't hate me when you think of that night, that's all." He shrugged.

"I needed you that night and you were there. That's what I remember."

A smile breezed across his face. "Can I see a picture of her?"

I reached for my phone and showed Josh my wallpaper image of his daughter riding her horse, Trixie. He smiled through some tears, not bothering to wipe them away. His jaw twitched and his breathing increased until finally he dropped his head in his hands and wept like a baby. I patted his back, which only intensified the bucking and the sniffling. I now understood where Ayla got her sensitivity.

We spent an hour together that afternoon sitting under the cherry blossom tree. I told him about her knack for tree house building and about how she loved to ride Trixie at sunset, how she adored reading mysteries and playing the game Risk. He laughed when I told him how she hated gummy bears because apparently, he did, too. He winced when I told him about the time her appendix burst and she ended up with a four-inch scar on the right side of her belly. He nearly died of laughter when I told him about the time when she was nine and packed a suitcase to run away from home, but not before asking if Aunt Marie could go with her.

When the sun sunk below the tree horizon, we stood up to leave. "I'm not ready, yet, but I think one day I might be."

"When you are, I'll be there with you. Until then, you've got my word. I won't tell her about Ayla."

He grimaced. "I'm not a bad person."

We were both so much alike in that respect, just two people trying to justify our lies.

"You're preaching to someone who already knows that."

145

Chapter Ten

Olivia

Chloe wanted to help orchestrate the construction of a new wing on the facility. This new addition would cut out some of the fenced yard, a minimal reduction when compared to the lives we would save.

Chloe showed up to our first meeting with the architects smelling light and romantic and dressed up like a New York professional straight from Wall Street in a tailored suit, heels, and delicate jewelry that enhanced her overall look.

During the meeting, she argued her points of concern like a well-trained lawyer. She represented the shelter with eloquence, and never once fell into an emotional tirade whenever something didn't go her way. She simply remained poised and in the one-up position alongside the men with their pencils and sketches.

We met alone in my office later to discuss the details. She lounged back with a lazy smile, shining her chocolate eyes at me one minute, the next snapping back into serious mode to discuss business in detail. Adept, she swung between flirty and professional with tremendous ease. She knew the delicate terrain and traversed it fluently, like a tightrope performer with perfect precision. When I stiffened against a lingering glance, she'd pull back on her smile and her sultry ways and pop back into businesswoman. When things got too business-like and serious, she'd lighten the mood with a blink of her eyes and a flash of her breezy smile. This dance permeated our time together, keeping me panting and wanting for more.

She spent a great amount of time at the shelter those first several weeks. She wanted to understand everything from front desk management, to adoption rules and regulations, to promotions, to fundraising, to cleaning, to handling the animals. "I want to understand the needs so we can put together a solid strategic plan," she said on more than one occasion. I nodded each time, fumbling against her beauty and business savvy.

Keeping my guard up required hard work. Chloe tempted me with everything—with the smell of her freshly shampooed hair, the minty coolness of her breath, the way her cheeks shimmered in the sunlight or under the glow of soft lights.

Always around, Trevor and Natalie protected me from launching a full-scale attack on this beautiful girl who sat across from me twirling her hair and blinking her eyelashes. Their presence unknowingly kept me in full control, and from falling into the demise of lust.

I found myself worrying about silly things I hadn't worried about since high school, like if my lips shined enough or if my eyes sparkled. I wanted her to notice the extra squats I suffered through every morning and how my jeans fit me just right as a result of them. I wanted her to compliment my new highlights and my new perfume. But, she focused in on business, mostly every second while in my presence.

Disappointed, I obsessed over getting her attention. One day, I even cut clinic visits shorter just so I could run into her more often throughout the rush of the day. I even invited her out to dinner one night, only to be more disappointed when she'd also invited Trevor, Natalie, and Melanie.

I lost myself in her all over again, and I didn't like it. What would happen after more time? To a certain extent, she controlled the shelter. She morphed into our sugar mama. She managed to strangle my heart in several short weeks. She stole my focus.

One day, she had sunk into my chair during a meeting, smiling lazily at me as I talked on and on about Melanie and her housing predicament. Her eyes soothed me and released me of worry, which really only served to rattle me later when my body still quivered from her small, innocent blinks and smiles.

At moments, she would speak in words wrapped in silk as if sharing a secret. Her warm breath would swim in front of me like a summer breeze and, despite my best efforts to block the rush, I'd get all tongue-tied and flushed. I worried that I'd morph back into the old Olivia, let down my defenses to the woman who swooped in and saved all of our life dreams.

I figured if I could get past the construction phase, I could deal with her as the sugar mama to the shelter for many years to come and be unclenched by her sexy vibes and unconcerned with who she slept with and how she lived her secret life outside of the times when she was wielding a clipboard or pointing to a misplaced molding.

So after a few short weeks of working with her, and after another half dozen visits from contractors, I hugged her to thank her for helping me to get the Clark Family Shelter back up and running with a future that looked bright for our furry companions. I melted into her embrace, ignoring consequences. I massaged her back, and pressed her harder into me, not wanting to let go of the magic in the moment. Her heart pelted against mine. Before I knew it, I lifted my head and kissed her. She pulled back and I wouldn't let her. I reeled her in and soon she softened in my arms, and melted into my kiss, matching my passion. I hungered for her and didn't care if I got lost forever in her. I wanted nothing or no one else in that moment.

She pushed off of me. "I can't do this." She exhaled, her face beaming red. She bent over, hands on her knees taking in air.

"Why not?"

She raised her head and looked me in the eye. "I've got a boyfriend."

I collected myself, stood up taller, and secured my arms by my side refusing to transform into that lanky tomboy too consumed with the girl's beauty, left hanging by a thread while she moved on without me, unwilling to stop in her pursuit for better. "I see."

She rose and traced my arm. "I want to. I just can't."

I wouldn't play the fool. "It was just a kiss. We'll just forget it happened."

She poured me a smile as smooth and creamy as honey.

I could steer this back to normal. "How about we go get something to eat with the gang before you head home?"

"Ah," she said, "that sounds perfect."

I pushed her towards the doorway. "Well, get going, then, girly," I said giggling, wrangling away the awkward kiss with friendly banter. "My tummy's growling."

She giggled along with me.

I followed her, trying to reclaim my lost sense of dignity with a couple nudges and giggles.

Disappointment plagued me. A guy had once again managed to take over Chloe's heart.

~ ~

Two days after my kissing fiasco, Melanie called me and told me to come see her right away. Something big happened with her house. Too wrapped up in emotions, she couldn't drive. I left Trevor in charge and ran to my best friend's aid not sure what I'd find when I arrived.

When I pushed through her front door, she was sitting on her velvet couch, hands folded in her lap, jasmine tea steeping in her cast iron teapot on the coffee table. I rushed towards her. "What's wrong?"

She folded her lips inward, shook her head, and then laughed. "Relax. You look like you're ready to faint."

"I thought I'd come here to find your house vandalized or burned down to the ground. You sounded emotional. You're never emotional."

"Well, today I have reason to be. Someone bought my house."

I dropped beside her. I hung my head and braced it between my hands. "Ugh, I feel terrible."

She placed her hand on my back. "Don't."

"But, I do." I pulled at my hair, and even that didn't relieve the pressure mounting. "It's so unfair." My words garbled under my anguish.

"Hey," she said, lifting my chin with her finger.

I looked into her soft, reflective eyes filled with gratitude instead of hatred. I sniffed back some tears.

She circled under my eye to catch them. "Why are you crying, my friend?"

"Because I just ruined your life." I ground my teeth, adding to my pressure.

"Because of four walls?" She swung an arm over my shoulder and pulled me in. "Oh come on, now. You know me better than that."

I rocked side to side with her. I could paint a rock for her and she'd act no differently over it than she would if I presented her with a diamond necklace. "How long before they kick you out?"

"I'm not going anywhere."

I snapped up. "What are you going to do? Hang out with the new family while they play X-Box on the weekends and offer them reiki treatments in between their turns?"

"I'm not being kicked out."

I shrugged away from her arm, frustrated with her need to drag everything out at snail's pace. "What the fuck is going on?"

She laughed. "Seems you're not the only one Chloe has a soft spot for." She winked. "She really surprised me when she told me her plan. Please don't ask me to go into the details because I wouldn't remember. She spoke like an investor and I pretended to understand just to be nice, but that lingo goes right in one ear and out of the other."

"Chloe bought your house?"

"Technically, I think so. I signed some papers and she brought those over to the county office and filed some paperwork, paid up the back taxes and mortgage and is the owner on paper, but I still get to have my name on the title. I don't know it all. Too confusing. I just know that I don't have to go live with Phil and give up my independence."

"You could've lived with me."

"Well, I started dating Phil again once he got back from his mother's. It was the wisest choice. The last thing you need is me clinging to your couch every night. Besides, I really did need a proper reiki room."

"So you were going to use Phil?"

"It would've been an even exchange. I give he gives. We all win."

I winced. "So, what do you do with him now?"

"He'll probably be thrilled that he doesn't have to rearrange his life for me and my candles and sage sticks. He's a sweetheart, truly. He'll remain my friend."

Phil would be heartbroken without the romance. "I really thought you two were adorable together."

"Well, it's your fault, really. You got me all crazed up about Jacqueline and finding her again."

"As a bisexual, I would imagine, it must be hard for you to choose between a man and a woman."

She tilted her head and mocked me with a smirk. "Being bisexual has nothing to do with who you love. Love knows no sexual boundaries."

"I don't buy it. You and Chloe are both wishy-washy."

"I can't speak for her. For me, if I ran into Jacqueline again, I wouldn't let go this time."

"Then, that's a mighty big lid to uncover. What if she's still married?"

"That's why I'm not opening it. Imagination is key. I can live in my dreams. Just as long as they're not clouded by unnecessary baggage, like men I don't care to live with if I don't have to. Speaking of baggage, this means I won't have to pack up all of my crap."

"So, what's in this for Chloe?"

"Once my credit is back up and functioning, I'll be able to get a loan and pay her out. I'm sure she'll get some money back on her investment of me, eventually."

No words managed to filter through the questions running around my brain. *Was this a scam? Could someone be this generous? What did she want from me if not my love?*

153

When I got to my truck thirty minutes later, I texted Chloe to thank her. She replied with a smiley face and the simple message, "I know you would've done the same."

How did she go from being the selfish one to being the redeemer? Why did she bother? One minute she's tossing flirts and the next she's stepping back into the arms of a boyfriend.

I wanted her to flirt with me. I wanted to kiss her again. I wanted her to work by my side every day and not just on Saturdays now. I liked seeing her face during the day. I loved eating sandwiches and potato chips in my office with her.

I feared losing her again. I couldn't pretend I enjoyed being alone anymore. I wanted to snuggle up in bed with her and watch movies on cold, rainy nights. I wanted to go hiking with her and a couple of the dogs and picnic on a rock. I wanted her to want me again. One thing was for sure, she would be tied to me for a long time if she waited on Melanie's credit to increase.

A frothy mix of euphoria bubbled over in me. *Get a hold of yourself, girl.*

~ ~

Josh visited me that night at my apartment, like he did most every Tuesday night since our parents died. He offered me a Corona from the twelve-pack that he carried in, and I took it from him much like a weary child stole back her baby doll after a punishment episode.

"What are you so stressed out about?" he asked.

"I shouldn't be stressed out." I wagged my head side-to-side. "I'm just overwhelmed by some things."

"Let's hang out on your deck." He walked straight through my living room, past the mess of clothes I'd left on my recliner that morning and right out of the sliding door onto my deck, which overlooked the quiet terrace below. Of the twelve apartments in my complex, Josh and I, on his routine visits, were the only ones who enjoyed the peace of the fake palm trees, climbing ivy and bright stars.

Before my parents' accident, Josh avoided me. He treated me like one of the unpopular kids in high school. On holidays, he'd arrive late just so he wouldn't have to engage in small talk. At his wedding, his wife, Bridget, invited our cousin, Marilyn, to be a bridesmaid instead of me. When I graduated with a four-year degree, he didn't even bother to mail the RSVP back. He just didn't show and didn't bother to tell anyone. He treated me no better than he would treat a bum on the street. I always assumed his coolness rose out of his jealousy over how our parents treated me like the sane one and him like the dumb fool. I was the golden child, he the reckless lunatic.

Our father especially treated Josh like shit. The two could barely sit through a dinner together when Josh and I were in high school. My dad would take his plate into the den and eat on a tray table in front of the television set as he watched reruns of the *Dick Van Dyke* show.

Josh didn't care much for our mom, either. He once slipped to me that she annoyed him, especially the way she cackled whenever she spoke.

I happened to love that most about her.

Things weren't always strained in my family. Things turned around for the better just about the time we were setting to graduate high school. Josh made All-America and colleges up and down the coast were recruiting strongly for him. I remember my dad peppering his finest advice to him throughout all of this recruiting. He wanted Josh to choose his favorite team, Notre Dame. Josh wanted Florida State because he wanted to live in a warm climate. My mom begged him to choose somewhere close by so he could still drive home for dinner on the weekends every once in a while. Josh eventually caved to our mother and chose College Park.

This thrilled them because not only would he play for a great team, but they could easily get tickets and see their son in his glory.

Then after a few wild party nights and groundings, he acted out and backed out of his decision to go to College Park, instead deciding to go to his first choice, Florida State. But he decided too late. Florida State rescinded their offer and scholarship because they'd given the opportunity to another bright star. So, Josh, to the surprise of many, rescinded on a full ride to College Park and ventured to a third division school in south Florida.

The next time I saw Josh was on his wedding day when my dad handed him a cigar and a brandy and begged him to do a shot with him. Josh obliged, looking very much like an older man now towering over our gray-haired dad. That was the last time I could recall seeing the two of them sharing a pleasant memory together, smiling, arm-and-arm, caring about one another once again.

The next time I saw the two of them together, Josh knelt beside his coffin blubbering away, hugging me tight as we mourned the death of both of them.

Since then, Josh had been the epitome of the perfect twin brother. My parents' death jolted him back to life, to responsibility, to the great brother I remember him being as a kid. He watched over me, protected me, guided me to make the right decisions and to constantly be aware that this world was a terrifying place filled with people just vying to take over the control.

So, as Josh sat down next to me on my deck, it surprised me when he said how blessed I should feel that Chloe showed up willing to help, and that I shouldn't have been confused by it.

He lit a cigarette, a habit he picked up in college and never quit. He offered me one. I reached over and stole one from his pack. He lit it for me. The good brother. We sat smoking on my deck, one cigarette leading to three, then four, then five. By cigarette number six he had me fully convinced that Chloe was a genuine friend, and I should be happy for her that she loved some guy.

"Don't waste your time obsessing over her. She's involved with someone. She's complicated. She's moved on with her life and so should you," he said to me, crushing out his final cigarette.

I trusted Josh. "You don't think it's possible that she's still in love with me?"

"After thirteen years?"

I drew on my cigarette and pondered this. "I need to get laid, don't I?"

He stole my cigarette from my fingers. "Now you're speaking truths." He inhaled the last bit of it and tossed it into the fountain below. "You need to get the control back. You're sounding like the old, desperate Olivia. That's painful to listen to. Get out of that mode and find some hot chick. Go have some fun."

Later as I retrieved the cigarette from the water, I shook my head. He hit it head on. I had zero control over my feelings for her. Chloe steered this ride, and I loved the rush of it all too much to get off. I liked sitting beside her and watching her kick it into high gear. She revved my engine. The rush powered me. Her sex appeal could drive me from point A to point B in a flash. I wanted things to go right back to how they were before, before she stomped on my heart like she was crushing out a cigarette.

~ ~

To get my mind off of Chloe, I turned to Google and researched Melanie's former lover. Scrolling before me were listings of Jacqueline LaFleur's book in various online stores, including Amazon. I clicked onto her author page and stared at her picture. Her face was smooth and barren of makeup, her eyes happy, and her jaw strong and square. Boxy and masculine, she sported a short silver hairstyle. A gorgeous red-haired dog sat next to her, sporting a leather doggie vest, a smile planted on her face.

I clicked on her Facebook link and landed on her fan page. Her timeline showed her in many pictures with her red-haired beauty named Penny. She was tagged. Curious ever more, I scanned Penny's page, too. Jacqueline had written a long biography. Ah, a woman with tremendous heart.

"My special angel, Penny, is a mixed-breed; a cocker spaniel, beagle, golden retriever mix with a cubby bear snout. I adopted her on March 6, 2010 at age two. Penny lived in a foster home with my friends. I first learned of Penny when my friends sent me a picture. I fell in love with her instantly. I drove immediately to meet her. When I arrived, Penny laid curled up on the couch next to my friend, Kyle."

I adored this woman.

"Here is how Penny came into my life. Penny, docile and loving, was being fostered because a local no-kill shelter was overloaded. The shelter took in dogs from the south who were rescued and sent north for adoption. When Penny arrived, she had an ID tag on her collar with someone's information. At home with my sweet baby girl, I stared at her tag and contemplated calling the number, hesitant of losing Penny. One night, I called anyway. What I heard, I truly didn't expect. Sure enough, the woman on the other end of the line knew Penny. She told me that she lived in South Carolina, where "kill shelters" were a tragic reality. She decided to go into a kill shelter one day and ask which dogs faced euthanization within those twenty-four hours. Included in that group was Penny. This lady adopted all of the dogs who were scheduled to be killed, four in all. She brought them to a vet and had them all fixed and immunized. Then she brought them to a groomer and had them shampooed and primped. After that, she contacted the shelter up north and had them

158

shipped there and put up for adoption in a safe place where their lives weren't threatened."

Melanie needed to contact this lady.

I continued reading.

"She attached her name and address to the ID tags of the dogs, just in case they were lost in transit. The lady didn't do this for any reason other than altruism. She saved my Penny's life, and I will be forever grateful to this angel on earth who brought my ANGEL to me! So, PLEASE consider adopting a pet from a shelter. They are filled with angels just like Penny."

When I stopped crying, I clicked into Penny's photos. Penny obviously enjoyed lounging by the pool and eating ice cream cones. I loved how Penny's face lit up when she sat next to her mama in the sidecar of her motorcycle. Jacqueline and Penny could roll. I liked them already.

Jacqueline looked like she'd be a blast to down a few beers with. A real and true person. I could picture Melanie and her together, walking down the street— Jacqueline the protector with her hand pressed against the small of Melanie's back guiding her to the ice cream stand despite Melanie's argument against such artificial treats.

I wanted them to reunite.

I clicked back on to her page and read over her information. Widowed, she lived in Pennsylvania and had two kids in master's programs at Delaware State. Pennsylvania wasn't that far. My mind raced with scenes of the two reuniting after all of these years.

I sent her a quick message telling her who I was and that Melanie, not a technical person, asked me to touch base and see if they could chat.

If they were meant to meet, so be it.

159

Half an hour later, my cell rang. "You should come to the shelter," Melanie said, her voice cracking.

"Why?"

"It's Snowball. She's had a relapse."

Chapter Eleven

Chloe

The staff suffered from work overload and the construction of the new wing hadn't even begun. People dropped off more animals than the shelter could handle, and Olivia refused to turn them away. She called foster parents and other no-kill shelters scrambling to find temporary housing for them. She spent fifteen hours a day working at the shelter, and that didn't include when she educated crowds on animal rights and responsible pet ownership issues. She answered the phone more curtly, trembled, and dashed around the shelter like her feet had transformed into roller skates. She looked ready to crack under the pressure. I'd never seen someone as dedicated and strong-willed. I told her she needed to hire more people. She told me she didn't have time.

People scuttled in with their pets, dropping their leashes in our hands and walking out alleviated of all responsibility, like we ran a five star resort. The number of people willing to discard their family pets like they were nothing more than trash saddened me.

On Saturday, I helped out at the front desk and handled the dogs so Natalie could train a new volunteer. Olivia ran back and forth between clinic visits, caring for a relapsed Snowball. Melanie and Phil sat vigil by her side, hoping for the best.

161

With an IV hooked up to her arm, the poor little girl slept most of the time. Melanie sat beside her, holding her head in her lap, petting her, feeding her energy, no doubt. She kept saying how she should've visited her at Phil's and kept up with her daily treatments. "This is why she relapsed. She was too weak to be on her own. My treatments were keeping her strong."

Phil patted her back and twisted his face into a sad smile shushing her and telling her not to blame herself. She leaned against him, anguish spreading across her face.

The place felt more like a morgue than a place of hope. Men and women would walk their dogs into the shelter, hand off the leash to me, Natalie, or Trevor and ask us to find their beloved pets a good home. *Are you freaking kidding me? What the fuck was wrong with people?* I could see the death of a master being a good excuse, possibly even financial hardship if the dog suffered malnutrition because the family couldn't afford to feed him anymore due to a job loss. Any other excuse sucked. A family pet should rank above smoking cigarettes and eating cheese doodles.

Yes the accommodations were pretty, comfy, and safe for these abandoned pets, but they certainly weren't home. No one spoiled them with constant love and petting and walking. These babies craved devotion not much differently than we did. We could've hired triple the staff, and we'd still lack the time to devote the kind of love they all deserved.

People browsed the kennels and cat room as if browsing furniture. *Not this one, he's too curly. Definitely not this one, she looks too sad. This one is too tall. This one is deaf.* Why couldn't they see the love like the rest of us could? Maybe the beige walls looked too institutional? Department stores understood this philosophy. Dress up a display with fun colors and designs and the people will come. Maybe this place just needed some art.

I went up to the front desk to where Natalie prepped a family about adopting a cat, and I called a friend I had met at a benefit dinner a few months back. I asked about the artist they had hired to paint a mural at a children's hospital. Within minutes, I called the artist. He would arrive in three hours to consult. Before hanging up, he already fed me his ideas. He envisioned painting colorful birds, hopping rabbits, happy dogs, and curled-up cats all among a lush green field of wildflowers.

After the family left, cat-less, I asked Natalie, "Do you go home and bawl after working this front desk?"

"You get used to it, unfortunately. I used to leave here and think about the dogs shaking and shivering in their kennels alone all night long with no one to hug them or cuddle up to them. I wanted to take them all back to my house with me and spoil them with table scraps and Milk Bones and long walks on the carriage trails in back of my home. As it is, though, I already foster four of them. But too many are being dropped off, and even with the expansion, we're still going to find ourselves running out of space."

"Sounds like you need more help in here."

"You think?" Her voice cranked out a soprano note. "Thank goodness for the foster families. They volunteer their homes, their food, and their time to care for these doggies until a family arrives to bring them home. If it weren't for them, we'd never be able to remain no-kill. It only gets worse with time."

"Olivia said she had everything under control."

"Olivia always says that." Natalie rolled her eyes. "She's consumed with clinic visits from people who can no longer afford to take their dogs to their family vet office for routine shots. So, we now have a busy clinic on top of an overloaded no-kill shelter. Olivia can't refuse any creature." She pulled open the file cabinet and dug out a new folder. "In fact, this one time, this boy came in with a turtle and said he found it in the middle of his road and was afraid it'd get run over. The turtle was hurt and dehydrated and needed care. Most shelters as over capacity as we were would've turned the poor boy away. Not Olivia. She took the turtle off the little boy's hands, reassured him she'd fix him up and return him to where he belonged, in the woods."

I smiled at the vision of this.

"She babied that turtle, nursed him back to health, and we walked down to the creek behind the old drugstore on Main Street and released him into the wild. She cried when he crawled out of our sight."

I could see Olivia muddied up to her knees in a creek, releasing this turtle into the wild, hoping he'd become king of the creek. "She's certainly committed."

"Too much sometimes," Natalie said. "Though, she needs to wrap herself around a task during all waking hours or else she'd start pulling her hair out or banging her head against the wall. Some people just thrive in chaos."

She needed help, and I would help her. I would set up interviews and start hiring her some staff.

So, the following week when I returned, despite her fighting me over placing ads in newspapers without her consent, I reassured her that the two interviews I had set up would be worth her while. I told her that if she disagreed with me after, I'd volunteer to clean the kennel runs for a week.

She smiled at that one.

God, I loved her smile. I loved her laugh. I loved her soft eyes. I loved everything about Olivia Clark. I wish I could've told her. I wished I could've told her the truth about Josh and have her tell me the years smoothed over the hurt and that she couldn't wait to meet her niece.

Later on that day, she granted me another peek at that smile when I lifted a leash from the peg and volunteered to take a very hyper Mr. Chipper for a walk. Two of the volunteers had called out that day and everyone else was drowning in tasks. Trevor and Natalie introduced families to some of the cats, and in between vaccinating dogs in the clinic, Olivia had been dashing in and out to check up on Snowball.

"You'd make me a very happy woman if you could walk him," she said, relaxing into a sweet smile. "That front door has been opening and shutting all day with visitors and vendors and drop-offs. I haven't had a moment to eat a string cheese or pee."

"I'm glad to help whenever. Just let me know when you're overwhelmed."

"It's been busy, but, nothing I can't handle."

I studied her twitching eye, her tense stance. "Hmm. Okay. I didn't mean to insinuate anything. I'm just here to help, that's all."

She pointed her eyes in Mr. Chipper's direction. He wagged his tail and perked his ears. "Someone's waiting for you."

I looped part of the leash through the handle to form a collar. "I best not keep him waiting, then." We locked eyes for a moment, then Mr. Chipper barked. She smiled again before I tore away to unlock Mr. Chipper's gate. I wedged my hips in between the gated door to block him from escaping as I looped the leash around his fluffy head and pointy ears. The two of us took off towards the waiting area.

"Don't forget poop bags are outside of the front door," Olivia yelled.

"Oh, I know. I placed them in there first thing this morning." I winked and strutted forward, swaying my hips more than usual. "Come on, Mr. Chipper." I pulled him closer to my side, walking tall and in full command of this furry, strong beast of a doggie who, no doubt, could easily take over as leader with a simple

165

nudge. "We'll be back in a bit." I turned for one last wave. She stood in front of me, hands on her slender hips, with a small, sexy smile resting on her lips.

I turned back and my tummy rolled in delight.

~ ~

The artist had stuck to his word and arrived in time for Trevor to unlock the shelter's door at eight o'clock the night before. He created a masterpiece, just as he had envisioned in our meeting. He painted happy, tail-wagging pooches enjoying lush fields with purple, yellow, and pink flowers in all sizes and shapes imaginable.

About an hour after I received a picture message of the freshly painted accent wall near the kennels, I got a call from Olivia. "I don't know whether to yell at you or lavish you in praise."

"You're such a control freak, that I wouldn't blame you if you wanted to yell first and lavish second."

"I don't know how to thank you." Her voice drew out long and breezy.

"Sure you do," I teased.

She snickered, and this sent my heart into overdrive.

"Let me guess," she said. "Peanut butter and banana on rye?"

"Yeah," I copied her long and breezy tone. "Something like that, sure."

"Mom," Ayla yelled out running into the den. "I can't find my new jacket."

I shushed her. "I'm on the phone."

"Is that your daughter?"

"Yes, that's Ayla." I frowned at her and waved her away.

"But Mom, Scott and Alexia are coming in like five minutes and you're not even ready."

"Is Scott your boyfriend?" Olivia asked.

I didn't even like Scott anymore. He bored me now. "I guess."

166

"Well, I don't want to keep you. Have fun, and thank you."

I wanted to stay on the phone with her all morning. I missed her. I wanted to work by her side tending to vaccines and socializing dogs all day long. "Call me if you get overwhelmed."

"We'll be fine."

"Olivia?"

"Mom," Ayla begged me, pulling at my sweater. I pushed her away and pointed my finger like a real authority. She rolled her teenage eyes at me and stomped.

"Yes, I'm still here."

"I'm going to be back up this week to check out the mural."

"I was hoping you would. I'll have that sandwich waiting for you."

"Counting on it." My daughter's eyes bore into me.

"Chloe?"

"Yeah," I said, pushing past Ayla's patience limit at this point.

"I'd like to meet her."

"Ayla?"

Ayla shot me a dirty look.

"Bring her with you next time," Olivia said.

"Mom, this is getting ridiculous."

"I've got to go," I said. "I'll talk with you soon."

I hung up and Ayla pulled me up the stairs and into her room to find her jacket. "Who was asking about me?"

"The lady who owns the animal shelter."

"*The* lady?"

I coughed. "Yes. Now shush and let's find your jacket."

167

"I don't see why you can't just take me with you there," she said, tossing clothes from her bed to the floor. "I'm not a little kid. I know how to deal with animals."

"It's just been kind of crazy there. As soon as things calm down, maybe I'll take you."

She stopped tossing. "Really?"

You would've thought I told her we were visiting Disney World for a month. "Yes, really."

She jumped up and down like a five-year old.

If I didn't complicate my life, then my name wouldn't be Chloe Homestead.

Chapter Twelve

Olivia

Snowball improved each day. Melanie and Phil both attributed her miraculous second recovery to reiki. I couldn't deny the treatments had benefited all three of them. Melanie and Phil looked more like a couple, looping their arms around each other's waists and singing their high praises to the other's resilient spirit. When I asked her about their status, she told me, "I was wrong about him before. He's great to have around."

"I found Jacqueline on Facebook."

I'd never seen my friend pale. "Oh wow."

"She's adorable."

She looked ready to pass out. She clung to Max's kennel gate. "Why did you do that?"

"Are you mad?"

"Well, things are good now with Phil. He's got my heart fluttering all over again."

I loved that my friend's heart fluttered, but the playful side of me wanted it to be because of Jacqueline. So, I had to press. "I could send her a quick message about you if you want."

"Absolutely not." She shook her head, as if knocking the fluttering right out of it. "Now, don't we have a spay/neuter program to organize for Sunday?"

I laughed, swinging an arm around her. "You are the most complicated woman I know. One minute you're in love with a woman, the next a man. You're spinning my head."

"Don't get involved with a bisexual. We're all fucked up."

"I thought you said love had nothing to do with sexual preference."

"I don't know what I feel anymore."

I leaned into her as we walked. "I'm sorry," I said, swallowing a chuckle. "But, really, at least one of us is getting some flutters."

She stopped. "What are you talking about?" She scoffed. "You're fluttering all over the darn place when Chloe's here."

"She's out of the question. She's got a boyfriend."

"Yeah, and so do I. That doesn't stop my curiosity from piquing over a woman I haven't seen in over twenty years."

~ ~

The day the construction started, Chloe showed up at the shelter armed with a smile and a take-charge attitude.

Trevor, Natalie, Chloe, and I stood arm-to-arm out in the fenced yard staring at the enormous hole in the ground where the foundation for the addition would be poured. The contractor showed his blueprints again, and my heart leapt. I stared at the proposed new space with pride swelling from every pore. Sixty new kennels all equipped with doggie doors that led to fenced in runs. The blueprints swaddled me in hope, renewing my dreams and erasing all fear.

"Now all they need are comfy beds and flat screens, and I might be banging on the door asking if I can move in." Chloe wrapped an arm around my shoulders and hugged me to her. She smelled like fresh shampoo and mint gum.

"Can I give you a hug?" Natalie asked already throwing her arms around Chloe, knocking me from the embrace.

Once Natalie backed down, Trevor shook her hand. "You freaking rock."

"I adore what you do here," Chloe said, her face brightening. "I'm just glad I could become a part of it."

"We're thrilled to have you a part of our team," Natalie said.

Too shy to admit out loud just how much I enjoyed her being a part of our team, I simply nodded.

Over the course of the past weeks, she had remained friendly and helpful, always eager to jump in, roll up her sleeves and get her hands dirty if need be. The dogs and cats and ferrets adored her, possibly as much as Natalie did.

I no longer filled the position of Natalie's crush. That baton passed rather quickly over to Chloe once she began shadowing Natalie. Chloe wanted to learn everything and anything that had to do with the shelter, from inventory, to watering, to feeding, to cleaning, to socializing, to training, to walking, and even to assisting me on vaccine days.

As we neared closer to the concrete pouring and walls going up, I started to let my guard down. I no longer circled in search of myself when with her. I found my footing.

We were friends. I could trust her in that way.

When she asked to help with hiring new staff and planning new educational programs, I didn't hesitate to say yes. She jumped right in and followed my lead, eager to spread her help around to me, to Natalie, to Trevor, to Melanie.

As the drywall and plaster went up, and the artist came back in and painted a second colorful mural, we were able to start piling up new inventory.

"Here, let me help you with that." Chloe secured her hip under the forty-pound bag of kibble and carried it in like a construction worker heaving a bag of cement. I hid my laughter under the weight of my own forty-pound bag of kibble, following her to the new storage room.

"We can place these at the far end," I yelled to her.

When she arrived at the empty shelving, she opted to drop the bag at her feet. I dropped mine on top of hers and we both sighed as if we'd just trekked a mile hauling them.

"Please tell me you have a cart back here." She blew a wisp of her hair off her flushed face before bending over at her knees.

My mind wandered. I imagined throwing my arms around her back, cradling her to me and her looking up at me with those brownie eyes, a tease in them.

"I never purchased dog food in massive bulk like this before, except for before the dreadful storm."

She rose. "No cart?"

"I'm afraid not."

"I know what I'm buying you for your grand opening gift." She patted my back, like one friendly sister to another.

~ ~

Chloe walked into my office one day as I checked my Facebook for a message from Jacqueline. Still none. I told her about my secret quest to get them in touch.

"Jacqueline LaFleur," she said. "That is such a pretty name. It sounds like she should smell like a garden of flowers, wear bright pastels and write memos on delicate, flowery cards."

172

I loved how she embellished the world. "She's into leather, mostly."

She curled up beside me and whispered, "Mmm, even better."

I squeezed my legs together, enjoying the tremble.

~ ~

Trevor helped me work a spay and neuter presentation at the Howard County Festival a few days later. I dredged up ruthless details about the sad consequences of not spaying and neutering pets, sparing no emotion in my voice as I talked about overcrowding, euthanasia, and animals suffering on the streets from malnutrition as a direct result of overpopulation. Mouths hung open as I dispelled facts, and Trevor forwarded through slide after slide. I always set out to point out the truth at these educational events, especially the ugly truths. People sometimes walked out, huffing and disgusted that I would go into such details, others wiped their eyes the entire time, and others thanked me profusely at the end. I always ended on the point that we needed to take care of the animals in need now and not add to the issues by purchasing pets through puppy mill supporting pet stores. I emphasized the importance of spaying and neutering our pets to avoid bringing more puppies into the world that could be potentially abandoned.

Howard County thanked me in a follow-up call a few days later and asked me to join them at their next county executive meeting so they could gift me with a community award for my work in ensuring positive lives for all domesticated animals. In addition to the plaque, they also donated five thousand dollars to fund additional educational programs and advertisements aimed at communicating the truth to those who would be willing to listen. Within an hour, I called the reporter who first interviewed me and asked her to line me up with a sales rep. I spent the entire donation on a commercial spot to target households with the intent to breed their domesticated animals for money and at would-be purchasers of puppies from dishonorable pet stores who supported known puppy mills.

After that call, I visited Melanie at her home reiki studio so I could tell her the good news.

She was reading Jacqueline's letters again.

~ ~

Chloe invited us all out to dinner to celebrate my award from Howard County. Melanie had called me up to warn me that I had better wear something nicer than cargo pants and a t-shirt because Chloe had planned something downright awe-inspiring. Melanie refused to elaborate.

When Chloe arrived at my condo, she sizzled, wearing a sundress with large colored beads on the shoulders and rainbow splatters of springy pinks and greens and yellows. She looked like she belonged on the set of *90210*. She had sleeked her hair back and the ends curved up just above her shoulders. Long silver strands that resembled tinsel hung from her petite ears down to the ends of her hair. She wore a pair of platform sandals and her toes glimmered in a sparkly pink.

Thanks to Melanie's warning, I had run out to the mall and, with the help of a few clerks at Nordstrom's, I purchased a respectable outfit: taupe silk pants, a collared blouse that buttoned just low enough to expose a little tease, and a fitted navy blazer. When the clerk handed me a matching clutch bag, I refused. "I'll just stick my wallet in my pants pocket," I said to her.

"Wow," Chloe said, circling me, tracing a finger along my fitted jacket. "Lecture a few hundred people on the importance of getting their pets fixed and I get this gorgeous sight? Sign me up."

"This doesn't happen often." I massaged one of the shiny colorful beads on her shoulder, admiring the way it balanced on her soft golden skin. "You look so elegant."

She plucked up my hand and led me outside. "You haven't seen anything, yet."

I locked my door, turned and faced a limo. The driver opened the door for us and we climbed inside to the plush leather seats and chilled champagne.

Three glasses of champagne later, we arrived at the harbor. The driver opened our door and when we climbed out, we faced a grand silver and white yacht with three levels of shiny, polished beauty. A cool breeze blew across the water and added an element of mystique, intrigue, and freedom to the moment. Melanie, Phil, Trevor, Michael, Natalie, and a pretty black girl with wild curls piled on top of her head, smiled at us from the lower deck. They looked dressed for a night out to the Academy Awards.

Vivid silver predominated the yacht, and pristine white draped the rest of this magnificent boat lover's dream. A welcome mat greeted our first steps onto the ramp. A crewmember greeted us and ushered us inside and up the stairs to the second level deck area where white couches draped in white cloth awaited us.

"Isn't this incredible, Olivia?" Natalie rushed towards us, spraying the air with her colorful voice and puppy-like enthusiasm. She hugged us both.

"Oh, and," she turned and waved over her striking friend, "you told me to bring a date if I wanted, so here she is, my friend Tina."

Tina extended her hand and smiled shyly. "Congratulations on your community award," she said. "I adopted my cat, Punk-a-Doodle, from your shelter two years ago."

"Nice to meet you." I winked at Natalie as they walked away hand-in-hand towards the table overflowing with appetizers and more champagne.

We toured the yacht, following the man who bore a serious, respected personality. The yacht boasted everything a sun-seeking guest could wish for – loungers, a bar, banquettes, and tables. A pool with built-in sun pads and everything a group of friends celebrating under a night sky could want—grace, sleekness, and a sexy vibe—adorned the top deck.

Inside, everything whispered "rich" and "comforting" with white and cream color schemes giving way to a deep combination of chocolate brown and gold and hints of Art Deco.

The main deck provided a saloon with a sociable seating space and a dining area with an oval table big enough for twelve. A walkway with a highly-polished teak floor and large windows led to a galley where a chef wearing a white apron and sporting a mustache that had to have been more than two years old prepared our dinner.

Moving forward from there, an impressive, light-filled passageway ran along the centerline to the galley and crew mess. It had a high-gloss varnished teak floor, white painted walls and tall ovoid windows on each side.

We retreated to the upper deck and sat on loungers. A man dressed in a white tuxedo carried a tray with champagne flutes. Chloe handed me a glass and saluted it with her own. "Cheers to you and the fabulous work you're doing every day."

Everyone clinked glasses and cheered.

We sipped lots of champagne as the yacht set off from the ramp and onlookers from the dock waved us off. Above us birds circled and beside us boats sailed. As I waved, I couldn't help but think that the money invested in this night could've fed the shelter pets for a year. I mentioned this to Chloe mid-wave and she placed my heart at ease by telling me one of her clients owned it and wanted to treat all of us to a grand night to thank us for our efforts.

After learning this, I slipped into the night like I would a set of satin sheets.

We ate ceviche and figs wrapped in bacon, and then crab dip with asiago bread, rosemary-encrusted potatoes, and prime rib. We laughed as a team and dreamed up a world where all animals had a home and a lap to curl up on as we stared out at the setting sun over the harbor.

Before long, Chloe and I stood arm-to-arm, looking out over the rippling water, cocooned in a moment together. I didn't care what the world dumped on me later, for that moment in time, I surrendered to the flutters, to the love swarming, undeterred by needless anxiety of the moments that would follow when she rejected my flirts and showered me in only friendship. Under the bright blanket of stars, under the spell of ever-flowing champagne, under the blessing of her adoring eyes, I resisted the fears of loss and hurt. I let go of everything but the moment, breathing it in, embracing it, savoring it.

We laughed, we tickled each other, we teased. I let my guard down, if for no other reason than I wanted her to reciprocate. I opened up to her about the past thirteen years of my life, and how I became the passionate vet. She genuinely listened to me hanging on my words like they were prisms dangling and flirting with her. She asked me about vet school and how I survived the grueling studies. She asked me about the first day I worked as a real vet at Pet World. She asked about my first surgery and about the first time I had ended a dog's misery on earth. She wept along with me when I told her about the time I had to put my sweet cat, Honey Bear, to sleep, and how peaceful she looked when she drifted to a place far better than this one.

Somewhere in between talks of anatomy class, dog baths, nail trimming, and long dog walks, we bonded again, and my walls slowly started to crumble from her bright and sunny interest.

177

One moment I poured my soul to her, and the next we stood on the rails of the yacht, laughing and yelling out to the open Chesapeake Bay unaware of where everyone else had taken off to. The night turned cooler, the breeze blew stronger, and the scent of fish and sea air swam around us. New hope hung in the balance, sweet and fresh, untarnished.

I tapped her shoulder. "I'm glad you came back."

She blushed. Chloe never blushed. She traced the back of her hand down my cheek. "Likewise."

We stood arm-in-arm and enjoyed the last bit of the open bay before docking again, landing in the limo and eventually, reluctantly, calling it a night.

~ ~

When Chloe worked at the shelter, it ran smoother. The five of us handled the weekend tasks like a championship team, understanding each other's strengths and working in harmony. Chloe faced each task with an expert eye, stepping up to even the most unpleasant ones with surety. The animals loved her. The clients loved her. The vendors loved her. During the week when she worked her other business affairs, the place crooked to the side like a hapless house knocked off its foundation. With the expansion complete, we were busier than ever. We had more floors to clean, more kennels to sanitize, more dogs to walk, more cats to groom, more birds to entertain, more ferrets and hamsters to feed and more paperwork to log.

We needed more staff.

The chaos overwhelmed me.

Then this one day, Melanie noticed just how overwhelmed I was. Trevor and I had been working hard at organizing a co-promotional event with a hair salon that just reopened since the storm months ago when she waltzed up front and stared at me with that motherly look, pointing her eyes at me in disapproval. "You're going to give yourself a heart attack."

I waved her off and continued riffling through a layer of files on a mad search for the graphic designer I had hired a year ago to create some postcards for a photography fundraiser event.

"You need to get back into balance." She pulled me towards the kennel area and back towards the shelter's new reiki treatment room. The smell of lavender, bergamot, and citrus seeped from under its door tugging on my senses.

I stammered the whole way, pulling backwards like a toddler on the verge of a tantrum. "I don't have time."

She pulled me forward anyway. My feet skated across the shiny cement floor.

The dogs barked and howled as we passed by their rows. Melanie stopped in front of Max's row. He stared at us, head hung low, expecting a treat no less. "Did Natalie tell you about how the owner came back for him?"

I snapped my hand back from her and readjusted my ponytail. "No. She didn't. That owner was an idiot. I'm glad to see Max still here."

"Me, too. Apparently the guy's cat got run over by a car the other day, so now he thought it was okay to come back and get him."

I stared into his warm, chocolate eyes. His short stub wagged as if powered by its own electrical circuit breaker. "How did Natalie tell him no?"

"Well, she called Phil for backup because the guy took off to the kennels after she told him about our abandonment and adoption policies."

Not only did we need more handlers, but now we needed security, too? "Was Natalie okay?"

"You know Natalie. She chippered right up as soon as Phil escorted the guy out of the building with a stiff warning. She turned to me and asked if I wanted one of her brownie cupcakes."

"I need to do some hiring," I said. "I don't have time for a treatment. I've got to get cracking on this to-do list. It's out of control." I rushed back to the front, and Melanie caught up. Just as I opened the door, she spun me around.

She swept the back of her hand across my burning forehead. "You're hot, which means you're fighting. The animals are agitated because you're agitated."

We stared each other down. I wanted to sit down on the cement, close my eyes and shut the chaos out for two minutes. She took my hands in her own and squeezed them. Dizzy and feverish, I surrendered to her healing touch.

"Fine. Make it better," I whispered.

An easy grin stretched across her face. I followed her into the reiki room like an obedient dog.

We entered the new treatment room. It smelled like green freshness, with refreshing and transparent wafts of lotus and honeysuckle. She had painted the walls a serene whisper blue and hung pictures of beach scenes—Adirondack chairs with flip flops and oversized beach bags sunk in the sand alongside them, tall sea grass swaying in the breeze, the sun rising up over a tranquil morning, seagulls swooping in over a fresh low tide. Breathing in the vanilla lavender candle scent from a trio of them on a silver tray on the Formica countertop, I slipped into a relaxed state.

She dimmed the overheads and turned on the small lamp on the counter. She raised the table, typically reserved for large dogs. "Take off your shoes and lay down on your back."

I obeyed my friend, tossing my sneakers to the side and sidestepping the buildup of tasks, of stressors, and of barking, agitated dogs. The table, not more

180

than six inches off the ground at its lowest setting, cooled my hand. I sat on it and then spread out, exhaling a lifetime worth of kinks.

Melanie lit a stalk of sage and began her cleaning ritual, waving it around the room to rid it of my stress. She hummed, and circled the table, raising it up to her hip level. "Try and relax. Breathe in. Hold it. Now exhale, long, steady."

I stretched out on the table, staring up at my holistic friend through narrowed eyes, trying hard not to giggle at the sight of her strange room-cleansing routine. "The cat and dogs really relax?"

She ignored my question and headed to the sink, dropping the burning sage stick in it. She turned on some gentle music of birds chirping, a harp, and a hooting owl. She rubbed her hands together, and then stood above me at my head. She rested her hands an inch or so above my forehead and circled them. She started at my head and carried her circles down to my feet with small, but dramatic patterns.

Within a minute, I began to relax, allowing the music and the sage and her energy to take me off to lala land where no dogs were barking their stresses, and tropical birds were not screaming out their frustrations. The crickets and the rain filtered out of the surround-sound speakers and serenaded me while heat from Melanie's hands caused a trail of sensations through my limbs.

In my reverie, I floated above all of this and drifted along energy pockets that allowed only free-spirited indulgences, the kind rooted in deep-breathing and healthy mantras that always started with *I am* and ended in some happy, joyful emotion.

Melanie stopped above each chakra point, steadying her hands and energy for several minutes, drawing energy to me, allowing it to release the pressure, and rebalance my system. At one point, when she circled her energy in my stomach area, it warmed and tickled under her healing hands. I saw purple light through my closed eyes and let the moment carry me away. I floated on a magic carpet ride away from the chaos, away from the concerns, vacationing for several necessary minutes in euphoria. I cried. The emotional turmoil of which I couldn't control was being brought out of me and to the surface where it dissipated and allowed me the sweet release I'd been begging to come and wash over me ever since the storm, the increase in orphaned pets, and Chloe's announcement that she had a boyfriend and had gotten on with her life. Melanie traveled her hands above my body, pulling the negativity out of my cells, on past my vital organs, and down to my feet where she pulled them out of me, leaving room only for healing energy, the likes of which tingled and cleansed me like fresh mountain rain.

I escaped into the free moment.

Chapter Thirteen

If it weren't for Chloe, I would've surely earned the title of most boring high school student. Before becoming close with her, my idea of a fun Friday night consisted of completing a five hundred piece puzzle by nine o'clock, with the help of a couple of root beers and a bag of Doritos. But, once Chloe started hanging out with me, the puzzles landed under my bed and sugar-free soda and carrot sticks replaced the junk food. I started to care less about how delicious good sweet and salty food tasted and more about how that indulgence would land directly on my hips.

Chloe was a chiseled beauty. Her cheekbones arched perfectly. Her collarbone was sculpted expertly. Her arms and legs were artistically molded to show off the delicate balance of muscle and curve. As we began to sleep side-by-side I became increasingly aware of my body and I wanted it to be perfect for her so when she would caress it as I did hers, she would melt and fall into a fit of lust equally as powerful as I did.

So, every chance I could, I dove into leg squats, sank into crunches, pressed into pushups until finally the day had arrived when she circled my belly with her tongue and she stopped to admire the muscles I worked so hard to create. I'd never

183

felt so alive and sexy as I did in that wonderful moment when Chloe stared into my eyes and told me I was beautiful.

I wanted to be a fun person, too. So, when she challenged me to climb the water tower with her after she'd heard Molly Sanford and the rest of the popular clique were going to be climbing it that night as well, I agreed like I'd wanted to climb that thing since the day I could walk. Her eyes grew large and her smile radiated from a place deep inside her. Chloe Homestead smiled at me like I was the coolest girl on the planet. So, off we ventured up the side of the water tower next to the Ford dealership, spray cans in our back pockets and bandanas wrapped around our heads like biker chicks ready to rock and roll and get crazy. A bunch of us girls mounted the side of that thing looking like a dozen secret agents on the hunt for criminals. My heart knocked around in my scrawny chest, sputtering as if fueled by bad gasoline. My knees buckled, refusing to cooperate like they had every time I bent down to squat for my dear Chloe. I flexed like Gumby, all elastic and rubbery, unable to press into the ladder rungs with much certainty. My fingers trembled, my head pounded, my stomach rolled against this plight to enjoy myself on a wild Friday night.

I never wanted to solve a puzzle as badly as I did on those last ten or so ladder rungs to the metal landing at the center of the water tower. I sandwiched in between Becky, the hot red-headed co-captain of the cheerleader squad, and my dear Chloe. The other girls were already hooting and hollering like a group of derelicts from atop their perch, and I clung to life, praying to God for his mercy that I might actually survive this wild trek to the center of the water tower. Five steps or so to my destination, I started promising things like, *If my feet land safely on the landing, I will study extra hard for three weeks straight. If I end up coming out of this without any injury, I will mow my parents' lawn five times without asking for extra allowance.* And, *if I get out of this stupid adventure alive, I will never embark on another careless outing again, regardless of how Chloe might interpret the refusal.*

My prayers were answered. I landed safely on the metal surface and even managed to spray paint a cute smiley face with my initials. I also fell against Chloe, as she hugged me from behind erasing my fear, allowing the brush of the cold wind to tickle me, and the spectacular view to sweep me away to a place of wanderlust instead of fear. Looking out onto the town below, I snuggled up to the comfort and thrill of my new life. Chloe swaddled me up in her arms, her beautiful, sexy, fun-loving arms, as we stood on top of the rest of the town and all its silly phobias and boring ways. I tangled up in her love, fearless.

Several things happened after we landed safely back on the ground hours later. I laughed at all of my shaky promises from when I dangled like a hooligan from that ladder rung. I never spent another Friday night working on a puzzle. Instead, Chloe and I explored life, one big adventure after another – diving into deep waters from tall cliffs, running hand-in-hand through dark woods, getting drunk under the stars and skinny dipping, and best of all, getting all decked-out, driving to the city, and crashing fancy parties at the Hilton.

Chloe, always fun-spirited, taught me how to live life outside a shag-carpeted bedroom littered with empty root beer cans and crumpled Dorito bags.

After all of these years, Chloe hadn't changed too much in the fun category. She still managed to inject her larger-than-life juice into days that could've just passed as ordinary. She sprang to life at the shelter, whipping up joy for the dogs through long, sudsy baths amidst water fights with Natalie or me or Trevor. She sang to the cats in a, albeit, terribly tart soprano voice. She greeted potential adopters similar to the way a fan would greet a celebrity.

Chloe carved fun into life.

I couldn't get enough of her.

I found myself aching when she left for the week, wanting desperately to beg her to just leave her usual business stuff to someone else and come hang at the shelter full time. She never talked about her life outside the shelter. She never talked about Scott, thankfully. She also never talked about her daughter. I wanted to meet her. I was ready to meet her.

"You have to bring Ayla in here soon," I said to her before she headed out of the front door. "Bring her next time."

She hesitated, nudging the glass door with her foot. "I'll bring her at some point."

I stepped up to her, propped up her chin with my finger. "You're not allowed back unless she's with you."

She ran her fingers through my hair, lounging on my order, a tease playing out on her face. "We'll see."

Several days later, when she walked in the door leading a mini version of her, I choked up, too emotional to speak. I simply opened up my arms and welcomed her with a hug. She fell into my arms like she'd known me her whole life. "Thank you for inviting me here today," she said with a sunny voice that matched Chloe. She was every bit as adorable as I pictured, long, black hair that hung in loose waves to the middle of her back, big brown eyes shaped like almonds, skinny arms and legs and a smile that stretched beyond her face and engulfed her entire being.

"I'm so happy you could join us. I've got so much to show you," I said.

She beamed up at her mom. "Can I see General?"

"You have to ask Dr. Olivia." Chloe swung her glance my way.

I reached for her timid hand and led the way. "So, I hear you like to ride horses."

"I've got one. Her name is Trixie. She's an American Quarter Horse."

We walked through the kennel door and were hit with the sweet echo of excited dogs.

Ayla giggled and her mouth drew open wide. "Trixie would hate it in here." She let go of my hand and opened her arms up wide and spun. "But, I love it." She darted off down one of the rows, her black hair flapping around like a horse's mane. "Oh, my gosh, look at all of these cute babies." She bent down in front of Tiger's gate and he greeted her with a romp and a wag.

"You should feel special," I said. "It took me all day to get a wag from him when he first arrived.

"So, he lives here?" She placed the back of her hand up to the gate and he sniffed her out, wagged his tail more excitedly.

"Yup, just like the rest of them."

She rose. "Can I walk one of them?"

Chloe placed a hand on her daughter's shoulder, pulling her back. "Ayla, I don't know if—"

"Of course you can," I said, jumping in and rescuing her from a fearful mom. I arched my eye at Chloe, "Maybe not Tiger because he's just eaten, but maybe another one."

Ayla walked onwards and Chloe tapped my arm and mouthed a thank you.

I lingered on her gaze a moment longer than I probably should've and then galloped after Ayla. She landed in front of General's kennel. He slept, snoring on his bed.

"Oh," Ayla whispered. "He is so adorable." Her voice rolled out affectionately.

"Do you want to sit with him?"

187

She nodded. "Hey big guy," she said, tapping on his gate. She tapped again. "Hey big sweetie."

"Honey," I said, unlocking his gate. "He's not going to hear you. He's deaf."

"Aw. Poor thing. How did that happen?"

"He was probably born that way. It doesn't bother him any. He doesn't know any different."

I opened the gate and Ayla tiptoed over to him anyway.

I trailed her and sat down first. "With a deaf dog, you want to approach carefully so you don't scare him." I placed my hand on his back and he snorted, opened his eyes halfway and stared up at me with his usual red, inebriated expression. His cuteness warmed me. He wagged his tail, and in his typical mellow mode, remained sprawled out on his pillow. His whole body wriggled as he stretched his head up, snorted some more and kissed Ayla's face.

She knelt forward and let him shower her with doggie kisses and she giggled.

"Ayla, meet General, the shelter's official friendliest resident."

I stood up beside Chloe and we watched as the two morphed into a bubble of joy together.

Ayla spent two hours with General. She brushed him, fed him treats, held his water bowl as he lapped up water, took him on a walk around the fenced yard, and pet him as he laid his head on her lap and snored off into a gentle nap.

Hours later, long after they left, I soaked in a tub with a glass of wine and reflected back on how perfect a day it had been. I had been afraid of the day I would actually meet her daughter, afraid that it would conjure up jealousy and hurt. Instead, she jolted me with joy. She took to General like a perfect angel, caring for him, petting him, and talking with him. She understood dogs in a way most kids her age couldn't. She reminded me a lot of myself at her age.

I rested my head back on the bath pillow, grateful to have met such a wonderful little girl with such a candid, giving heart.

~ ~

Chloe had helped us hire two new vet techs, three handlers, and six rotating volunteers. We still lacked for a permanent, friendly receptionist. This person needed to handle the range of emotions required to deal with the drop-offs, the line of questioning that drop-offs involved, the greeting of potential adopters and the ability to educate them on our process in a friendly, non-assuming way, and the paperwork.

Chloe had sifted through two dozen applicants and only one stood out. She arranged for the candidate to come in early the following Saturday morning. I sat in front of my office computer, sending Jacqueline another Facebook message at the request of a curious Melanie, when Chloe announced the girl had arrived for her interview.

"I'll be right there. I'm trying to get Melanie's ex to respond to me. Melanie's hounding me about it, but the lady hasn't posted any activity for six months now."

"Jacqueline LaFleur," Chloe mimicked her name like it was an exotic, rare flower.

"How do you remember her name?"

"It's beautiful. It reminds me of Victorian times. If I ever write a book, I'm going to name my lead character after her."

I shook my head, signed my named and sent off the message to the elusive Jacqueline LaFleur."

I walked out of my office, past the kennels, and up to a spot just in front of the door to where I could peek at the candidate through the window. The girl sat tall in the waiting room chair, her hands folded up nicely in her lap and her hair gathered in a neat ponytail at the nape of her slender neck. She couldn't have been more than twenty. She wore a smile. Read the literature. Crossed her feet at her ankles. She'd probably answer all of my questions with a nod and a smile, dotting her great comebacks and can-do attitude with an intelligence that mirrored NASA scientists.

"She's perfect for the receptionist spot," I said.

Chloe planted next to me, her arm resting against mine. She peeked at her through the kennel door window. "Easy does it." She trailed her finger down my arm. "Not everyone is beautiful and intelligent."

My chest twirled.

"Well," I said, backing away. "I can tell a winner from a loser."

"Tell me your method." She leaned in, whispering. "How do you determine from under the beauty if she's the real deal or not?"

Her light fragrance danced in my head. "It's not like I have a system. It's just an instinct thing."

"Okay, but how can you know for sure if this girl is someone who possesses the right traits just by asking a few pointed questions about her past jobs and what she studied in school and how she sees herself in five years? Do you really think a person's true colors come out in that process?" Her eyes sparkled and her finger circled my wrist.

"I'm guessing not."

"A person's true colors come out when no one is looking."

"Enlighten me."

Her lip curled up into a sneaky smile. "Follow me to the desk. But, under no circumstances are you to pay any attention to me. Just go directly to the desk and sit down. Pretend to call someone."

I walked out with her and pointed myself towards the desk. I picked up the phone and pretended as instructed. Chloe meanwhile, read a stack of medical records she had just plucked up from the front desk. As she rounded the edge of the counter, she tripped. I popped up. She shot me a look that told me to back away. So, I did.

The medical records had flown all around her, landing in a scatter at her feet. She knelt down and giggled over her clumsiness. The girl giggled along with her and continued to sit in her chair, propped like a statue, watching as Chloe picked up paper after paper with her pretty long fingers, the same fingers that just tickled my core.

Once she gathered all of the paperwork, she stood up and faced the girl. "Sarah is it?"

The girl stood up and smiled broadly. "Yes, that's right. I'm here to interview for the receptionist position."

"Yeah, about that. You can go now. This isn't going to work out."

The girl's smile faded. "What do you mean?"

"You're the last person I'd hire to be a helpful receptionist." She pointed towards the door. "Sorry."

The girl stood, pointed her head down and walked out of the door.

Chloe faced me with eyes wide open. "Well?" she asked, her face beaming.

She looked so darn cute and happy with herself. "Have fun setting up more of these." I tapped her shoulder and bounded for the cat room.

~ ~

Josh asked about Chloe again on his latest Tuesday visit. "Does she ever mention me?"

"Why would she?" I sipped some beer.

"I don't know." He shrugged. "I figure at some point she might, that's all."

"She's preoccupied getting my shelter fully staffed and comfy." I dangled my feet on top of my banister.

"Cigarette?" he handed me his pack.

I stole one and lit it. I only smoked with Josh. In a strange, unhealthy way, it bonded us. His wife had no clue and neither did anyone in my life.

He lit his cigarette and propped his feet up, too. "How's her boyfriend?"

I stared out over the horizon, inhaling, trying to picture what kind of a man she'd be with. Tall? Short? Sporty? Businessman? "She never brings him up."

"So things are friendly between you both?"

"I guess." I drew another drag. I'd always been honest with him. "I have to say, the more I see her, the more I miss her when I don't."

"Be careful with that."

"Sometimes I think she feels the same way."

He stared out at the stars. "I don't understand how a bisexual can be happy choosing a man over a woman or vice versa."

"Melanie says when it's love, it doesn't matter. Love apparently sees no gender."

He inhaled and laughed on the exhale. "Whatever."

"She introduced me to her daughter last week."

He dropped his feet and sat up tall. "What?"

He looked about ready to throw up.

"I told her to bring her by the shelter. I wanted to meet her."

"Why?" Panic stretched across his stubble.

"Why wouldn't I?"

"Hell, I don't know." He sat back, resting his elbow on the arm chair. His cigarette shook. "What was she like?"

"A mini Chloe."

He drew one last drag, flicked his cigarette over the edge to the fountain below and stood up. "Listen, I have to go."

~ ~

The next day, as I checked my Facebook for a message from Jacqueline, Trevor handed me an envelope. "She's up to it again, I guess."

I opened it and stared at a check for five thousand dollars made out to the Clark Family Shelter. A typewritten note read, 'To Whom It May Concern: This check represents a portion of my business proceeds and serves as a donation to use however you see fit. I am committed to donating this amount to your shelter monthly because what you are doing is absolutely selfless and necessary. Yours truly, a fellow animal advocate.'

I tossed it down and picked up my phone. She barely said hello before I laid in to her. "Under no circumstances are you doing this to me again."

Melanie cleared her throat. "What are you talking about?"

"I'm looking at your foolish attempt to ruin your financial life again and it's not necessary. So, really, five thousand dollars? Where is that coming from?"

"I have no idea what you're talking about. Breathe and start from the beginning."

"You didn't mail me a check for five grand?"

"I don't have one grand. Where would I get five?"

"Who the heck is sending me five grand, then?"

"Maybe someone who saw the news segment?"

"Maybe." I lingered on this thought, comforted by it. Every dollar helped. Especially five thousand of them.

~ ~

Chloe helped me bathe a white pit bull named Bumblelina. Mid scrub I asked her, "Did you send me a donation for five grand?"

"Someone sent you five grand?"

"So, you're saying it wasn't you?"

"Can't claim that one."

The bubbles rose above Bumblelina's belly, continuing to inflate. They threatened to overrun the basin. "I've got to call the plumber," I said to Chloe. "I keep forgetting."

Bumblelina shook out her bubbles, drenching us. Chloe backed up and laughed. That's when Bumblelina attempted to climb out of the tub. Chloe quickly jumped to the rescue and secured her in the foot of soapy water that smelled like a bowl of passion fruit, mango, and papaya.

"Once we're done with her, I'm going to take a look at the drain," Chloe said.

"I've already done that. I've poured gallons of liquid plumber into it. I've reached into it with a screwdriver and pulled out some gunk, but still, it clogs."

"Which one of us grew up with a drunk stepfather incapable of anything more than fucking himself over and over again in front of the television set?" She swiped her hand down Bumblelina's back, releasing another round of suds and water into the tub.

I reached in front of her to wipe suds from Bumblelina's mouth. Chloe tugged at my ponytail and snuggled in closer to me. "You're very cute in suds."

I plucked up a pile of bubbles and plopped some on her nose. "So are you."

We stopped bathing Bumblelina and stared into each other's eyes, gazing past the suds and into that forbidden place. She touched my cheek with her soapy hand. I closed my eyes and drank up her feathery touch, drawing my hand on top of hers and caressing it.

"Why does this have to be so difficult?" I asked her.

She blinked, long and thoughtfully and then Bumblelina shook, spraying us in soapy water. We both jumped back and broke out into a fit of laughter, bent over at our knees, clinging to the light-hearted gift of distraction.

A few minutes later, and a whole lot more dazed and drenched, we managed to complete Bumblelina's bath. Eventually, the suds and water receded. We bounced right back into our platonic roles. Chloe insisted on tackling the issue, and I stood back and let her. I walked away leaving her to work. I snuck a look back at her every few minutes and watched as she knelt below the big basin, her toned arms reaching above her, her butt resting nicely in the crook of her ankles, and her tongue sticking out the side of her mouth. She looked adorable and I wrestled to steer my gaze away from her.

A few minutes later, she called me back to her. She ran the water and it flowed right down the drain. No clog. No suds. Just flowing water. "First pickup trucks, now clogged drains. What can't you fix?"

She arched her eye up and clicked her tongue. "More than I'd care to explain." As she passed me, she tapped my lower back.

I wanted more.

"Hey," I called out to her. "Care to help me give Fido his shot?"

She waved me forward. "After you."

"It's not going to be easy."

"I don't care," she said, walking by my side towards Fido's kennel, our arms brushing softly.

A few minutes later, Chloe braced herself over Fido as I stuck the needle filled with antibiotic through his tough fur and under his skin. He squirmed and Chloe pressed all of her one hundred and twenty pound frame on top of him, cooing and stroking his head. He didn't like this and snapped at her. She jumped off just as I removed the needle. "I don't get it. All Trevor has to do is play with his scruff and Fido melts like a lovesick hopeless romantic." Her eyes watered up as if taking Fido's behavior personally.

"Don't you dare start crying on me," I said, watching her chin quiver and her eyes start to brim with moisture. "I warned you this wouldn't be easy. Yet," I circled around her, closer than necessary, to get a treat for Fido. "You still wanted to come in here with me."

She moaned and toyed with the string to my lab coat. "I love shots. How could I resist?"

I wanted to flirt. I wanted to enjoy her heat. I wanted to be wrapped up in her arms. I leaned in closer to her, breathing her air. "You're playing with me now."

"You must be mixing up my signals." She chuckled and pulled away. She reached into the treat jar and plucked one out. "I just want the dogs to like me. I'm starting to get a complex."

"Show it to him with your palm open, and let him take it when he's ready."

She waited to breathe while Fido's large snout sniffed her hand and moved in for the treat. She giggled at his touch. "See I'm not going to bite you, you big, silly thing you." She patted the top of his head and he pulled away.

I moved in to Fido and petted the underneath of his neck. "Most dogs don't like to be petted on the head. They much prefer under the scruff." I opened my stance

196

and welcomed her into my and Fido's bonding moment. "Try." I rested my hand on the small of her back as she attempted my move. With great care, she circled her fingers against his scruff and he raised his head and relaxed his tail a bit.

"See!"

"Ah," she said so low I barely missed it. She leaned back against my hand and I left it there, cradling her in the bond, not wanting to let go of her and this innocent opportunity to be close to her without worrying of a mixed signal.

"Remember the time we pet-sat Mr. Mercer's cat and she spent the entire time clawing at our ankles?" she asked.

"Correction. Your ankles. Mine were perfectly fine."

"That was a fun night." She turned to me, and back came the smolder in her eyes.

That night we had sex under the stars of their patio while Sinatra crooned in the background. "Indeed, it was." I slipped into her spell so easily.

Chloe must've read my signal correctly because she left town right after Fido's shot, citing something about needing to take care of something important. When I asked her what was so important, she shrugged and said she'd fill me in soon enough.

~ ~

Chloe arrived back in town the same day a family came in and adopted Max, our Rottie. Chloe and I bawled as the family strolled out of the front door, walking their new family member by a shiny leash and collar bedazzled with silver and emerald jewels, handcrafted by his new sister, Desiree. She latched onto his leash and skipped down the front walk with him and he trotted alongside of her like a brother always meant to be by her side. He adored her already, and I just knew before that little girl closed her eyes to sleep that night, Max would be snuggled up to her, happy to be alive and happy to be loved by such a beautiful family.

No more nights spent alone in his kennel. He trotted with his head high and a happy skip to his step.

Chloe stepped in and cradled me, and I allowed several months' worth of anxiety over Max to unleash. She swooned and cuddled me closer. "Come on. Let's get you a hot cup of tea."

I walked with her, sniffing and carrying on like a mother sending her child off to college. "I'm going to miss him," I said as we got to the pharmacy area and stood beside each other at the counter staring at a box of Advantix Flea and Tick medicine.

She touched my hand. "That's what I admire most about you," she said in a whisper. "I don't know anyone with as much compassion as you."

Exhausted from the emotions, I fell into her comforting embrace. "It's so hard sometimes."

She massaged my shoulders. "You're awfully cramped."

I moaned. Her deep kneading relaxed me.

She circled behind me, warming my neck with her hot breath. "I can't promise Melanie's magic healing power," she whispered, "but I can promise to try."

I melted under her feathery touch. "Melanie wouldn't approve of that being a chakra point."

Chloe closed in tighter, her breath bathing and tickling the side of my neck. "Well, it's a good thing she's not here, isn't it?" Her voice strolled out all flirty and seductive, a sound I welcomed. "You're starting to relax."

I swayed, delirious from her light fragrance. Her seductive touch swept me away again, just as it did years ago. Her delicate touch, her sultry voice, her light-hearted vibe combined to form a spell over me. My toes and legs numbed, and I could barely manage a breath.

She cradled my shoulders in her strong hands and massaged down my arms, flinging nervous energy off of me like she was clearing rainwater from the hood of a car. My defenses disappeared along with my resolve to stay strong. Then, she circled me towards her, cradled my face in between her two soft hands and stared deeply into my eyes. "I've missed you so much."

What was I doing? I could hear Josh's echo of how I needed to be careful. I didn't care. I wanted to give in to her. I wanted danger. I wanted to stand on that ledge with my feet half-dangling. I wanted to lose focus if only for an hour, staring into her pretty eyes, getting lost in her shiny hair, inhaling her delicate scent. My heart twirled around in a gazillion circles. For just one moment, I wanted to be free.

I grabbed her hand and led her back past the kennels, past the free roaming cat room where cats were hanging out together on carpeted podiums, past the exam rooms, past the colorful mural of dancing doggies and hopping rabbits and straight towards my office. I turned back to her, a familiar smile spread across her face, danced on her lips, played on her eyes. The spark in her eyes intensified as I lifted my free hand to her soft cheek. I caressed her face, longing for more. She closed her eyes and drew a visible breath. Her chest bellowed in and out, an obvious heartbeat in check. Her eyelids fluttered and her hand trembled in mine. When she opened her eyes, I moved in closer wanting her breath to wash over my face. I closed my eyes now, sealing in this moment when love tickled my core. Her soft skin, her delicate summer scent, her strong fingers caressing mine, a sweet combination that lured me to seek more. Just as she had done to me so many times, I drew her to me this time and kissed her with a new hunger, one that stirred every nerve in my body to full attention. She placed her hand on the back of my head and pressed me harder against her, vying for that control that raised her to a level unparalleled to anyone of her stature, her beauty, her grace. She backed up towards my futon, never taking her lips off of mine, pulling me along with her, past the file cabinet, past the printer, past the floor lamp with an oil ring that smelled of vanilla and clove. Once at the futon, we tore off each other's shirts, shorts, and bras, hungry to feast, famished from years of starving ourselves from each other.

We landed on the futon couch and tossed aside leashes and collars and dog toys. I caressed her, cradled her to me, and grazed her in kisses, wrapping her in love. I pulled her tight low ponytail out of her hair and let it flow. My fingers laced in her sleek black mane. I twirled it round and round my finger, staring at it, mesmerized by its shine, its vibrancy, its strength. I twirled a piece and slid my finger to its edge, then gently down to her breast. I circled her nipple, aroused by the way it hardened. I reached out for her hair and placed it atop both of her shoulders, cradling her like a stole. "Why don't you wear your hair down like this anymore?" I whispered into her mouth.

She kissed me sweetly, her tongue lingering on mine. "If I would've known you liked it like that I would've worn it this way more often."

I couldn't kiss her hard enough now. I pressed her to me, stroking her back, enjoying the tickle of her bare breasts against mine. I melted into her embrace, savoring her delicate, sweet taste. I couldn't press against her hard enough. My hunger for her overpowered my ability to control the intensity.

Chloe commanded the scene, rolling me over on my back and grazing my skin with her lips, soft caresses planted carefully and gingerly from my neck to my shoulder to the curve of my breast. She swooned her way down my cleavage and onto my belly button, circling it with a reverence she'd yet to show me. I moaned, unable to keep the pleasure to myself. She responded with a stronger grip on my hips and a firmer, more seductive kiss traveling down past my bikini line and into a place of extreme highs. I clung to her thick hair, twirling it and stroking it between my fingers as she planted her tongue, her love, in me, taking me to new heights, new pleasures, new ecstasy.

Chapter Fourteen

Chloe

We had dozed off for an hour after making love. When I woke up, Olivia's arm was draped around me, her leg entwined in mine. I kissed her hand, and she stirred, moaned, and pressed closer into me. I pulled her arms tighter around me, not wanting this moment to get away from us. I wished I could've sealed us into a cocoon, not permitting the rest of the world and all of its hurtful truths from entering. Josh popped into my mind. Then Ayla. Then I saw Olivia taking her love back from me. I clung tighter.

"You're trembling," Olivia said, brushing wisps of my hair away from my neck. "Are you cold?" She caressed my neck with her warm lips, cuddling up closer to me.

"I'm not cold," I said. "Just really happy right now." I turned and faced her, brought her hand up to my lips and kissed it, staring deep into her loving eyes. If only I could keep this love intact.

She kissed me. We lingered on our lips, each teasing the other with a flick of our tongues. She giggled and I squeezed her. She giggled more, and I tickled her belly. She kicked and wriggled out of my arms. I didn't stop. I pressed on with my tickles to her flat tummy. She responded with a bold grip of my wrists and a wrestling stronghold with her legs. Paralyzed beneath her now, I convulsed into laughter, squirming, kicking, and pushing against her grip.

We giggled and lost ourselves in each other all over again.

A few hours had passed since we had first sealed off from the rest of the shelter. We emerged back out to the kennel area, a bit disheveled. Trevor took one look at us and a lopsided grin propped up on his face. Natalie couldn't meet our eye. She danced around the obvious with a pressing request to work with a new collie who had just arrived and needed some guidance on how to sit and stay when one of us entered her kennel. Olivia turned right back into serious mode, fully taking back command of her shelter and any suspicion that she had just let her hair down and gone a little wild for once.

When Olivia walked away from Trevor and me, he winked at me and turned red. I punched his arm and told him to get his head out of the gutter.

~ ~

Later that night, back when the shelter cleared out and Olivia sat in her office at her computer, I snuck in and locked the door. I scooted up around behind her and placed my arms around her neck, dangling my hands at her breasts. "What are you doing?" I asked.

"Look at how adorable Jacqueline is. She rides a motorcycle. Melanie would totally love riding along with Penny in her sidecar."

I kissed her neck, hungry for more of her. "You are stalking her."

She craned her neck into me, causing my lips to press even harder against her skin. She smelled like Dove soap. "Melanie's the one who keeps asking me to dig up more."

I traveled my lips down her neck onto her collarbone. "Why doesn't Melanie just stalk her, then?"

"Melanie doesn't own a computer. She doesn't have an email address. She only knows what Facebook is now because I showed her Jacqueline's pictures. I think she's in love."

"Come here." I pulled her away from the computer and back over to her futon again. She stole position with me and pushed me down on it.

She straddled me, pressing my arms down with her delicate hands. I wriggled under her, and couldn't budge.

"You are a class-A control freak," I said to her.

Olivia giggled, flipped her head backwards and then landed on my lips.

"That's sexy," I told her.

She commanded control of me for the next hour, weaving her tongue back and forth across my skin as if creating an invisible shield that only she could penetrate. She circled my body, inside and out, sending warm tingles and surges of pleasure through me, making me her prisoner. I surrendered to her control over me, allowing her to bring me back and forth to that point where pleasure and hunger met and formed pure energy, perpetual fire, steamy bliss where all one could do was fold in on herself and cave in to the moment.

~ ~

When I arrived back home, Aunt Marie was preparing fried rice and shrimp for dinner. I sat on the stool and confessed my afternoon to her. She arched an eye, tossed some soy sauce in the fried rice mixture and said, "You need to tell her."

"I'll tell her in time." Pleasure still swam through me, tickling me between my legs, around my nipples, and deep down in the farthest reaches of my tummy.

"The longer you wait, the more shocked she'll be when you tell her." She stirred the fried rice. It sizzled in the skillet and smelled like heaven. "She's not going to trust you if you continue to toy with her."

"It's been thirteen years. What's another couple of days or weeks?" How would I come out and say *I not only cheated on you and got pregnant, but your brother is the father?*

She cracked an egg over the rice just the way we all loved it. "Ayla," she called out. "Come and get it while it's hot."

Aunt Marie wiped the counter with the dirty dishrag. I hated when she did this. "That is full of germs."

She rolled her eyes all knowing. "I've been doing this for years. Have you died, yet?"

Ayla appeared wearing her pink and gray sweatshirt and blue jeans. She looked adorable. "Can I go back and see General?"

I couldn't look my teenage girl in the eye. I had just made love to her aunt, to her father's sister, sister of the man who disowned her, sister of the man she desperately wanted to meet.

"We'll go soon." I smoothed her wild hair. "I figured we could eat dinner together tonight and maybe watch a movie." I bowed down to scoop up a spoonful of rice.

"But Scott's taking us to the basketball game, remember?"

Scott. I still hadn't told her I'd broken it off with him the past weekend after Olivia and I bathed Bumblelina. "I won't be going."

"Mom. You're never around to do anything anymore."

Aunt Marie peeked up at me as she shoveled a spoonful of rice in her mouth. She cocked her head as if to say my little girl had a point.

"I've just been really busy."

Ayla rolled her eyes. "I know you broke up with him."

"Did he tell you?" I asked, mortified that a grown man would do that.

"Alexia told me. She heard him crying. Well, she said sobbing. So she asked him what happened and he told her."

"Sobbing?" This annoyed me more than saddened me.

"Yes." She squared off with me, standing not more than a foot from me. "He loved you."

We both stood, arms folded across our chests, battling her desire for a father figure in her life. Hurt brimmed my little girl's eyes.

"I wasn't in love with him."

"I know," she said, softening.

"You know?" I smoothed her hair again, exercising my maternal right.

"You like Dr. Olivia."

"No, I don't." I was ten-years-old again, brushing away rumors that I liked Amanda Hodkins.

She scoffed and hightailed out of the kitchen. "Whatever, then."

"Hang on," I screamed out. "You can't talk to me like that, young lady."

"Whatever." she screamed back at me and stormed off.

Fifteen minutes later, with me fuming in the kitchen with Aunt Marie, Scott beeped his car horn and Ayla ran out of the front door without saying goodbye.

I ran after her, opened the front door and screamed out to her like a raving lunatic mother. "Ayla, I want you home by eight o'clock sharp."

Ayla turned to me before getting into the backseat of Scott's SUV and waved at me like we'd just shared a nice ice cream cone before she bolted out of the house. "Sure thing, Mom. See you at eight." She hopped in and closed the door and smiled at me like a good daughter should.

Scott waved.

I waved back.

I turned to go back in the house and Aunt Marie shrugged and flashed me a knowing smirk.

"Too much?" I asked her.

"Overload." Aunt Marie twisted her mouth in pain. "Screaming is bad enough to do in front of your recent ex. Not so cool in front of your daughter's friends. She's not one who likes to be embarrassed."

I exhaled and dropped my shoulders in defeat. Aunt Marie swooped in and led me back into the kitchen. "I am totally in love with Olivia and she's going to hate me when she finds out about Josh. I am screwed." I tapped the counter with my fist. "What am I going to do?"

"You're going to start by having a mango martini with your favorite aunt, followed up by a good game of Rummy."

A competitive card game, alcohol, and fruit answered to everything and anything stress related with Aunt Marie. "Why do you put up with me?"

She squeezed me. "Because I love you, kiddo."

"I can't lose Olivia again."

"I didn't know you had her again."

I smiled and flushed.

"Did you fuck her?"

I laughed at my aunt's boldness. "I didn't fuck her. I made love to her."

"You don't miss having a guy's, you know…"

"Penis?"

"I hate that word. It's so clinical," she said.

"Dick?"

"Worse. That sounds dirty."

I chuckled at my aunt's innocence.

"Vagina has a much better ring to it," she said. "I need to think up a good name for a man's thing."

"Or how about we just don't talk about a man's thing. Unless of course there's a man with a thing who we need to be talking about?" My aunt would never disengage from her independent life. She loved reading books on her Kindle, watching *Dr. Oz*, polishing her cherry wood furniture and eating Doritos while playing a challenging game of Spider Solitaire.

"You're right. No need to name it." She bent down and took out the blender from underneath the counter. "Can you pass me the mangos in the basket?"

So ended one of the strangest, most awkward conversations I'd yet to have with my dear Auntie Marie.

~ ~

I snuck into Ayla's room later on. She snored gently, covered up with her pink blanket and cuddling up to our two cats, Tom and Jerry. She woke when I sat down. She groaned and stretched. "What are you doing in here?"

"I missed you, that's all."

She plopped her head back down on her pillow and I rubbed her back until she fell back asleep.

I couldn't deal well with people hating me. The look of disgust, the scoffing, the finger-pointing, all knotted up in my stomach and rendered me incapable of sleeping, eating, sometimes even breathing. That's why I ran away from Olivia thirteen years ago. I couldn't face hurting her. Back then, I thought, I'd come back when I had adopted out the baby and she'd never even have to know I hurt her. I could chalk up my disappearance to bad choices over an acting career in New York City. Back before I knew how deeply I had gotten into trouble, I thought I could play off my disappearing act like I'd spent countless months touring the city's bohemian and theatre sections, living recklessly. I could lie and say all of the wild carousing taught me that wanderlust didn't define life—love did—and then we'd make up for the lost time. But then, I gave birth to Ayla. I saw that beautiful face, those tiny little fingers, and perfect toes, and I couldn't give her up. I couldn't lie and say I'd spent the summer traveling through New York to get work as an actress. I couldn't act for shit, so that lie would never have panned out. I could hardly get an audition, never mind a part.

I fell in love with Ayla the second I held her. How could you explain this love to someone who would ultimately be hurt by it? You couldn't. You waited it out for the perfect moment when surely you could come back to town and all would be forgiven in a split second. At least when you're eighteen, that's how you thought the world operated. Then, you turned twenty, and by the time you turned twenty-five, and had dated every loser walking the face of the earth, you wished more than anything you could be standing in front of that girl you hurt and she'd take you in her safe arms and hug you and tell you she forgave you for being so silly and not trusting her. And, then you'd approach your thirties and you'd still be single, raising a teenager on your own, and you'd wonder where that lovely girl, who was way too special to litter with lies, placed her heart.

Lies sucked the life out of great moments. I couldn't lie anymore. I couldn't look into Olivia's eyes and mess with her trust for one more second. This one big lie was snowballing and quickly avalanching out of control. I had to grab hold of it and smash it into pieces.

I stared at my cell for three weeks trying to figure out how to face her, how to tell her my dark secret, how to live the rest of my life without her in it. She would hate me for leaving her in the dark, but I needed time to plan how I'd convince Josh that now was the time.

Chapter Fifteen

Olivia

When Chloe hadn't called me that whole week after we made love in my office, I blamed it on her busy schedule, being a single mom and an entrepreneur. Maybe Ayla had horse competitions. Maybe she forgot to tell me about a busy week of new business dealings she had to tend to. Her absence could've easily been explained, had I bothered to try and call her, too. I couldn't bring myself to reach out for fear of rejection. The entire week, I checked my cell several dozen times a day for missed calls or messages, and each time I didn't have one I fell deeper into an abyss where the walls slicked over in a slippery, impenetrable coating.

Melanie offered me a reiki treatment. I snapped and told her to treat Phil instead. She tried to change the subject and asked about Jacqueline again. I told her to drop it and be grateful for what she already had. When Trevor and his boyfriend invited me out for drinks at Decoupage, a trendy gay bar a few towns over, I blew them off. And poor Natalie. She suffered the brunt of my attitude as we entered week two with no call from Chloe. Natalie waltzed in and asked me to sign an adoption contract, something I did often. I tore it from her hands, crumbled it into a ball and tossed it out of the door. "I don't have time right now," I yelled. "Go sign it yourself."

She ran out of my office in tears.

Halfway through week two of no Chloe, Missy, Chloe's top pick for a receptionist, started her first day. I hated her instantly. Even Natalie, the sweetest girl in the world, agreed that Missy sucked at the front desk. Firstly, she walked in to her first day on the job wearing a Patriots football jersey and jeans with a hole in the ass pocket. Secondly, the girl flirted with every good-looking man who entered the shelter, winking, giggling, even offering her number to one.

She didn't last two days. I tossed her out of the door.

I called the girl who failed Chloe's test instead and invited her to come back for another interview appointment. When she asked why I changed my mind, I told her my mind had never changed in the first place. I added that Chloe, the girl who kicked her out, would not be conducting the interview and would not have a say in hiring. Chloe might've strangled my heart again, but she certainly didn't control the reins.

I needed to hire this girl.

When Chloe first left for New York thirteen years back, I dove into studying hoping it would set me free from the wraths of her memory. I studied anatomy and psychology, even Spanish, hoping to find strength and a break from the empty, lonely pit that sat in my stomach until it wretched. Fellow classmates would invite me to parties, and I'd go only to return to my dormitory miserable or frustrated with the guys who would ask me out and get an attitude when I turned them down. Soon, the few friends I managed to meet took offense to my declining their offer to set me up with great guys who were friends of theirs. So, I'd end up back alone with no one to talk to who understood me or cared to.

I'd think about Chloe often during that first year of studies. Every time I'd see a cute girl with black hair, it'd take me several weeks to get back on track with my emotions, my determination, and my focus. During my second semester mid-term period, things got so bad that I flunked out. I'd lost so much control that I ended up right where I started, back in my bedroom at my parents' house. One very bad night, I got drunk on cheap red wine and started smoking cigarettes. I sat on the rooftop outside of my bedroom window, staring up at the stars and wishing I could just die and be done with this world. Then, Floppy stuck her head out of my window and attempted to climb out onto the rooftop with me. Well, one clumsy paw after the other she managed and sat beside me letting me smoke my cigarette and wallow in a sea of red wine pity. She leaned against me, and I spoke to her about how much better life could've been had I just died right then and there. I could just jump, I told her. Screw school. Screw girls. Screw everything. Floppy looked up at me with her sad eyes and pleaded with me to end the silly talk and get a hold of myself. I balked and slapped the roof in some sort of crazy protest and then I slipped. I slid down the roof one slow agonizing shingle at a time, clawing for my life, clinging to an edge only to be greeted with more velocity. My arms dragged against the grainy shingles, cutting them up. Then, my chin got in on the punishment when it, too, scraped and failed to save me from falling ten feet into a holly bush. Floppy barked like a junkyard dog from the top of the roof. Next I remembered my dad carrying me out of the bush like a firefighter rescuing an innocent victim. Only I wasn't so innocent. I caused this. My lack of control caused this. My inability to focus caused this. My weakness over another human being caused this. I broke an arm and a leg that night, suffered a concussion, and battered my skin pretty badly. My father later told me Floppy warned him with her incessant barking. My parents were fast asleep, and I would've frozen to death out there once the temperature dropped to its ten degrees. Thanks to Floppy I lived. She saved my life.

I guess she owed me. And, I had owed her again to rise above my challenges and get on with my life. So, school became a breeze. I just focused in on how much Floppy and other dogs would need me. My purpose needed to be greater than worrying about how some girl had screwed me over with careless abandon. I had maintained control ever since.

Now that Chloe was back in my life, I found myself veering close to that edge of reckless abandon again, though. I cared too much again. I lost myself in needless anxiety over what she could've been thinking, who she spent time with, and why she hadn't called.

I couldn't stop obsessing over her.

Melanie noticed this first. During a reiki treatment on one of our older dogs, Ben, a graying German shepherd mix with not a whole lot of energy left in his pocket, she asked me about Chloe.

"Why do you ask?" I asked as I helped drain the weak energy out of Ben's body by envisioning a flood of positive light shining from my hands into his neck and traveling down to his feet.

Melanie focused in on Ben's hips. "The photographer called here this morning expecting to have a phone conference with you. I told her you were out sick. I've never had to lie for you before."

"Shit. I completely forgot about her." I blew out a sharp breath. "We were supposed to go over the logistics for the Walk for Paws event."

"I'm not judging you." She peeked up over her flowery frames. "I think it's fabulous that you're letting yourself feel some emotions for this girl."

214

We continued work on Ben in silence until he dozed off, snoring like an old man. The whole time I couldn't focus on anything but why Chloe refused to call me. The shelter needed me to stop this ridiculous, childish behavior. I couldn't handle focusing on both.

~ ~

Chloe called me three weeks from the day we last saw each other. Josh and I were sitting on my deck smoking a cigarette. "This isn't a good time," I told her.

"I'm really sorry I haven't been around. I promise to tell you everything when I see you."

I rolled my eyes at Josh who had inhaled deeper. "I'm not going through this again, Chloe."

"I didn't mean to freak you out. I just needed time to sort through some things."

"If you can't be honest with me, this will never work. I don't play that game."

"Can you talk tomorrow at the shelter?"

"Just come by. I'll be there." I hung up.

"What was that all about?"

"We fucked each other three weeks ago and she's finally coming around to call me. So, now she wants to chat. What now? Did she murder someone and spend the last thirteen years in a jail cell?"

Josh clicked his tongue and tossed his half lit cigarette below. He exhaled with force. "God only knows." He stood up and opened his arms for me. "Come here, kiddo. Let me have a hug before I leave."

I drew a drag and flicked my cigarette down below, too. I walked into his arms and he held me tight, rubbing my back like my dad used to do when I'd get flustered over a homework assignment.

215

"Whatever happens in the future, I hope you know how much I love you and care about you."

I pulled away and saw concern. "What's this all about?"

He grasped my upper arms and spoke slowly. "I just wanted to tell you that." He walked away. "Get a good night's sleep, sis."

Chloe

Josh called me shortly after I hung up with Olivia. "We're hurting Olivia more by keeping her in the dark now."

"I love her, Josh."

"I think it's time we tell her, then."

"Are you sure?"

"I'm ready if you are."

"Would you mind if I tell her alone?" I asked.

"I was kind of hoping you'd say that."

The next morning, I drove up to the shelter and sat for a few minutes with my window opened to take in the barking, the rustle of the leaves, the cool breeze, my last moment of peace before unleashing myself into the unknown.

With Josh's permission after my call with him the night before, I set out to tell Olivia the truth.

I emerged, shaking and dizzy. I stopped to straighten a lopsided sign about a family picture event, praying it wasn't the last thing I would do for the shelter, aside from sending in my anonymous donation every month. I'd never tell her. Regardless of what happened, I'd never stop sending it.

I walked in the front door and Sarah, the girl I tossed out of the interview for failing the paper pick up test, stood behind the receptionist's desk. Olivia stood beside the display of leashes and collars with a satisfied smirk on her face.

"Hi," I said, extending my hand to the girl and smiling through the embarrassment.

"Hello to you, too." She shook my hand without meeting my eye and then escaped back into a stack of prescription orders.

I looked to Olivia who ignored me as she fiddled with a row of leashes that had fallen. I bent down to help gather them. We collected them, our knees brushing together and then stood to meet the tension. I turned to Sarah. "See, that's how it should be done." I winked, grabbed Olivia's arm and led her to the door that would lead us to the conversation that could ultimately destroy all we'd worked so hard to rebuild.

Chapter Sixteen

Olivia

Chloe stood before me in the fenced yard wearing no makeup and wrinkled clothes. General sniffed the ground beside us, brushing his face against the grass to scratch his dry nose. As if he sensed we needed privacy, he looked up at me, locked eyes for a moment, and walked away far against the perimeter of the yard, a place he never ventured alone.

Chloe stood with her arms wrapped around her like a strait jacket. This jumpstarted a series of tummy flips. I bounded towards the back fence, dodging holes and dog balls along the way.

"You have every right to be mad at me for not being here," Chloe yelled out to me.

I cringed at her need to point out the obvious. I turned and faced her. Giant tears pooled in her eyes and streamed down her porcelain-smooth face. "Don't flatter yourself."

She bit her lip and bowed her head, kicking up dirt with her sandals. "I was afraid to come here, because I need to tell you something that's not going to be easy to hear."

"Stop with the drama. Stop wasting my time. Just come out with it."

"It's so hard. The last thing I want to do is hurt you."

Exacerbated, I walked away to the edge of the yard and stared out over the valley below. She followed and stared out over the wild grass with me. She bucked, sniffled and started bawling, clinging to herself as if ready to confess that she murdered someone and buried him in the yard. I didn't step in to console her. I let her buck and bawl waiting for news that would surely rattle my world.

We stood side-by-side for several long minutes. She sniffled, shook her head a few times, sighed, and finally said, "I still love you, and that's why this is so difficult for me."

"Just tell me."

She inhaled and trembled under the pressure.

"Are you married? Is that what this is all about?" I asked, staring her down.

"I wish it was as easy as that."

"Did you kill someone?"

"No." She twisted her face.

"I can't imagine what could be worse," I said. I looked back down to the valley. "Did you steal the money for the shelter, and now someone's expecting payback?"

She swallowed hard before looking up at me with her tear-stained eyes. "Josh is Ayla's father."

All sounds vanished. The rustling leaves, the barking dogs, the chirping birds— all gone and replaced by a void so deep and profound, that it swept me up in its swirling vortex and spun me against gravity itself, funneling me into what I could only explain as the blackest, deafest, space imaginable.

I fell to my knees, bent over with my face in the grass, unable to win against the force of truth. It shackled me to the ground and blindfolded me to a nightmare of tangled webs with spiders digging their fangs into every square inch of my body,

220

piercing me with poisonous lies, engorging my cells so they could no longer sustain against the pressure of reality. I couldn't shed a tear. I couldn't open my mouth to yell. I couldn't swallow to rid the awful taste of grit.

I had no idea how much time had passed. I glued to that spot in the grass, comforted only by General's embrace as he leaned against me and fell asleep snoring. I clung to him and that's when the tears sprang and my voice returned. I finally looked up and forced out a tough question. "Does Josh even know?"

"He knows."

My heart clenched. I buried my head against General again. The two people I cared about the most in this world betrayed me. Of all the guys, she chose him. I looked up at her. "Why Josh?"

"He was just there. It was just a moment. A blip in time."

"But, I was there," I said. "Why wasn't I enough?"

She inched up to me, hands in her pocket, head cocked slightly to the right, her toes pointing like a ballerina with each slow, methodical step. "Of course you were, but..."

"But what?"

She dug the tip of her toe into the dirt refusing to meet my anger. "It's just that night..." She paused and shook her head.

"Go on."

"That night that it happened, Josh helped me stand up for myself and I guess that opened up a whole new set of experiences for me. Up until that moment, I'd always been the weak one; the one who turned to you for protection."

"The night you went with him to return the ring?"

She nodded.

That night returned to me like a slap. I begged Josh to go with her. When she returned, she curled up in bed, stiff and different. "I should've been there."

"No," she said. "See that's just it. You were always there for me, protecting me."

"Why was that a bad thing?"

"By protecting me, I was weak."

"So what happened that night that made you fuck my brother?"

She winced. "My stepfather came after us with a baseball bat. Josh stole it from him and handed it to me. He told me to stand up to him. I swung and for the first time, my stepfather fell back, and I stood tall looking down on him. I told him off. I kicked him. I stood up for myself, finally. I was no longer the weak one."

"Did I make you feel weak?" My voice reeked of bitter spices.

"You enabled me. You took care of me. You protected me. So, yeah you sort of did."

I crossed my arms over my chest demanding more.

"You pitied me. You viewed me as a weak person, and so I became that. Each time we got together, I became weaker in your eyes. Do you know how terrible it feels to look into the eyes of pity?"

"You think I pitied you?"

"Can you honestly deny that?" Now she crossed her arms, standing up to me, challenging me. "I wanted you to adore me as much as you said you did. I wanted you to love me because you loved me, not because you felt guilty that you were blessed, and I wasn't. I wanted you to look into my eyes and feel challenged, not empowered that you controlled my safety."

222

I blinked more times than normal, settling in on her words, truly comprehending what she said without passing judgment. "I never meant to pity you."

She closed in on herself, avoiding my gaze.

I inhaled deeply. "You know after my parents died, strangers flocked to me, baking me fruit cakes and casseroles, inviting me for coffee and to participate in book clubs and card games, offering up their services for free to see me through the tragedy. I hate pity. I'd rather someone yell in my face and tell me how much they can't stand me than pity me." I looked up to the tree branches and then back at her. "I did pity you, and I'm sorry."

She turned away from me still tightening her arms over her chest as if afraid I'd start to fight her.

"You always smoothed everything over for me instead of helping me to face things. You did everything for me and I couldn't do anything back," she said.

"I loved you."

"Did you love me? Or did you do nice things for me because you felt sorry for me and you lived to be the savior?"

The years spread out in front of me like dominos. I pushed through, standing on my toes to see over the memories, the hurts, the embellished times, and I couldn't tell truth from lie. Of course I loved her back then. But, maybe I did want to control the situation for her like I attached to controlling my shelter, my diet, and my future. "Maybe a little bit of both. I don't know. It was a long time ago."

"Exactly."

The invisible strings that connected us strained under the pull of my indecision. I wanted to take back my answer and sweep it in the corner so that later I could collect it, study it, and look for virility. The winds of change blew around us,

223

snapping string after string, unbinding us, leaving no fasteners intact for later use. Plink, plink, plink. I sank into my lap, wrestling with what-ifs and maybes and absolutely nots. I focused more after drinking a bottle of sangria than I could at that moment.

I wanted to be angry with her. "I can't believe you fucked my brother."

She squeezed the bridge of her nose, exhaling sharply. "I was a different person back then full of fears and insecurities. He didn't feel sorry for me that night. He saved my life by treating me like an equal. And, then the adrenaline took over, and before either one of us knew what we were doing, I was paying him back for pulling me out of a life that would've trapped me."

"You've had plenty of years to justify this to yourself, haven't you? I suppose Josh did, too." I wanted to throw up. "This is exactly why I choose to not get involved with anyone."

People sucked.

"Neither one of us wanted to hurt you."

"Hurt doesn't even begin to explain it."

She pulled in her lower lip and blinked up at me. "I love you so much, Olivia."

"You love me?" I scoffed. "How can you say that?"

"I've come back for you twice. Doesn't that prove anything?"

I bolted out of the yard faster than a line drive ball. I didn't need her anymore. I could fund the shelter on my own like I did before. With the new donation check coming in I could use that to pay incidentals, my clinic hours to pay staffing, and continue with fundraising for extras. I would pound on every door in Maryland if I had to. I would not place myself in this muck, always looking over my shoulder to catch blame for being too loving.

As I headed towards the door, I pictured the three of them together, Chloe, Josh, and their adorable Ayla, the look-alike Chloe with pretty sandals, shiny black hair and brilliant eyes.

Ayla was Chloe and Josh's daughter, their unbreakable bond, the miraculous result of a moment of passion. I wondered if Chloe had been staring into my eyes this whole time thinking how much I reminded her of her daughter.

I sped up trying to outrun the vivid pictures piling up in my brain. I didn't want to think about any of this. I just wanted freedom. I had piles of work to get through at the shelter. I looked back and she was following.

"Fuck off!" I yelled out to her before slamming the door to the back room. I now had all the proof in the world that human beings could never be trusted like animals. Animals would never screw me over like this. They'd never cloud my judgment. They'd never cause me to question my place in this world. With them, I knew my place. They needed me. I needed them. Reciprocity at its finest. What human relationship could ever equal to that level of trust?

Obviously not one that involved Chloe Homestead.

~ ~

I arrived at Josh and Bridget's and he was grilling burgers on their pool patio. Josh flipped a burger when I charged toward him. Bridget poured pink lemonade into tall flowery glasses that I just knew Josh despised but would put up with anyway because that's what he did with Bridget. He cowered to her to keep her smiling. She wore a string bikini and looked way too good for a thirty-five-year-old who had given birth to a jumbo, watermelon-sized baby nine years earlier. She waved at me. I cringed, wishing she would disappear.

I pounced on my brother. "We need to talk."

Panic traced his eyes. "She told you?"

225

"She just did."

He pressed his lips into a thin line and nodded. "Okay." He avoided my eyes and stared down at his grill. "Let me just take these burgers off the flame." He scooped up the burgers, one agonizing, shaky flip at a time. He piled on the last one and it fell to the ground. He bent over, picked it up, and tossed it in the trashcan.

I watched him, searing my eyes into him. "How could you?"

He exhaled, looked up to the awning and blinked back at me. "I should've been there when she told you." He peeked over at Bridget who was standing poolside dunking her toe in the crystal water.

Just then, Thomas bolted out of the door and ran directly towards the pool, launching himself to the sky. He tucked his knees and he hit the water like a cannonball, splashing water to within feet of Josh and me.

"Leave the freaking burgers where they are and come with me." I pulled at his tank top.

He trailed behind me without a fight. Thirty seconds later, we sat down on his leather couch and his bottom lip started to tremble. He stared down at his Bermuda shorts and shook his head. "I don't know where to start."

"I trusted you," I cried out.

"And, I'm a fuck up." He lowered his head into his hands and pulled at his reckless strands.

"No, you don't get to do that." I shoved at him. His face remained planted in his hands. "You don't get to call yourself a fuck up. I get to do that." I spoke through clenched teeth. "I need to do that." I wanted to punch him.

He looked up at me, sorrow rested along the fine lines around his eyes. "I don't know how to make this right."

"You can't make this right. You fucked up, Josh."

He stretched his neck to see out of the patio sliders. Bridget was tossing Thomas a ball. "I didn't know you were in love with her," he whispered.

He didn't. I made sure he didn't back then. "I can't get past the part about you keeping this from me all of this time."

He pressed his fist into his forehead. He circled it half a dozen times. "I was ashamed." His voice stretched.

"Ashamed?"

"Yes, ashamed." He unfurled his fist and dropped his hands to his side. "Ashamed for being such a coward and not doing the right thing."

Tears drained from his eyes. Pain etched along his stiff jawline. I stared into the eyes of a stranger.

"Does Ayla even know?"

He shook his head. The tears sprang like a leaky faucet. Red blotches popped up on his skin. Panic riddled his eyes. "She'll know soon enough now."

"All of those times I carried on about Chloe." I paused. "I feel like a fool now. How did you think it would all end someday?"

"I just thought she'd live her life and be fine."

"So you were okay with fathering a kid and letting her wander through life without you?"

He groaned. "You make me sound like such a monster."

I wanted to pull his straggly hair, stomp on his bare feet, and punch him in the gut. "Well, who does that?"

He fell back against the couch dazed. "Assholes like me, I suppose."

"I need to go. I can't deal with any of this anymore." I jumped up and ran past him wanting to throw up.

He pulled me back.

227

I snapped back at him. "I really hate you right now."

His mouth creased in on itself. "How do I fix this?"

"Were you ever going to tell me if she didn't?"

He stretched his eyes and sighed. "For the longest time, I struggled with this. I went back and forth on whether I was even worthy enough to be Ayla's father. I kept thinking that if I stayed silent on this, no one's life would be screwed up. You know?"

"Well, everything's so screwed up now."

"Just so you know, I never wanted this," he said. "I made one mistake and all of these lives are screwed up forever. The best thing was when she went away and I could deny that I ever even had a child. I wasn't ready to be a fucking father, and especially not with her!"

"But, she was good enough to fuck though, wasn't she?"

"Give me a fucking break. I was a horny kid alone with a hot girl. If you would've been honest with me back then about being a lesbian, I wouldn't have ever slept with her. What kind of a person do you think I am? The fact that you could ever think I would stoop that low just really pisses me off."

The sincerity of his words slammed into me. They branded me in fault. "Screw you!" I turned and ran to his front door.

He whipped me around again. "This is ridiculous. I'm not an enemy here. Okay." He lowered his hand. "I just want to finally do the right thing. And, I need to know you're with me on it. I can't have you hating me."

My heart knocked against the hollow of my chest, rattling my core, cutting off vital flow, causing me to convulse in choking tears.

He pulled me into his protective arms and rocked me back and forth. "I'm so sorry. I really am."

I emptied all my anger in the form of tears, imagining the introduction. I'd be angry with them all, even innocent Ayla. I'd be most angry with Chloe and her lovely, soft smile, the way she'd be gently holding her daughter's hand as she pushed towards Josh. I'd be even angrier with Josh for crying. He'd look at his daughter like she was a rare gem dug out of the earth and presented to him like he deserved her. Their daughter, delicate like a flower, would be smiling, too. She'd look fragile in a pretty sundress, so fragile that she'd look about ready to break before she even got to hug her father.

He'd move towards them, to his precious new family. They'd be within a foot of each other and Josh would no doubt throw his arms around this little girl who had his same shiny hair and big eyes. Chloe would be weeping and shaking. I'd want to throw up. Instead, though, through no control of my own, I'd be weeping, too, succumbing to compassion and wishing with every morsel of my being that I could control moments like these when I turned into a sap.

I told him, "I want to hate you."

He drew a painful breath, and then tossed his head back, blowing many years of regret, no doubt, into the air. "You should. It's much easier to move on when you hate someone."

He might've been a jackass on the outside, but inside of him, a heart did tick. "In some warped way, I can't hate you."

~ ~

I took General along with me to my parents' gravesite. I needed the company and friendship more than ever. General, my hundred-pound furry friend resembled a regal leader with his jowls and mighty chest. He was every bit the snuggle buddy I needed. He sat in my passenger seat like a person, strong and stoic, his chest bellowed out and proud, his front paws supporting his upper body into an upright angle. We traveled the country roads, past the rebuilt country store that still sold penny candy; past the farmers' market where local farmers sold beefy, juicy tomatoes and big, red bell sweet peppers and hung signs written by hand with misspelled words touting great deals on the freshest veggies; past the funeral home where we held my parents' wake several years ago. General looked over at me as if he knew I needed his one blue eye and one brown eye to tell me life would be okay as always.

I reached over and patted him and he responded with a tired yawn. General was my buddy who had seen me through my fair share of mild breakdowns and major shakedowns over the past few months. He'd never seen me this upset before, though. He shifted his body so that he could lean on me, all one hundred pounds. He rested his head on my shoulder, not bothered when I had to turn my wheel. He just pressed into me, licked my face gently with his big, wet tongue and yawned again.

Instead of turning down Highland to get to the front gate of the cemetery, I drove a few miles south to Lakeview Road and turned into the parking lot of the baseball field that I had ventured to almost every night last October when Thomas's team fought to defend their championship title. I parked alongside the broken, rusted fence and sat staring at the pitcher's mound. General snored with his eyes open. His big head rested in the crook of my shoulder and neck. I scratched at his scruff behind his ear and he snored louder. I sat for some time hugging my big furry boy, taking comfort in his loyalty and friendship. I hugged him so hard at one point, he snorted loud like a foghorn had bellowed out of his massive barrel chest.

So many nights I'd sat in this same spot, windows rolled up to escape the mosquitoes, cheering on my nephew and his championship team. The smell of fresh greens, vibrant floras, and pungent roots permeated the car anyway, wafting from the overgrown woods circling the field. My brother would often look back at me and smile and wave and urge me to stand next to him and Bridget. Bridget swatted gnats, smiling all the same, proud of her little family, unknowing and innocent to the fact that the man she stood beside fathered another kid.

On Thomas' big night under the grand lights, I did venture out of the truck and stand alongside my brother and his faithful wife to cheer him on. That night, my brother and I huddled against the fence screaming out cheers like Thomas' life depended on his team winning. When he positioned at the plate and choked up on the bat like his father taught him, a swell of pride flowed through me that reconfirmed if I really wanted to, I could have a kid, too, and be equally as proud of him. A wave of jealousy washed over me that night, one that engulfed me, spun me up and down, panicked me, that I might never make that come true. I thought of Chloe at that moment, and how she had screwed me up. She angered me by planting the seed of doubt in me. That seed had grown into one hell of a strong vine, choking the trust in relationships right out of me, leaving no room for drama, for commitment, for dreams of a life that included more than solitude, lonely nights, and angry resentments. I remembered wondering that night as Thomas banged out a line drive right up the center of the field past the pitcher and second baseman, and into the shallow circle of center field, how many more years would have to pass before I could let go of how Chloe had hurt me.

Later, after Thomas had struck out, and my brother and I spent the following two hours consoling him with oversized cones of butter pecan ice cream dipped in chocolate, I never thought that years later I'd be sitting here in my truck alone without even a brother I could trust.

The ice cream had helped us all heal from the blow of the strikeout and lost attempt at winning the championship that night. Well, it helped Thomas at least. My brother took a little longer to heal from that. He had big dreams for Thomas's future. These dreams had Camden Yards stadium written all over them.

My brother, the father of the year, coveted the role of Thomas' big hero, and mine, too. I viewed him as my staple, my guard post, my foundation. After our parents died in the accident, he nestled me under his wings and protected me from all things hurtful. I relied heavily on him to get me through the rough patches when grief would come to me and strike me down. Only he could shake me out of the grip of sadness when it struck. Only he intimately understood my pain. He protected me and carried me through those moments that still happened far too often. I wondered how he'd protect me now that he had turned into the cause.

Instead of driving to the cemetery, I headed for Melanie's.

~ ~

Melanie scrubbed her kitchen floor on hands and knees. Her house smelled like pine and lemons. She pushed and pulled a wet rag around, grunting. "I will never put laminate tile in my kitchen again. This is not work for anyone over the age of fifty." She wiped her forehead with her cotton sleeve. "In my next life, I am hiring a cleaning lady."

I joined my friend on the floor, knee-to-knee, elbow-to-elbow, pushing, pulling, and grunting, dispensing the ugly secret of how my brother and ex-girlfriend destroyed any possibility of me trusting any being that didn't grow fur. Instead of lecturing me about my pessimistic attitude, Melanie listened, nodded, handed me more rags, and pointed out other areas of her kitchen that needed my energy, my attention, my anger. We moved the fridge, we opened up the radiator covers, we pulled out the chef's carts to banish dust bunnies and grime. We even huffed and puffed our way through the grueling task of scrubbing her oven clean and rebalancing her dishwasher. By the time we finished, we could eat dinner off of her

232

floor if we chose to do so. Instead, we pulled up a spot alongside General in the living room and collapsed on top of him. I summed up my entire conversation with Chloe, about why she slept with Josh and about how I made her feel less-than—all of the ugly details—which only brought on more anger.

"If you've still got some anger in you, my bathroom could really use some help."

General snored under our weight. I moaned, sore from hours of using muscles that hadn't been challenged in years. "She's not worth it."

"If I wasn't so tired, I'd disagree with you."

I patted Melanie's hand, and General snored again. "I'm too tired to laugh at that."

An hour or so later, I woke up when General jumped to his feet, alerted by the smell of fresh meat cooking on the polished stovetop. Try to get him to walk on a leash for a relaxing stroll in the park, and he acted like a ninety-year old man with arthritis. Yet, open up a package of chicken tenderloins, and he'd sprint a freaking marathon to get to it.

I strolled into the kitchen and jumped into making a salad. I sharpened the chef's knife and began slicing a garden-fresh tomato when I asked my friend, "Was Henry your soul mate?"

She stopped poking the tenderloin. "He cheated on me and never apologized for the initial tears I cried over it. So, I reciprocated and he didn't care. Soul mates would never hurt each other like that and not care." She returned to poking the tenderloin, flipping it over in the skillet with a fork.

I sliced down hard on the tomato and it squished under the pressure. So, I smashed it even more, chopping it, smacking it, pounding it. "I can't believe I was stupid enough to believe she was my soul mate."

She turned on the fan above the stove, then opened her seasonings cupboard and took out a container of Adobo rub. She sprinkled some on the chicken. "She is, honey."

"I'll never trust her again."

"You're just angry right now."

"I'm so angry that I lost control over myself out in the yard. I wanted to punch a tree. I wanted to stomp my feet. I told her to fuck off. I've never told anyone to fuck off."

"That's what love will do to you," Melanie said.

I stopped chopping. "How dare she come back into my life again knowing this would eventually have to come out? Were the two of them just going to skip around the idea that they have a kid together?"

General scooted up to Melanie and sniffed the air. She plucked up a small piece of chicken, blew on it and dropped it in his mouth. He smacked his lips together, chewing the inch cube like he would chow down on a massive piece of juicy steak. "I don't think either one of them had a clue how to handle this." She turned back to her chicken, browning it in its apple cider juice. "Don't leave out the cucumbers, please."

I chopped those cucumbers and tore the head of lettuce into shards quickly. We chowed down listening to Barry White under the watchful eye of General, who took up residence on my left foot. His eyes never left my food. I stuck firmly to good health for all animals, but I also understood the complexity of wanting something you shouldn't be wanting and how if you didn't stymie that with an indulgence from time to time it could consume everything. I tossed General a few bites of my chicken. I couldn't help myself.

"If Phil ever hid something like this from you, wouldn't you hate him?"

234

"I couldn't hate Phil."

I rolled my eyes. "Do you love him?"

"Love is fleeting to me. Some days I give in to the emotion. Other days I'm preoccupied with other pressing stuff."

"You're just afraid to commit because you're still interested in finding out if someone better will come along."

"Life's too short to get tied down to one person. That's my philosophy. I love Phil in the moments I'm with him. When he's not around, I love other things like the trees, the bees, Mozart. Love isn't one of those feelings you can ever run out of. I can love whatever is present right now, not back when or way in the future. Right now."

General snapped a piece of chicken from her fingertips. "Yes, by right now, I mean you, General." She bent over and kissed his dry nose. "I'm going to treat that little spot for you in a little bit."

He licked his nose and sat down, perched and ready for another scrap to hit the floor.

~ ~

I couldn't get Chloe out of my mind and this pissed me off. Whenever I closed my eyes, I saw her sunny smile, felt her warm hugs and soft breath on my face, and heard her flirty whispers. She taunted me. How did I ever allow her to gain so much control over me again?

I caressed the anger. Whenever thoughts of her roamed freely and clenched my desires, I willed the anger back into being. She would not hurt me again. The anger served as my guide and helped me to focus. Without it, I could easily sink into a lonely, dark place void of colors, of butterflies, of cute puppy dogs, of sneaky cats, of purpose. Anger, my tool of choice, my loyal companion who stood tall and carved a path through thickets and brambles, primed my path in the past and would still in my future. Anger was my fuel to get through the day, to justify my presence in the world, to drive me forward so I wouldn't get left behind in the muck of bad memories, of poor choices, of misguided actions.

I could live this way forever. Nothing would change my resolve. Nothing. I meditated on this thought most seconds of the day, calling it into being so it permanently engrained itself in my subconscious framework.

Then, Chloe called.

My heart galloped, my head buzzed, my toes and fingers tingled. I inhaled deeply and ignored the ringing. I let her call go to voicemail. Meanwhile, I sat at my office desk and hyperventilated as I waited for the ding, hoping it would come, pretending with no success that I didn't care.

Then, my cell dinged, notifying me of the message.

~ ~

Chloe tracked down Jacqueline. She researched one trail after another and landed at Philadelphia airport three days prior. She rented a car, drove to Jacqueline's house, and discovered that the reason she had not messaged me back after all of this time had nothing to do with her not wanting to speak with me or Melanie, but rather because she didn't even know such a message sat in her inbox.

Instead of coasting along pretty country roads with her dog, Penny, in the sidecar next to her, and later posting pictures for stalkers like me to find, Jacqueline was busy running from one appointment to the next getting chemo beads shot into her failing liver as a last-ditch effort to save her life.

"She says she's going to be fine, that the chemo treatment is working, and soon she'll be back up to riding. She wants to see Melanie," Chloe told me later when I caved in for Melanie's sake and called her back.

236

I listened with great restraint, protecting myself from her soft voice, her perfectly executed inflections, her kindness for taking this upon herself. She led me with open-ended questions and I followed with short snaps. The friction mounted in her voice, and I blocked it out with extreme success. We were just two women helping a couple of deserved women to reconnect under dire circumstances.

An hour later, I showed up at Melanie's studio. She chomped on a peanut butter and jelly sandwich with Phil on the sundeck. They laughed and carried on about Phil's latest funny arrest involving a naked man by the lake whose wife had kicked him out of his house and forced him to drive without clothes.

This went on for an hour. Finally, Phil cleared our plates and left us alone.

"Jacqueline wants to see you."

"What?" Her face flushed.

"Hey," Phil said, coming back too swiftly with a couple of flavor packets in his hand. "Would any one of you ladies care to try this new strawberry zinger punch? You just toss them in your water."

"Phil, let's take a walk." She stood, took Phil's hand and started to walk away.

"Want to join us?" he asked me.

"She's got to run, sweetheart." Melanie pulled him. "No need to lock up, dear. Just close the storm door."

Back in my car, I called Chloe, putting on another great performance of control in the wake of a soothing, friendly greeting. "She's not interested."

"No way," she said. "We've got to get her interested. This poor lady could be dying. Did you tell her that?"

"And make the visit be out of pity?" I asked.

"Point taken."

"I'm glad you understand."

"I'll let Jacqueline know," she said, disappointment trailing her words. "I guess some things are just better left to fate."

"Yeah, I suppose so."

"Olivia?"

I caught my breath. "Yeah?"

"I miss you."

I squeezed my free hand into a fist and kneaded it against my forehead. "If she changes her mind, I'll let you know."

~ ~

A day later, I cornered Melanie in the reiki room at the shelter. "Chloe talked to Jacqueline and she really wants to meet up with you."

Melanie closed her eyes and drew a deep breath. "I'm not opening up that part of my life again."

I tugged at her sleeve. "Hey, I understand. It's unnerving. That's a normal reaction."

She opened her eyes. "Normal isn't digging up the past and hoping everything will be just as you remembered it. Normal is living life presently, and presently I am happy with my life, with Phil, with my memories."

"She's dying."

She collapsed onto her treatment table.

~ ~

Three days later, I faced reality for Melanie's sake again. I agreed to meet up with Chloe and Ayla. We would drive to the airport together to pick up Jacqueline.

Ayla sat in the backseat curled up next to General. He panted and enjoyed the lavish praise, resting his front paw on her lap. Chloe drove. I rode shotgun.

"Melanie's not thrilled with me right now," I said trying to center the conversation around anything but us.

"They'll both need this closure."

"I hope you're right."

Chloe hightailed it towards the airport. "I'm glad that Ayla got to see General once last time before he goes home with his new family."

Ayla hugged him. "I'm going to miss you so much, big boy. I wish my Aunt Marie wasn't so afraid of dogs." She kissed the top of his head and he burped. "Aw, you are such a goofball, General!" She pushed him and he responded by panting. "Are the people nice?" she asked me.

"They are," I said. "I screened them myself. They've got lots of big trees in a fenced in yard and the mom will be home with him all day long. They are very excited to welcome him to their family. They're vacationing in Florida until the end of the month and then he gets to go home with them."

She wrapped an arm around him. "I'm going to miss you."

"Me, too," I said. General was the only dog I'd brought home with me at night for most of his duration at the shelter. I just couldn't bear to leave him in his kennel when I left to go sleep in my comfortable bed. He was special. He acted like a human being sometimes the way he sat tall and scanned a room, the way he reciprocated a hug, the way he watched over me.

"Thanks for letting General tag along," I said to Chloe. "Melanie loves him, and whenever he's around its impossible for her to be anything but elated and loving."

"Jacqueline adores dogs, so she's excited to meet him."

She snuck a glance in the rearview mirror. "You are not feeding him too much, I hope?"

I peeked and General smacked his lips together, chewing.

"It's just one treat," Ayla said. "Geez."

We arrived at the Southwest passenger pickup point and Chloe pointed her out. She looked frail, bony, and pained. She dragged her wheeled luggage behind her and smiled when she saw Chloe.

"She looks like a corpse," I said.

I climbed out to greet her. She smiled at me like she'd known me all of her life. "You must be Melanie's friend, Olivia?" She opened her arms and welcomed me into her delicate embrace. She patted my back. I feared breaking her brittle bones.

I had her sit up front next to Chloe, and I climbed in next to General who sat in the center of the backseat with this chest bowed out, staring at the new car mate with a curious, relaxed eye.

I stared at the back of Jacqueline's pink turban wrap, sad that I opened up this can of worms for my friend. I wished I could've texted her and warned her. I couldn't, though, because she didn't know how to text.

~ ~

Time knew no boundaries. Love knew no boundaries. Disease knew not what love could do to it. According to Melanie, love could heal souls, bodies, broken hearts and severed relationships. With love as the guide, anything was possible. The firestorms that once rained down on earth could not constrict the power in love. No force rivaled its great power. Love knew nothing about distance, about years, about lies, about pain, about sadness. Love only knew how to connect, how to lift, how to thrive. In love there was no void, no lag, no wrinkles, no fat, no disease that could outshine it.

When we arrived and Melanie took Jacqueline into her arms and held her, we all witnessed the true essence of love. Even Phil. He linked arms with me and cried,

240

too, as we watched love fill a dying woman's heart with life if even for that short moment in time. Even Ayla and General respected the moment and sat quietly on the front porch steps staring out at the bright blue sky that kept watch over this unadulterated slice of time.

~ ~

A week had passed by and Chloe had called several times to ask about the shelter operations. Each time, I dodged her calls. I emailed the answers to her questions instead. I wouldn't allow the emotions of the past week to carry me away in a fog of stupidity. By week's end, Chloe stopped calling with her silly questions. I managed to sidestep the empty feelings by pounding some old concrete patio bricks on the side of the existing shelter building with a rubber mallet. And, when that no longer worked, I hit the streets for a long jog.

Two weeks following her visit, Jacqueline landed in the hospital. Melanie and Phil rushed to her side. They rented a room at an inn and visited with Jacqueline every day for two weeks. When I received the call from Phil that Jacqueline would die any day, I picked up the phone and called Chloe. "She's dying."

Chloe dropped Ayla off at Josh's. I dropped off General a few minutes later. My brother knelt down to pet General's big head. "I guess you come along, too, huh?" General bathed him in a wet lick.

Ayla giggled and leaned in for one herself.

"The two of them are in good hands," Josh said to us both.

~ ~

Chloe and I flew to Pennsylvania to be there for Melanie.

Jacqueline's two sons stood on the other side of their mom's bed, and Jacqueline's dog, Penny, rested her head on her heart. Chloe and I stood in the hallway, amid the smell of anesthetics and air fresheners.

241

Phil placed his hand on the small of Melanie's back, supporting her past and bracing for her future. Melanie leaned over the bed and whispered into Jacqueline's ear. No doubt, she whispered Jacqueline's words, *until we meet again*. Jacqueline opened her eyes wide, smiled at her, and then closed her eyes. A moment Melanie would surely relive in her mind for the rest of her life.

A few minutes later, surrounded by her children, her beloved Penny, and the woman she loved, Jacqueline LaFleur drew her last breath.

Chloe and I stood outside the hospital room and watched as Melanie broke down hugging Jacqueline for the last time. Phil's hand remained on her back as she relinquished her sadness for the loss of a friendship, a lover, a decade or two of unborn memories. My friend heaved and sobbed releasing feelings she'd spent her whole life suppressing as she lived out her role as the healer instead of the one who needed healing.

Chloe cradled her arm around my waist and I resisted for as long as humanly possible before falling into her embrace. She hugged me and we sobbed.

~ ~

Later on, we picked up General and Ayla from Josh's and headed back to the shelter. Ayla hugged General and broke down, clinging to him. "I wish you could've come to live with me." She looked up at her mom.

"He's going to a good home, sweetie."

"He is," I chimed in.

We left Ayla alone with him for a few more minutes. We walked back to my office so I could give Chloe a copy of the financials from the last month. I handed her a flash drive.

Our fingers touched, and I let mine linger.

"Thanks for inviting me to go," she said, cradling my fingers.

I pulled back my hand. "It was the right thing to do."

"The right thing to do?"

"Yes. The right thing to do," I said matter-of-factly.

A question sat on her face. "Will you ever be able to let go of all of that anger?"

I stared at her, long and hard, trying to imagine a time in the future when I wouldn't remember the past. I couldn't help but judge from my jilted reference point. She lied. She cheated. She hurt me. "Probably not."

She glared. "I'm done trying to prove to you that I am a good person. I screwed up. Well, so haven't we all. I was eighteen, confused, and didn't understand what regrets would come to mean in my life. I'm a grown woman now and I've got feelings. I won't apologize for Ayla anymore. She is my daughter, and I love her and am proud of her. So, if you can't deal with that, then I don't know what to tell you. Your pride gets in the way. You're not perfect, either, you know. You're too stubborn to admit it."

She ran off and I let her, too stunned to move, numb from my head to my toes.

Chapter Seventeen

Picking myself up and dusting off remnants from Chloe's firestorm, I busied myself with the shelter. I scrubbed the kennels more. I walked each dog longer. I held the cats longer. I organized the pharmacy shelves. I trained Natalie and Trevor on assisting me as vet techs. I filled my days to the brim without any success of adding joy to it. Several weeks had passed since Chloe unleashed on me, and I still couldn't erase the power, the control, and the command in her voice.

How dare she?

Line one rang. I ignored it.

How did things flip so fast? She wronged me yet, I fidgeted like the guilty one. I collapsed onto my futon couch and tossed a pillow over my head.

"Olivia," Natalie sprang into my office. "Oh, are you okay?"

I peeked at her from under the pillow, protecting my eyes from her bright and cheery face. "Not now, Natalie. I have a headache."

"Oh," she rushed to my side and sat down. "Can I get you some tea?"

"No, just shut the light."

"You have a phone call on line one."

"Take a message."

"Hmm. I don't think so. You need to take this."

"Of for goodness sakes," I said, climbing to my feet. I picked up the phone and plopped in my chair. "This is Olivia."

"Dr. Clark. Hi, this is Peter Dayal, we met a few weeks back about General?"

I sat up taller. "Yes, Mr. Dayal, welcome back from your trip."

"Thanks," he said, stretching his voice out.

"So, General is going to be so thrilled when he sees you. What day do you want to come by?"

"Yeah, listen, um." He paused.

"This isn't sounding like a good thing." My heart ached at what I heard in his voice.

"We're going to pass on General. While we were gone my mother-in-law bought our daughter a puppy. A boxer. I'm afraid two dogs would be too much for us. Especially one who is deaf."

I dropped my head to the desk. "I understand." I hung up without saying goodbye. I flung the phone against the door and cursed at it, stomped my feet, punched my legs.

Natalie ran back in. "I overheard."

She opened up her arms, and I fell into them crying out my frustrations like a wailing baby.

I sat with General for the rest of the afternoon. He sat up tall on my futon staring ahead, as if contemplating his unfortunate life. "It's unfair, isn't it?"

He shifted and leaned into me. "All you want is a family."

He lifted his head and dropped it on my lap. "It shouldn't be that hard, should it?"

He snorted as if agreeing.

I cradled his neck, petting behind his ears the way he liked. He curled up closer to me, reciprocating the affection, not afraid I would walk out on him, break his heart, and leave him in a cage forever. He simply lived in this moment, cuddling up to it, not worrying about how others had wronged him in life, abandoned him, hurt him. He forgave them the moment they handed him to me, and I knelt down beside him and hugged him.

He forgave them and never looked back.

"You deserve more than this, more than an occasional nap on my futon, more than a metal gate as your window to the world. You deserve boundless love, hugs, and a lifetime of opportunities to lick the face of a master worthy of your love."

He fidgeted, propped up, turned around a couple of times and sat back down, even taller, leaning against me. I draped my arm around his shoulder and he turned and stared at me. "Don't give me that look," I warned. "This isn't about me." He kept staring. "I know you think I'm a fool. I know you think I should just call her. It's not that easy." I continued to ramble on and he continued to stare at me with his one blue and one brown eye as if questioning me and my stubborn stupidity. "Of course I care about her. It's just complicated. You wouldn't understand." He shifted, but didn't let up with his stare. "Fine, okay, you win. I do love her. Of course I do. And, yes, I know… I know… she loves me, too. We're just a couple of fools, aren't we?" I grabbed hold of his adorable mug. "Okay, fine, I'm playing the fool this time. I get it. What am I supposed to do? Call her and say 'hey'?"

He wouldn't lose grip on his stare.

~ ~

I placated to General's determination. I called Chloe.

"Hey," I said.

"Hey," she said.

I leaned against General and gave into the moment, shedding my pride, embracing humility, and taking a leap I had sworn off thirteen years ago. "I miss you, too."

She breathed deeply. "You have no idea how badly I wanted to hear you say that."

For the next hour, I leaned against General and spoke with Chloe about life, about the shelter, about Melanie, about Ayla, and about Josh. She listened and offered friendly insights, interjecting with her laughter and her sweet sarcasm. From time to time, General would prop his head on my shoulder and nuzzle my ear or tickle my cheek with his big mushy tongue.

I told her about General and immediately she jumped to his rescue. "We'll adopt him."

"What about Aunt Marie?"

"I adore my aunt, but her silly fear of dogs has to go. When she sees General, she'll get why Ayla came back in tears a few weeks ago."

"Poor girl."

"She's been crying herself to sleep ever since. She adores him."

"What if your aunt doesn't want him there?"

"I'm a millionaire. I've got options."

I hugged General, my heart swelling for him. "Can I bring him by tomorrow?"

"I'll have a bowl full of his favorite kibble waiting."

When we hung up I playfully punched his burly chest. "So, that was your plan all along, wasn't it?"

~ ~

The day smelled like fresh air and sunshine on a crisp spring morning. I pulled up with General in front of Melanie and Phil's. Penny and Snowball ran down off the porch to greet us. I stooped low to pet them. "Hey you." Penny ran in small circles at my feet, landing finally on a hop. I petted her soft fur and she cuddled up to me. Snowball barked and wagged her tail. "Do you two want to see your cousin?"

Both of them circled me and yipped. I opened the door and General crawled out. He sniffed them both, wagged his short stub and walked up towards Melanie and Phil on the front porch.

"It's a beautiful day, isn't it?" I asked looking up through the maple tree to the fluffy puffs floating against the bright icy blue sky.

"It's a perfect day." Melanie smiled, lulling me into peace. "Thanks for bringing him by. I need to give him some of his favorite treats before he hits the road."

General, Penny, and Snowball followed Melanie into the house.

"How's she doing?" I asked Phil.

"I'll let her tell you."

A moment later Melanie came back out with treats in hand and three very happy doggies at her feet. They stared up at her fingers, waiting. That's when I noticed her diamond sparkling in the sunlight. I grabbed hold of her hand and the treats fell. The dogs scattered to get them. Phil giggled like a kid and I stood with my mouth agape. "Well, I'll be darned."

"What can I say?" Melanie pushed the ring closer to me. "He's a keeper."

~ ~

I pulled up to Chloe's. "Well, big guy. Welcome home."

General stared out, pressing his nose against the window. I climbed out and headed over to General's side. When I opened the door, he turned and licked my face with his big wet, gritty tongue. I petted his barrel chest before leading him out.

We walked across the green grass and to the backyard gate as Chloe instructed. I unhinged it and we walked through. Chloe and Ayla were tossing a Frisbee. Chloe wore white pants and a fitted short sleeve silk blouse. Her feet were bare. Ayla wore pink shorts and a halter-top. Her skinny legs danced around as she dashed around in wide arcs to catch the Frisbee.

General barked.

The two of them turned to us and Ayla sprinted forward. "General!"

"Ayla stop running," Chloe yelled out.

I knelt down beside General to ease him into the arms of his excited friend. He sat tall and still like a gentle giant.

Ayla sprang towards us, her hair spraying all over her face, her neck, her twiggy arms. She flung her arms around his big head and hugged him, sporting a smile that reminded me of my brother's.

I handed her the leash and she took off with him, leaving me alone with Chloe.

"Hey you," she said, with her easy smile.

I shaded the sun with the back of my hand, taking in all of her beauty. "Hey."

Chloe turned and smiled at Ayla and General walking, Ayla talking his deaf ear off. "He's all she talks about."

We watched as Ayla ran through the grass with him. His stubby tail wagged, his ears perked. "A happy beginning for him."

"A happy beginning for us all." She hugged herself and admired the two of them. "Aunt Marie is going to love him, too. I just know she will."

I stepped in closer to her, supported by a new sense of awareness that this beautiful moment required freedom to breathe and to enjoy, not to be overlooked. "He gave me a good reason to come by and see you."

She turned to me and waited for me to say more.

"I, um—" I took a hold of her hand and moved in closer. "Um—"

"What is it?" she asked, whispering, prodding me along.

I placed my finger to her lips, looking into her eyes and latching onto the love in them, resting on their beauty and the truth of the moment, of the only moment that mattered. I leaned in to her and brushed her lips with mine. "I love you, Chloe."

She tickled my cheek with her feathery touch. "Third time's always a charm."

I caressed her hand and cradled it against my cheek, losing myself in the sweet breaths that connected us, savoring them for everything they represented in that moment of time when nothing else mattered but her hand on my cheek and the love on her lips.

NOTE FROM THE AUTHOR

This story is an important one for me to tell because it's one that is close to my heart. As an avid animal advocate and lover, I feel it's critical for human beings to protect the welfare of animals. They rely on us, trust us, and remain by our sides with loyal, unconditional love.

If you are considering welcoming a pet into your life, please consider adopting a shelter pet!

As with all of my books, I enjoy giving a portion of proceeds back to the #lgbt community. For this book, I will also be donating a portion to Hearts United for Animals, www.hua.org.

Made in the USA
Charleston, SC
19 July 2012